THE ROOK
VOLUME SIX

by **BARRY REESE**

PRO SE PRESS

THE ROOK, VOLUME SIX
A Pro Se Press Publication

Cover Illustration by Ed Mironiuk, Interior Illustrations by Anthony Castrillo.
Rook Logo Art by Bill Carney, Production Design by Sean E. Ali.

Edited by Tommy Hancock

This book is a work of fiction. All of the characters in this publication are products of the author's imagination or are used fictitiously. Any resemblance to actual persons, living or dead is purely coincidental. No part or whole of this publication may be reproduced or transmitted in any form or by any means, graphic, electronic, or mechanical, including photocopying, recording, taping or by any information storage or retrieval system, without the permission in writing of the publisher.

Pro Se Productions, LLC
133 1/2 Broad Street
Batesville, AR, 72501
870-834-4022
proseproductions@earthlink.net
http://www.proseproductions.com

The Rook, Volume Six
Copyright © 2011 Barry Reese
All rights reserved.
ISBN: 978-1463548995

Dedication

to Cari and Julian

TABLE of CONTENTS

INTRODUCTION	
THE SCORCHED GOD	1
THE SINS OF THE PAST	124
DARKNESS, SPREADING ITS WINGS OF BLACK	138
THE SCORCHED GOD - AN INTERVIEW WITH AUTHOR BARRY REESE	187
THE ROOK - A TIMELINE	190

FEATHERING A NEW NEST:
an introduction to THE ROOK: VOLUME 6
By Tommy Hancock

Pulp is an interesting bird. Whether you see Pulp as a genre or a medium or a medium that's become a genre or a classification or a waste of time, it doesn't matter. Pulp is obviously here to stay in several forms, including collecting the classic tales, researching the history of authors and artists, and most notably in the creation of New Pulp stories and creations to people these original modern tales.

Recently one of those New Pulp characters has taken flight. Noted New Pulp author Barry Reese's THE ROOK winged its way from its very successful tenure with Wild Cat Books and has roosted here, with Pro Se Productions. Speaking for Pro Se, I'd first like to say that we are very fortunate to get a property that has been treated so well by Ron Hanna and the team at Wild Cat. The five previous volumes of THE ROOK have captured the imaginations of New Pulp fans everywhere and will likely prove to be future classics of The New Pulp Movement, thanks to Barry's awesome creative abilities as well as to Wild Cat's wonderful treatment of the property.

When the discussions initially began about THE ROOK making a transition to Pro Se, it was all very positive, both the conversations about where Max and company had been, both creatively and publisher wise, and about where Barry and Pro Se would take THE ROOK in the next couple of years. Barry wanted THE ROOK and all related concepts to spread its wings and Pro Se Press intends to assist the masked Mr. Davies and all the wonderful tales to come from his adventures in doing just that.

The stories in this collection show just how versatile the concept behind THE ROOK is and is a wonderful testimony as well to Barry's inimitable skill as a New Pulp writer. The tales take Max all over the globe, across the lines of the supernatural, and even introduce a brand new character, Lazarus Gray, to the world. Yes, THE ROOK has settled well into his new nest.

As for just how far those wings are going to be spread, keep your eyes to the sky and watch what Barry Reese and Pro Se Press has in store for THE ROOK.

Tommy Hancock
Pro Se Editor in Chief
5/19/11

THE SCORCHED GOD

An Adventure Starring The Rook
Written by Barry Reese

Trouble is a friend
But trouble is a foe
Oh, oh
And no matter
What I feed him
He always seems to grow
Oh, oh
- "Trouble Is A Friend" by Lenka

Chapter I
The Man of Destiny

April, 1942 – Off the Coast of New Zealand

The zeppelin moved through the stormy skies with an almost majestic grace. The winds were powerful enough to buffet the ship slightly off its chosen course but the German engineers who ran them pushed the mighty engines within its belly to their limits.

The commander of the vessel, Wilhelm Mueller, stood on the command deck. His posture was ramrod straight and he kept his gloved fingers clasped tightly together behind his back. He wore a monocle over his right eye, a well-pressed German military uniform, gleaming black boots, dark gloves and a long coat that brushed against the metal surface beneath his feet. He was forty-seven years old and a firm believer in Hitler's government. Before the rise of The Fuehrer, Mueller had feared that Germany was growing soft, having been whipped like a dog after the Great War. But Hitler had revived a sense of national pride in his people and once again men and women were proud to be Aryan.

"The island has been sighted below," a man said from Mueller's side. Horst was a good man and had been with Mueller through one posting after another for over twelve years.

"The coordinates are exact?"

"They are. It's just as the Jew said: the island is virtually invisible except when sighted from directly above."

Mueller knew the coordinates of this place by heart: 34°57'S 150°30'W. The island was 2,500 km east of New Zealand and was a cliff-bound volcanic location that seemed to defy all rational description. Ships and planes passed it by on a regular basis, never noticing the inhospitable strip of land.

"Shall we ready a landing party, Sir?"

Mueller's eyes flickered. Normally, he would lead such a mission himself. He was a man of action, prone to taking the most dangerous tasks for himself. Such instincts had led to numerous scars all over his body and more aches than he could count, but it wasn't something he would ever hope to change. His men admired him for his bravery and willingness to put his own life on the line.

"Inform the Furies that we have arrived," Mueller said dryly. Horst could see the disappointment in his commander's expression, but he merely clicked his heels together and spun about to do as he was ordered.

Horst moved through the interior of the zeppelin, the almost overwhelming noise from the engines no longer causing him the stress they had when he'd first joined the crew. Some of the men wore earplugs but others – like Horst – merely welcomed the loss of hearing that made the job bearable. The engines were growing quieter now, as they were used primarily for forward thrust. Now that the ship had reached its goal, there was little need for them except to prevent the vessel from being knocked out of the sky by the winds.

The Furies were an extension of the Fuehrer's Geheimnisvolles Kraft-Projekt, which translated as the Occult Forces Project in English. The OFP was dedicated to utilizing super-science and magic in the name of The Reich. They had successfully created a number of powerful agents, though as of late several of them had fallen in battle against Allied warriors. Just a few months prior, The Grim Reaper, one of the most feared products of the OFP, had been defeated in Atlanta, Georgia by the masked vigilante known as The Rook. Horst had been stunned by the news. How could a purebloaded product of Nazi science lose against a mongrel like The Rook?

The Furies were created as a gesture of goodwill from Germany to its major

Axis allies: Japan and Italy. A woman from each land was chosen, based on a wide variety of specifications, to become something more than human. They were all lovely enough to cause even the sternest of men to lose their breath in their company but these were no mere seductresses. They were as deadly as any man and were so ruthless that even Horst, a veteran of numerous interrogations and murders, balked at their actions.

Horst knocked on the door that led to the Furies' shared quarters. The three women seemed to do everything together and Horst was not alone in wondering about their sexual preferences. Were they lovers? He had no idea, but the thought had proved a titillating one.

The door opened before Horst could knock a second time. The Asian member of the trio stared back at him, wearing a light kimono that did little to hide the curves of her body. She was aware of his gaze but did not shrink from it. Like the other Furies, she regarded her sexuality as just one more weapon in her arsenal. Her name was Akemi, which Horst had been told translated as "red beauty." It was a fitting name, for she had dyed the front of her hair a crimson color. The red stripes stood out in stark contrast to the rest of her midnight black hair.

All three women spoke multiple languages flawlessly so Horst was not surprised to hear her answer in German. "What do you want?" she asked, showing him absolutely no respect. This attitude was common with Akemi and had not won her any fans amongst the zeppelin's crew, who believed that a proper woman should know her place.

"We have arrived at the island. Captain Mueller wished me to inform you of this."

Akemi opened the door further and Horst looked in to see the other two Furies in states of mid-dress. The German member of the contingent was wearing black leather, a riding crop strapped to her hip. She was Käthe, a name meaning "pure." Given the highly sexualized nature of her clothing and manner, Horst found that to be an ironic moniker. The third woman was the Italian named Imelda. Her name meant "warrior" and she lived up to it. Like Käthe, she wore a slightly sexualized version of her country's traditional military uniform. Her blonde hair was cut in an inverted bob, emphasizing the perfectly aligned features of her face.

The two women looked up at him with disdain as Akemi entered the room, dropping her kimono. She began to get dressed, seemingly oblivious to the fact that she was displaying her nudity to the German officer. Horst cleared his throat and attempted to maintain his own dignity, though it was difficult.

Käthe stood up after pulling on her boots. "Go and tell the Captain that we will handle the mission ourselves from here. We will parachute down to the island and retrieve the object."

Horst shifted uncomfortably.

"You have a problem with these orders?"

THE SCORCHED GOD

Käthe - Leader of the lovely and deadly Furies

Horst decided to not push the fact that Käthe had no military rank and thus had no authority to issue orders at all. He had a suspicion he would not live to complete those words. Instead, he cleared his throat and said, "Radio communication may be affected by the lightning storm. If you were to need emergency assistance, we might not be able to respond. My suggestion would be to take a small group of soldiers with you."

Imelda laughed coldly. She said something in Italian to Käthe, who smirked in response. Horst, who was able to speak only German, had a feeling that the words were insulting to him.

Käthe reached out and placed a gloved hand on his shoulder. She rubbed it affectionately at first, but then her grip tightened considerably and it was all Horst could do to not cry out in pain. "We are not the weak-kneed women that you're used to. Taking your men with us would only slow us down. Now go and tell the Captain what I have said. You wouldn't want me to report to the Fuehrer that our mission was delayed because you refused to listen."

Horst spun about and moved away, his face burning as he heard the Furies' derisive laughter.

The wind and rain made their descent difficult. The Furies' parachutes were caught in the updraft several times, sending them off-course, but each time the women adjusted, reacting like expert skydivers. While each had their own specialties, as a group they'd been trained in nearly every fighting style and military technique known to man. Those skills coupled with their indomitable will and keen intelligence made each Fury a truly terrifying opponent.

Akemi was the first to set foot on the rocky shores. She angled her landing so that she came down near a series of large stones that led toward the open mouth of a cave. As she was disengaging from the chute, Imelda touched down, followed closely by Käthe.

"That's it," Akemi shouted over the rain. Her pitch-black hair was plastered to her skull and water was running down her chin as she spoke. When they were alone, the three women generally each spoke in their native tongue, challenging the others to keep up with them. There was never any problem with miscommunication.

Imelda raised a hand over her eyes, squinting toward the cave. "Are you sure? We're good at this, but it seems unlikely we'd land right in front of it. Especially with this wind."

Akemi frowned, taking insult. She was the one who had plotted out their course. She was about to respond tartly when Käthe, ever the peacemaker in their group, spoke first. "Won't hurt to get out of this rain and take a look. If nothing else, we can get our bearings and figure out where we need to be. But," she added with a smile, her face illuminated by a particularly bright flash of lightning from above, "if I know Akemi, she set us down as close to our goal as possible."

Akemi nodded, placated by the praise. She reached behind her back and withdrew a katana sheathed there. Taking the point position, she led her companions through the muddy ground and up onto the rocks. Far off in the distance, a massive volcano dominated the horizon, smoke trailing up from its warm interior.

The Furies made it to the cave and entered, all of them shivering from the cold rain. It was very dark inside, prompting Imelda to take out a small flare and light it. The flames revealed something that made her wince in amazement. Glancing at Akemi, she whispered, "My apologies, sister. You were right."

Akemi smiled triumphantly. All along the rock walls were hieroglyphics. Even without knowing the truth of what they were seeking, the Furies would have been able to glean meaning from these symbols. They showed an island populated by tall, thin beings with golden hair. Pigments had been added to the drawings to give them color, making it clear that the people of this island were Aryan in design. The images seemed to show that the sea swallowed the island, forcing a few survivors to flee to safety. But then a bronze-skinned, blond-haired, blue-eyed man fell from the sky in what was obviously modern day London. This man was shown wearing pants resembling jodhpurs, calf-high boots, and a military shirt with epaulets and buttoned down pockets. He seemed the very epitome of the Aryan ideal. The next set of images were the most surprising of all: they showed the man raising the sunken land, bringing green grasses to a snowy plain, and then conquering what appeared to be a world within the Earth's interior.

"This is it," Käthe said, the sound of excitement making her voice husky with desire. "We've found it, my sisters. We've found the tomb of Sun Koh."

The Furies set to work quickly, ignoring the sounds of the raging storm outside the cave. Imelda took charge of preparing the floor, brushing back the dirt and grime until she'd formed a perfect circle. This she adorned with several mystical sigils, drawing each with her fingers with astonishing care. By the time she was finished, sweat poured off her body.

Käthe and Akemi pushed farther into the cave, having lit their own flares by this time. The cave went into the mountain another sixty or so feet and at the end of the passage they found a throne made of marble and gold. It was the most beautiful thing that either woman had ever seen and it filled Käthe with a sense of Aryan pride.

Akemi reached out and squeezed her friend's hand. "I'm glad that it's you and I who are doing this."

"Imelda is a loyal Fury," Käthe said, but she knew what Akemi meant. They were the closest out of the three and Akemi had listened patiently as Käthe had talked of her hopes and dreams concerning Sun Koh. It had been Käthe who had convinced the OFP to fund this expedition and it was she who believed most fervently in the cause. Her passion had proved infectious for Akemi and the Asian woman had quickly become a steadfast backer of the plan. As with everything, Imelda had proven the harder to convince.

As Akemi watched Käthe approach the throne, she thought back to all that Käthe had told her. She hoped it was all true… if it was, then this was the man who could ensure the Axis powers' victory!

Sun Koh was an Atlantean prince, sent from the past to salvage the Aryan race. He had arrived in 1932, dropping from the skies over London. The ideal Aryan specimen, Sun Koh was a genuine Übermensch. He possessed unusual strength and reflexes, along with an eidetic memory and a "danger sense" that warned him of imminent attacks. He had been sent from the past to prepare the Aryan peoples for the return of the Lost Continent before the arrival of a new Ice Age. He had embarked upon numerous adventures, claiming a cadre of allies, all of whom had become legends to the German people. Most of them were dead, killed in the course of their exploits alongside Sun Koh, but Käthe could recite their names with ease: Alaska-Jim, Jan Mayen, Rudolph Rauhaar, Rolf Karsten and Ludwig Minx. There were others, too, but those were Sun Koh's primary allies as he had battled agents of Zionism throughout Europe. Sun Koh had become a Nazi party member and an agent of German Military Intelligence, becoming a favorite of Adolph Hitler himself during the early days of Hitler's rise to power. Sun Koh shared Hitler's belief in eugenics and had been a steadfast advocate of destroying or enslaving the lesser races.

But then everything had come to an end in 1938. The stories that had come back to Germany had said impossible things: that Atlantis had risen from beneath the waves; that Sun Koh had managed to make Greenland lush and beautiful again; and had conquered the world inside the Hollow Earth. The Aryan race had been made secure, according to those outlandish tales… but Greenland looked unchanged and there were still plenty of enemies out there, looking to destroy the Third Reich.

And, of course, the new Ice Age had yet to come.

So where was Sun Koh? What had happened to him? And if he could be found, could he help end the war?

"It's here," Käthe said. She was kneeling next to the throne, reaching underneath. A section of gold at the base had hidden a small drawer. Käthe's hands soon held up a kingly crown, wrought of pure iron.

Akemi moved closer, gazing at the iron crown in mounting pleasure. Käthe had learned of the crown's existence while poring over all the reports of Sun Koh's final mission. A Jewish sailor had been quoted in the papers as claiming that his vessel had washed up on a mysterious island in the South Pacific. He claimed that a man named Sun Koh had been on the island, ranting and raving that something had gone horribly wrong. This island, he claimed, was actually Atlantis, newly raised from the sea. But it was all wrong… and Sun Koh had no idea why. According to the Jew, Sun Koh had led his allies into a dark cave, planning to take revenge on the peoples of the Hollow Earth. Sun Koh and his friends had vanished after Koh had performed some sort of strange ritual involving an iron crown and a throne that had once belonged to Sun Koh's father.

The Jew was believed mad by many, the victim of time too long spent on an island with no clean water to drink.

But Käthe believed otherwise. And now she was being proven correct.

Together, the two women returned to Imelda. The Italian beauty's eyes widened at the sight of the crown and Akemi felt anger blossom in her heart. The third Fury hadn't believed in the crown, either.

"Is the circle prepared?" Käthe asked, her eyes searching for any signs of imperfections in the sigils.

"Everything's perfect." Imelda glanced back at the drawings on the wall. "Hard to believe this is Atlantis. Where are the signs of the grand Aryan civilization that was once here?"

The way she said that made it clear that she was being disdainful of all the Sun Koh claims. Akemi sprang forward, her katana whistling through the air. Imelda was just as quick, ducking under the blade and drawing the handgun that had been holstered at her hip.

"Stop it!" Käthe shouted and both of the warring Furies slowly relaxed. "We stand on the precipice of a tremendous event… and the two of you are acting like two catty girls at a dance. I don't know what happened here, Imelda. But you see the hieroglyphs and you see the iron crown. This is where Sun Koh vanished. And we're going to bring him back."

"But even assuming that Jew was telling the truth about everything… how do you know which spell Sun Koh used when he left? And how do you know he'll be happy to be brought back?"

"I suppose we'll have to wait and see," Käthe answered and for the first time since this whole affair began, Akemi sensed there was some hesitation on her friend's part. "There's no point in waiting any longer. Let's go ahead and get started."

Akemi and Imelda both knelt on opposite sides of the circle, careful not to disturb the sigils. Käthe moved to the exact center, the iron crown in her hands. She lifted it high and began chanting, speaking in an ancient tongue that only the most powerful of mystics remembered. It was last spoken regularly when gleaming Atlantis stood proud and tall as the center of the civilized world. She ended her litany of words by placing the crown on the floor beneath her feet and then bowing her head, an action that was mimicked by her fellow Furies.

The storm outside seemed to pause and for a moment there was no sound at all. It was like some shroud of silence had fallen over the world and the Furies found themselves holding their breath, lest they disturb the perfect balance of the scene.

And then a powerful wind began to blow within the cave, nearly knocking Käthe off her feet. Dust began to rise up in response and all three women found themselves lifting up hands to ward off the tearing effect that the sand had on their faces. A golden light began to form in the center of the circle and Käthe squinted to see what was happening. The lights swirled around, slowly coalescing into the form of a man.

And what a man he was! Standing over six feet tall and possessed of a compact muscled frame, he was the perfect Aryan ideal. Sun Koh's bronzed skin, blond hair and blue eyes all combined with his well-chiseled features to make him worthy of female adoration.

When the lights faded and he stood once more in this place and time, Sun Koh looked slowly around himself, his eyes lingering on each of the women. Imelda and Akemi he regarded with open suspicion but he relaxed slightly when he saw Käthe, recognizing someone who shared his bloodline.

"When am I?" he asked Käthe, speaking in modern German. His words carried an unusual accent, but it was not enough to impair his ability to communicate. Käthe noted the way he'd phrased his question and responded in kind.

"The year is 1942. Your people still need you."

Sun Koh straightened his back, causing his broad shoulders to ripple. His beautiful blue eyes held Käthe's in an unbreakable spell. "I'm afraid our people have more need of me than they know."

"What do you mean?"

Sun Koh gestured for Akemi and Imelda to rise from their kneeling positions. His words chilled the very blood in Käthe's veins. "The Third Reich is doomed."

Chapter II
Dead Men Tell No Lies

The steam ship cut a swath through the choppy seas and The Rook knew he had only moments to regain control of the vessel before it smashed into the docks. In his true identity of philanthropist Max Davies, The Rook had taken this cruise in an attempt to spend some quality time with his wife. They'd left their son William in the care of their housekeeper Nettie and taken off for the tranquility of the ocean.

For the first week or so, things had been quite perfect, with good food, good company, and even better lovemaking. But then Max had noticed that there were several coffin-like crates in the hold and that various passengers on the ship were vanishing. The captain of the ship had not wanted to reveal these things, but Max had pressed him on it and he had finally confessed that some of the crew was beginning to believe that spirits of the dead were haunting the ship.

Evelyn had known it was a lost cost at this point, so she'd given permission to her husband to don his 'working clothes' – the well-tailored suit, long trench coat and domino-style facemask. The mask was peculiar in that there was a bird-like beak that rested against the bridge of Max's nose, giving him a slightly sinister demeanor.

As The Rook had suspected, mayhem soon ensued. One of the passengers, a dark-skinned man named Roberto, was traveling with four vampires, each of whom was sleeping in the ship's hold during the day. At night, the creatures were coming out to feed on the innocent.

Roberto had proven to be not much of a threat and he was now being held under armed guard in the ship's brig. But that still left the four vampires to be dealt with. Choosing when to strike against them was easy enough and The Rook was now hurrying into the hold in an attempt to beat the transition from daytime to the twilight of early evening. He held four wooden stakes under an arm, a heavy mallet clutched in his right hand.

As he approached the first of the coffins, The Rook couldn't help but think how strange his life had become. Slaying the undead was really not all that unusual an activity for him these days. Ever since he'd watched his father die for his beliefs, gunned down by criminals while Max was just eight years old, life had become a crucible in which Max Davies was forged into The Rook. He'd traveled the world as a young man, transforming his mind and body into weapons against evil. And aided by visions of the future, sent by his father from beyond the grave, The Rook was usually one step in front of his enemies.

But Warren Davies had sent nothing to help his son on this day. Max was on his own as he gripped the lid of the coffin and slid it aside. The stench of the grave filled his nostrils, making him draw back in disgust. The interior of the casket was filled with several inches of earth upon which a pale man laid, hands folded on his chest. The man was not breathing, but there was something about him that suggested animation, as if he might sit up at any moment. The vampire wore a white shirt and dark slacks. His receding hairline and slightly pudgy gut gave The Rook pause. This was hardly the typical killing machine he was used to when facing vampires. That didn't make him any less dangerous, however.

The Rook lined the stake up against the vampire's heart and brought the mallet down against it. The second strike was enough to pierce the flesh and crimson blood oozed up from the wound. The vampire's eyes shot open and he opened his mouth, releasing a gasp that stank so badly that it brought tears to The Rook's eyes.

The Rook slammed home the mallet once more and finished off the vampire, who expired with a small cry of frustration. The creature's body began to break apart, returning to the dust from whence it came. Max relaxed somewhat, thinking that all of this was going much better than he'd feared.

It was at that exact moment that he heard the lids to the other three coffins sliding to the floor.

The Rook whirled about to see the other three vampires clambering from their crates. They looked tired and somewhat bleary-eyed because their slumber had been interrupted, but they had somehow sensed the destruction of their brethren and that was enough to provide strength to their undead limbs.

The Rook briefly considered how he should proceed. In addition to the wooden stakes, he had two modified pistols on his person and one mystic blade. The guns were capable of firing nearly a hundred rounds each, meaning he rarely needed to reload. The bullets in the gun chambers were tipped in silver and had each been soaked in holy water, making them quite painful to creatures such as these. But his greatest weapon when facing the supernatural was The Knife of Elohim, a dagger that had once been soaked in the blood of Christ. The blade was capable of tearing through vampires, zombies, and other evil creatures with incredible ease. Seeing the looks of vengeance on the faces of the vampires he now faced, Max decided to discard the wooden stakes. He drew both the Knife of Elohim and one of the pistols, brandishing one in each hand.

Two of the vampires were men and both were slender to the point of being gaunt. One had long straggly hair caked with dirt and blood, the other had short cropped hair fashioned in a very modern style. Max suspected that the longhaired man was from another era entirely. The third member of the group was a woman and she was so lovely that Max felt an ache in his bones. She wore a black dress with a plunging neckline. Her blonde hair was pinned back, emphasizing her slender neck.

It was the woman who addressed him, the two men staring at him with a mixture of hunger and anger. "I know you," she said, her eyes drinking him in. "You're the one who halted the rise of The Kingdom of Blood."

The Rook's mind turned back to the events of 1936, when he and a small group of allies had foiled a vampire plot to fulfill a prophecy concerning the enslavement of the human race. "I would ask for your name," The Rook said with a cold smile. "But there's not really any point. You're going to be dust in a few minutes anyway."

The woman hissed like a cat, baring her fangs. Her male companions took that as their cue to attack. The nearest of the two, the longhaired man, lunged for Max's throat with outstretched hands. The Rook swung his blade, cutting off several of the vampire's fingers. The mystic weapon caused burning pain in its victim and the vampire howled, staring at his smoking stumps in shock.

The Rook meanwhile had spun toward the short-cropped vampire. He fired three times, each bullet piercing the monster's head and face. The vampire staggered with each impact, blood gushing from his wounds. It fell to the floor, twitching like a fish out of water.

The other male vampire had recovered by this time and he crashed into The Rook, slamming the vigilante against the side of one of the coffins. Max felt a sharp pain in his hip and he gritted his teeth, striking back with the Knife of Elohim. The blade caught in the vampire's belly and The Rook gave it a cruel twist before sawing up and down quickly. The vampire's open mouth, only inches away from The Rook's neck, opened and closed, the lips twisting in agony. The Rook had the monster pinned on the blade now and Max finished him off by raising his gun, placing the barrel between the vampire's eyes, and pulling the trigger.

The Rook shoved away the corpse, which lay unmoving next to his fallen companion. Both would need to be finished off with stakes, their bodies subsequently burned. The Rook had learned the hard way that even bullets to the brain weren't enough to prevent resurrections in the future.

The female vampire stood in the shadows, barely visible in the darkness of the hold. Max knew that outside late afternoon had begun to give way to early evening, making her strength all the greater. "Why do you hunt us, Max Davies?"

"Because you kill innocent people."

"We do what comes naturally to us. Do you hate the lion for taking down the gazelle? We thin the herd of humanity. We do you a favor as a species, removing the weak and the sick."

"Let's not play games. You aren't going around putting the infirmed out of their misery. You're hunting and killing people who are in the prime of life, stealing away parents and children from those who love them."

The woman took a step out into the light, her beauty fading quickly as her face twisted, becoming more animalistic and bloodthirsty. "The day you die will be a happy one in Hell, Max Davies. There are so many like me who will be waiting to greet you with open arms."

"What makes you think I'll be in Hell?"

"We both know that's where you'll be. You think God wants you to dress up in a mask and act as judge, jury, and executioner? You elevate yourself into His position, ruling on what is moral and just. He will condemn you to an eternity of suffering!"

The vampire's head suddenly exploded in a mass of bone and red tissue. The sound of a gun firing from the direction of the stairs caused The Rook to drop into a crouch, spinning around to point his pistol at the source.

Evelyn stood there in khaki slacks and a white button-up shirt. Her auburn hair fell in ringlets around her shoulders and there was a mischievous smirk on her face. "Did I give you a fright?" she asked.

"I thought you were staying out of this," he said, standing up and holstering his gun. The Knife of Elohim he slid into a protective leather casing, strapped to his left hip.

"I'm sorry, Max. Did I ruin your fun?" Evelyn sauntered over, ignoring the ruined vampire bodies on the floor. Before she'd met Max, she never would have thought herself capable of blowing someone's head off with a gun… but in the seven years they'd known one another, she'd been at his side for more weirdness than she could ever hope to catalog.

The Rook placed an arm around her waist and pulled her to him. They kissed there in the hold, the smell of rotting flesh and spent bullet shells hanging in the air. They'd been in worse smelling places. "Thanks for the assist, honey."

"No problem. Some of the crew heard the gunfire but they all did just as the Captain asked: not a one of them came down here to help."

"They would have been in the way."

"Right-o. But I assumed I'd be able to help out if needed… or I'd stay in the shadows and never make a peep."

"How long have you been down here?"

"I stepped in around the time you were stabbing that one in the gut."

"I bet that was a lovely scene."

"Very charming." Evelyn pulled away and cast a glance around their surroundings. "So what now?"

"We stake them and then we dump their ashes overboard."

"I'm not usually very domestic, but I can help you clean up if you want."

"I'd love the company," Max said and he meant it. Evelyn was far more than his lover or even the mother of his son. She was his partner and his confidante, as essential to the success of The Rook's mission as Max himself.

The grisly work was soon complete and Max took his wife's hand as they began to leave the hold. "Sorry for not sticking to my promise. I swore this would be one trip where I wouldn't wear the mask at all."

"It's okay, Max. I knew who and what you were when I married you. It's just like my acting career – you know that sometimes I have to be away for a while."

Max knew what she meant. When they'd first met, Evelyn had been a stage actress, but she'd soon graduated to B-Movies. As a result of this, she was sometimes off in California for weeks at a time, leaving Max to tend to the house and family.

It all made for an interesting arrangement but it was one that worked for them. As they stepped up onto the deck, the moon now beginning to peek out from behind the clouds, Max felt a pounding begin just behind his eyes. His vision swam and he released his grip on his wife's hand so that he could rush forward to lean against the rail.

"Max...?" Evelyn asked, though she recognized the signs of what was happening. Not long after witnessing the death of his father, Max had begun experiencing painful visions of the future. These visions usually centered on violent crimes of some sort and often took the form of enigmatic glimpses of potential events, rather than hard-and-fast depictions of what lay ahead. The knowledge that these visions came from his dead father did little to lessen the pain they induced.

Evelyn approached cautiously, knowing her husband was lost in a world she could not see. She tentatively reached out for his shoulder, but he jerked away from her.

In his mind's eye, The Rook was witnessing a number of things that made little sense to him, but which nevertheless filled him with dread:

He saw a man with bronze skin and blue eyes wearing a parka, trudging through the snow toward a strange emerald dome.

He witnessed himself being tortured by three women, all of them beautiful but cruel.

And he saw a wave of pure light washing over Washington, D.C., destroying everything in its path. He saw the White House reduced to cinders while the Lincoln Memorial was annihilated from the face of the Earth.

When his vision cleared and he was once more aware of his surroundings, Max turned his head and saw Evelyn watching him with obvious fear in her eyes. "It's okay. I'm okay," he said, though his voice shook a bit as he spoke.

"What did you see?"

The Rook reached up and removed the mask from his face. He dropped it into the pocket of his coat and began rubbing his temples with both hands. He summarized what he'd seen, but the words did little convey the horror of the images. It was always this way: no matter how he might try, he could never make someone else understand what it was like to witness destruction on such a massive scale. Thankfully, he'd been able to prevent most of the predicted disasters from occurring... but eventually, he was bound to slip up and fail. That thought kept him up at nights.

"You didn't get any idea who was behind it all? Was it those girls? Or the man with the blue eyes?"

"I didn't see those women and the man together. But I do get the sense that there's some connection between them. I wish these visions were clearer!" The Rook slammed his fist down on top of the railing and stared out over the water. "I have no idea who they are or where to find them. I don't know when the attack on Washington might come or how to stop it. Sometimes these things seem more like taunts than anything else, like my father is daring me to stop these crimes."

"You know that's not the case. Your father was... is... many things, but one thing you know is that he wants to see criminals punished."

"Yes. Even if it means torturing his son and turning him into an instrument for his vengeance." Max couldn't keep the bitterness out of his voice. He shook his head. "Enough self-pity. I've got work to do when we get back home. I have to stop those things from happening."

"Well, you know I'll do anything I can to help. And you have friends you can call on."

The Rook knew whom she was talking about. In recent years, he'd undertaken adventures with a wide variety of fellow heroes: the Russian superman Leonid Kaslov, the mysterious Black Bat, the supernatural detective Ascott Keane and the Domino Lady[1]. All of them would do whatever they could to assist him if he gave them a call... but he would hold off on that as much as possible. They all had their own problems and their own lives.

Evelyn squeezed her husband's hand. "You'll save the day," she said with a smile. "You always do."

"I hope you're right, Evelyn. Because the things I saw... I have a feeling that the entire world could be in danger if I don't."

---

1) *Leonid Kaslov debuted in "Kaslov's Fire" (The Rook Volume Two, 2008). Keane and the Black Bat met The Rook in "The Bleeding Hells" (The Rook Volume Three, 2009). Domino Lady teamed with The Rook in "Bloodwerks" (The Rook Volume Two, 2008).*

Sun Koh - Man of Destiny

Chapter III
The Daughter of Kali

Sun Koh lay awake, nestled in amongst warm female flesh. He was onboard the zeppelin, which was flying toward Europe. The Furies were all nude and covered with a fine sheen of sweat, their breathing deep and rhythmic. Sun Koh had exhausted them with his sexual prowess and they had fallen into a deep slumber immediately afterwards. This left Sun Koh in peace, allowing him to think things through.

Käthe lay with her head upon Sun Koh's chest, a faint smile on her lips. Akemi was on the other side, her cheek resting on The Man of Destiny's taut belly. Imelda was on the far edge of the bed, spooning with Käthe. All three women had been ardent lovers but Sun Koh had maintained a cool distance, even during the more intimate moments of their relations. Sun Koh knew all the ways to please a woman even though he regarded most of them as being lesser than a man and thus unworthy of his full attention. An Aryan woman was far above the men of the lesser races... but they were just as far below an Aryan man. Even a woman like Käthe, whose intelligence and skill were beyond reproach, would have better suited for her natural role: that of a mother, bringing new life into the world.

Only one woman had ever truly deserved equality with the men around her. Unfortunately, Sun Koh wasn't sure if she still lived. Of all his aides, she was the only one who hadn't accompanied him on his ill-fated return to Atlantis. All the others were now dead... but his beloved Ashanti might yet be out there somewhere, awaiting his return.

Ashanti Garuda, whose named translated as "The Daughter of Kali," was Sun Koh's mistress and his trusted assassin. Sun Koh had generally called her Shani, a pet name that no one else would have dared used. A true Aryan born and raised in India, Shani was a wondrous human being, defying the limitations of her gender. She had mastered alchemy, sorcery, Yoga, Siddha medicine, Kalaripayit and too many other Indian mystical arts to count. Thanks to Elixir of Life that she routinely drank, she was perpetually young and beautiful. Sun Koh had no idea how old she truly was, but her skin was also smooth and firm, her curves defying gravity in an enticing manner. A devotee of Kali, she had been gifted with the powers of pacifying, paralyzing, subjugating, obstructing, driving away and death dealing. She accomplished all these things with the temple that was her body, mastering all the pressure points that could be used to render men helpless, be it from pain or pleasure.

Her body, the dimensions of which Sun Koh could recall with perfect clarity, had been the canvas that displayed her devotion to Kali. In the center of her red tikala mark on her forehead was a tiny golden Swastika. Twelve more Swastikas adorned the rest of her body, located on the soles of her feet, the palms of her hands, the inside of her thighs, the inner portion of her arms on the outsides of her buttocks and the sides of her breasts. Sun Koh had traced them all with his hands and mouth.

The Atlantean slide from the bed, careful not to rouse The Furies. He found a robe that had been set aside for him and he slipped it on, cinching the belt in front. The hum of the engines was steady and consistent beneath his feet. He left the women's quarters and moved quietly through the zeppelin's hallways, finally entering the bridge. There were only four people present – three men who were studying gauges and charts and Captain Mueller.

Mueller, who had been sitting in his chair drinking a cup of coffee, stood up when he saw Sun Koh. "I trust the accommodations are to your liking?" the captain asked.

Sun Koh could sense the man's discomfort. "They are more than adequate. If I may ask, Captain Mueller, why is it that so many of your men seem uneasy in my presence?"

"Well, since your disappearance, your adventures have become a bit of modern folklore. I myself have a nearly full set of your heldromans."

Sun Koh nodded, suddenly understanding. During his last visit to this time, he had allowed several enterprising authors to fictionalize his adventures for consumption by the German masses. These pulp novels took certain liberties with the truth, but all of them were inspired by actual events. "Käthe told me of the last to be published. The one where I raised Atlantis, made Thule whole again and made the interior portions of the world safe for Aryans."

Mueller caught the tone in Sun Koh's voice. It was full of sardonic humor and it was quite apparent that the Atlantean didn't think much of the heldromans. "So none of it was true?"

"Oh, there were kernels of truth in all those tales, Captain. But I have not read my final adventure." Sun Koh smiled wistfully. "I would imagine that they would have changed some of the details so that I might have gone out as a hero and not as a fool."

"I don't understand."

"My companions and I journeyed to that location for the express purpose of raising Atlantis. That part of my plan worked exactly as it should have. But something was wrong… there were no remnants of our civilization, save for my father's throne, his iron crown, and a few hieroglyphs on a cave wall. It was as if… all of my life had been condensed into that one cavern."

Mueller pursed his lips thoughtfully. He wasn't at all sure what to say. He had always regarded Sun Koh as the perfect Aryan warrior – an ideal to which he could secretly aspire. But now he was seeing that the legend had feet of clay, eaten away by self-doubt. But almost as soon as he was thinking these things, he saw a change come over his hero's face. It was as if Sun Koh, too, had realized how he looked and sounded. Sun Koh threw off the shroud of sadness that had overtaken him and his face adopted the look of indomitable will that was usually associated with him.

"Captain, I would prefer not to journey to Berlin just yet. I have someone that I wish to look for."

Mueller was about to say that his orders came from The Fuehrer himself when a radio communications officer entered the room. After a quick exchange of salutes, the officer held out a communiqué with a stiff arm. "This just arrived, Herr Mueller."

The look on the young man's face gave Mueller pause. He knew that this message must have come from someone high-ranking enough to leave the man awestruck. Mueller glanced over the words, his jaw tightening. He looked at Sun Koh with an unreadable expression on his face. "New orders have arrived from Berlin. We are to return to the island and leave The Furies there to continue looking for anything from Atlantis that might remain. The Reich could benefit from the superior technology your people were rumored to possess."

Sun Koh sensed that the next part of the communiqué was what truly disturbed Mueller. "And what else, Captain?"

"We are to drop you off at the next Axis military base. You will be taken by plane on a covert trip."

"To where?"

"To the place where you entered our world: London, England."

"And for what purpose?"

"Because there's a woman there. A woman who somehow managed to contact the highest powers in Germany and convince them that she has to see you as soon as possible."

Sun Koh's lips twisted, beginning to form the faintest hint of a smile. "What is her name?"

Mueller fumbled with the pronunciation but Sun Koh didn't mind. Ashanti Garuda was alive… and she wanted to see him. He wondered idly why she was in England – her loathing of the British knew no bounds – but such concerns could wait.

Sun Koh was going to be reunited with his lover.

THE SCORCHED GOD

"I cannot believe this. We find him and revive him... and our reward is that we're dumped back on the island?" Imelda spat on the ground, her hands on her hips. The three women had rowed ashore after being deposited in a raft some three miles from the coast of Atlantis.

Akemi and Käthe exchanged a glance as they continued pulling supplies from the boat. It was Akemi who chose to address Imelda and her tone contained barely disguised loathing. "You sound like a cow when you moan that way. If your teats are so bloated, go and give them a hard pull!"

Imelda stared at her in shock. Then her face began to redden and she took several meaningful steps in Akemi's direction. The Japanese girl unsheathed her katana and adopted a battle-ready stance.

Käthe automatically opened her mouth, ready to try and soothe the wounds that lay between the two women. But then she decided to step back for once. She was disappointed as well and she found it hard to condemn Imelda for speaking out. Instead, she slung a backpack over her shoulder and began trudging toward the dense vegetation that covered the rocky terrain. The volcano was her ultimate destination. Sun Koh had been quite clear in saying that there were no volcanoes in ancient Atlantis and if the Fuehrer wanted confirmation of Sun Koh's stories – and Käthe was sure that was what this mission was now about – that seemed as good a place as any to start.

Akemi lowered her sword, staring at Käthe's back. The fact that their recognized leader had not intervened was not lost on either Akemi or Imelda. "She's hurting," Akemi said.

"And well she should be. How many months has she wasted on this? And this is how she's treated?" Imelda sighed and shook her head. "My apologies, Akemi. I am... tired."

The Japanese woman's expression softened and she sheathed her blade, providing her companion a brief nod. "Accepted. I should not be so quick to respond to your provocations."

Imelda frowned, seemingly unhappy with the lack of a true apology in response. She said nothing, however, and the two of them completed their task of packing up their supplies. They trudged after Käthe, trying to keep their footing on the slick rock surface. The rainfall had left deep puddles here and there, adding to the treacherous nature of the terrain.

They caught up to Käthe in a large clearing where a number of white-stoned ruins lay in various states of crumbling. There appeared to be four buildings in all, one-story affairs with multiple windows. In the center of the clearing was an old raised well. Käthe was staring down into it when Akemi stopped at her side, panting from the exertion. All three women were in remarkable shape, but even they were taxed by their rapid travel though the jungle.

"This is promising," Akemi said. "First signs of habitation we've found on this place, aside from the cave."

Käthe reached into the bag she'd set down at her feet. She pulled out a small coin and dropped it into the well. A splash was heard approximately eight seconds after she let it go.

"What do you think this was?" Imelda asked. "Looks too small to have been a village."

"I think it was a holy place," Käthe replied. "The priests lived in those two structures there and this one to my left was where their attendants slept. The final building was a common house where they took their meals and had prayer."

Imelda stared at her with a disbelieving grin on her face. "And how do you know all that?"

"I found a scrap of paper while the two of you were cresting that last hill." Käthe pulled it from one of her pockets and held it out to Imelda. The Italian studied the script and then shrugged. "It's in Atlantean," Käthe explained. "I translated it."

"I'm surprised Sun Koh didn't propose marriage," Imelda said. "You know almost as much about his people as he does."

"The only things I know are the scraps of information he gave German Military Intelligence." Käthe sounded slightly defensive and Imelda wondered if she hadn't hit on something. Had Käthe really thought that Sun Koh was going to make her some Aryan princess? "Besides," Käthe continued, turning away and looking around at the ruins. "Sun Koh has a lover. Or at least, he did."

"That didn't stop him from taking on all three of us," Imelda pointed out with a satisfied chuckle.

Käthe didn't bother replying to that. She knew that Sun Koh was a prince and was used to having multiple consorts. In fact, she'd read reports that had specifically mentioned his incredible stamina and sexual appetites. As such, she had certainly not been offended that he had wanted to include Imelda and Akemi in their lovemaking.

"We're not alone," Akemi whispered and both Imelda and Käthe responded without questioning. Käthe drew a bullwhip, keeping it coiled at the ready. Imelda was now brandishing two pistols of Italian design. They scanned the surrounding jungles, but saw and heard nothing.

Akemi sensed their confusion, but didn't rush into an explanation. Her senses were the most keen of The Furies and she was positive that she'd heard the crunching of leaves. It could certainly have been an animal of some sort, but so far they had seen nothing but birds and monkeys and both species were keeping high to the trees.

"Over there," Imelda hissed, training her pistols on a man who was staggering into view. The man was dressed in blood-encrusted Buckskins and a coonskin hat with the ragged remnants of a striped tail hanging off the back. He was huge, a veritable mountain of a man, with salt-and-pepper whiskers. He came to an abrupt halt when he spotted the three women, his mouth working in amazement.

"Who are you?" Imelda demanded, repeating the question in multiple languages.

"English," Käthe said. "He speaks English." She lowered her weapon. "You're Jim Hoover, aren't you? Better known as Alaska-Jim."

The hunter nodded slowly. "That's me." He swayed unsteadily on his feet. "You have to get off this island," he said. "This isn't Atlantis. Not at all...."

Akemi relaxed a bit as Käthe moved closer to the man. She knew of Alaska-Jim. He was one of Sun Koh's closest companions, a hunter and trapper from the Old West who sometimes worked for the Canadian police. A Canadian of German descent, Alaska-Jim had been very fervent in his defense of Aryan ideals. Akemi knew that true Aryans would look upon her own people as a lesser race but she allowed her loyalty to Käthe to overcome any distaste she had for such racial notions.

"This isn't Atlantis?" Käthe was asking.

"No! Not at all," Alaska-Jim repeated. He looked around, eyes wild with madness. "And I'm the only one left alive to tell the tale. Jan, Rolf, Ludwig, even Sun Koh himself. All gone. All dead."

"Sun Koh's alive," Käthe said and her words immediately caused Alaska-Jim to start.

"Alive? You've seen him?"

"We brought him back," Imelda said, drawing a glare from Akemi, who thought that Käthe should be allowed to handle this. "But we don't know all the specifics of how he vanished... or what happened to the rest of you."

Alaska-Jim fell to his knees, panting with exertion and hunger. "I will tell you all... but you must swear one thing to me."

Käthe stared him in the eyes and nodded slowly. "Anything."

"When I am done, you will take me from this place. You will help me escape it."

Imelda was at Käthe's side now. "If this isn't Atlantis, where are we?" she demanded.

The famed hunter looked at her as if she had suddenly sprouted a second head. "Little beauty... we are in Hell."

L ondon was greatly changed.

Sun Koh stepped from the small airplane that had carried him into the heart of the British Empire, his nostrils flaring as he sniffed the air. The airfield stank of not just gasoline and human sweat but also of despair and regret. He recalled similar things from the last days of Atlantis, before the Great Fall and before his trip through time.

He stopped in place, the pilot coming to a halt beside him. The man was watching him closely. Unlike Mueller, this fellow was unfamiliar with the legend of Sun Koh and thus had none of the hero worship that had infected the zeppelin's captain. "Are you unwell, Herr Koh?"

"No. I was just remembering the last time I was here. It was before the English people had become so dispirited."

"Ach. They are still fighters," the pilot said, shaking his head. His German was very common, Sun Koh noticed, and there were certain attributes about the man's features that suggested Jew ancestry. The Man of Destiny wondered how thoroughly the pilot's bloodlines had been investigated. "But The Blitz sent some of them into a deep depression, to be sure. At least, those that weren't bombed into oblivion!" The pilot laughed then, revealing yellowed teeth.

Sun Koh said nothing, continuing to study his surroundings. This airfield was a private one, belonging to a pro-Nazi airline. If anyone had known about their connections to the Reich, the entire affair would have been seized and those in charge locked away as traitors.

The Atlantean prince resumed walking, allowing the pilot to lead him toward a waiting car. A chauffeur was waiting there and he offered a crisp Nazi salute that Sun Koh half-heartedly returned. The pilot nodded his goodbye and spun about, leaving Sun Koh with the driver.

"Why have I not been questioned?" Sun Koh asked.

The driver, a solidly built man with a square head, blinked. "Sir?"

"Since I was brought onboard the zeppelin, I have only been asked the most basic of questions. No one has wondered where I went or the specifics of what happened to my companions. Why is that?"

"I'm just a driver, sir."

"You're a liar. You work for German Military Intelligence. Now answer my question."

"How did you know that?" the man asked, his jaw falling open in surprise.

"I can tell by the way your eyes move, the way you smell, and the way your heart rate remains perfectly steady, even now."

"You can… hear my heart beating?"

"Yes."

The driver relaxed his pose a bit, opening the door to the rear of the vehicle as he did so. "I'll explain everything while we're en route."

"You're taking me to see Ashanti?"

"Yes, I am."

Sun Koh slid into the backseat and watched as the driver got behind the wheel. "I am waiting."

The driver cleared his throat and glanced at Sun Koh's reflection in the rear view mirror. "From what I understand, the brains back in Germany know what happened to you, so they don't need to question you about it."

"Then they know more than I do. My memories are mostly a haze after I left this time and place. My friends came with me and I remember a terrible battle. I liberated an offshoot of Atlantis that was located within the Hollow Earth… but after that, all I remembered was fire and heat. It was like my flesh was being scorched right off my body! And then I was back, four years after I left."

The driver navigated through the streets of London, obviously knowing the city as well as any native could. "The Occult Forces Project has been partnering with a company called Bane Industries on something they call The Un-Earth Project. They're basically creating a miniature copy of the Earth, using telepaths to fashion the place. They're linking it the real world, making copies of people and places. Eventually, people who have psychic 'twins' in both worlds will be easy targets because those who are killed on Un-Earth are killed in this world, as well[2]."

Sun Koh found the man's words almost impossible to believe. He could recognize when someone was lying to him and he knew that there were untruths being said. "What does this have to do with me?" he asked, though he suspected he knew the answer.

"In 1938 when you and your friends raised Atlantis and you discovered that things weren't as you remembered, you performed a ritual, intending to transport your friends and yourself to the Hollow Earth. Correct?"

"Yes."

"But in doing so, you actually transported yourself to Un-Earth. The exploits you had in the Hollow Earth, the cleansing of Thule/Greenland… those took place in that other world."

"A false world."

"Not false… just one that was created by men on this Earth. It's going to be an Aryan paradise."

Something seemed to click in Sun Koh's mind, then, and it was not a pleasant thought at all. A false world created by Nazis would need for Aryan myths to become Aryan truths. A lost civilization of Aryan supremacy… Check. A time-lost hero, whose every mannerism and physical characteristic would imply Aryan superiority? Check.

Only one thing didn't fit: Sun Koh had arrived in London in 1932 and Hitler did not rise to power until 1933. So unless the Un-Earth Project predated Hitler and the Nazis, it would be impossible for Sun Koh to be a product of this other world.

Still, such a thing could explain the differences in Atlantis. If the lost continent on Un-Earth were the utopia that Sun Koh remembered, it would be confirmation that the Un-Earth was the planet of his birth and not this one. This one had possessed hieroglyphs and his father's throne… but even upon discovering them, Sun Koh had suspected they were forgeries. He had sensed that they were modern creations, designed to look far older.

These dark thoughts about his own origins kept Sun Koh from questioning his driver any further. In fact, he was so lost in his musings that he failed to notice the car coming to a stop in front of a hotel that catered to foreigners.

"We've arrived, Herr Koh. You will find her on the top floor, room 515."

---

2) *For more on the Un-Earth Project, see "Catalyst" (The Rook Volume Three, 2008)*

"Thank you." Sun Koh began to exit the vehicle but paused with his hand on the door. "Tell me… was I born on Un-Earth?"

The driver turned to face him. "I honestly don't know. I suppose it is possible that you were born there and that somehow, when you were thrown into the future, you accidentally breached the barrier and arrived in our world."

Sun Koh stared at the man, realizing that the fellow might be giving him the affirmation he needed… Ultimately, it did not matter. Whether he was born here or if his history had been sculpted on Un-Earth, all that he had accomplished since 1932 was real… and so was his desire to see the Aryan peoples protected. "Thank you," he said, exiting the vehicle.

He stood outside the hotel for several minutes before entering. The Daughter of Kali lay within.

Chapter IV
Truths and Half-Truths

The Rook slammed his elbow into the crook's face, shattering the man's nose. He then grabbed hold of his opponent's arm and swung him about, sending him tumbling into the arms of the other three thugs. All four men hit the ground and The Rook rushed forward, kicking two in their faces before they could defend themselves. He then raised the butt of his pistol and brought it crashing down onto the skull of another. That left only the one with the broken nose. The Rook regarded him for a moment before walking past him, leaving the man to whine in pain.

The door leading to the home of Phineas Glumm swung open and a cadaverous-looking man stood there, his hands on his hips. "The Rook," the man said with a most unfriendly smile. "You could have just knocked, you know."

Phineas Glumm was Savannah's most disturbing resident. A transplanted Briton, Glumm had made his fortune in the ivory field before retiring to Georgia. At one time, he'd had nearly a hundred poachers in his employ, all of them given a single task: hunt down and kill as many elephants as possible, depriving the dead and dying animals of their tusks in the process. It was nasty work but Glumm himself had never been witness to it: he'd remained in England the whole time, enjoying his three vices: wine, women and witchcraft.

"Your guards didn't seem to want to let me pass," The Rook said, stepping past Glumm. The interior of the house smelled strongly of incense. A massive oil panting of a reclining nude woman dominated the foyer and Max wondered at what sort of man would make sure that such artwork was the first thing his guests saw upon entering.

"They probably remembered you from your last visit," Glumm said, shutting the door behind him. He didn't seem overly concerned about his injured men. "I'm sure you remember... you burst in unannounced and demanded information from me. Much like now, I'd imagine."

The Rook kept walking until he'd reached Glumm's study. The room was wood-paneled with a tiger skin rug on the floor. The smell of incense was strongest here and The Rook winced a bit at the strength of the odor. His eyes drifted across the spines of numerous old books, some of which bore titles in Latin. "I had a vision and I want you to help me understand it."

Glumm smiled softly and sat down in a large-backed chair. He gestured for The Rook to take a seat on a nearby couch, but the vigilante answered with a shake of his head. "Why me?" Glumm asked. "I thought you usually consulted with Ascott Keane on things of a mystical nature."

"I really missed visiting Savannah."

Glumm laughed softly. "Very well, my mysterious friend. Tell me of this vision and I shall do my best to illuminate you about its meaning."

The Rook gave a detailed description of what he had seen, focusing particularly on the blue-eyed man and the destructive beam of light that was attacking Washington, D.C.

When the narrative was complete, Glumm sat back in his chair and steepled his fingers together. "Most interesting. I believe that you may be in luck… I do know some of the answers that you are seeking." Glumm stood up abruptly, crossing the room to a small shelf in the corner. It had escaped The Rook's notice earlier because, unlike every other bookshelf, it was not filled with arcane tomes. This one was stuffed to overflowing with popular materials, particularly those tattered-edged magazines known as the pulps. Glumm picked through of a few of these until he found what he was looking for. He held out one for The Rook, who took it gingerly. The front cover depicted a blond man falling from the sky with the words *Ein Mann fallt vom Himmel* plastered beside his body. Max knew enough German to translate: "A Man Falls From Heaven."

"What does this German magazine have to do with what I saw?"

"Heldromans. That's what those sorts of books are called in Germany." Glumm tapped his chin and began pacing, eagerly embracing the discussion. "A day or two ago there was a disturbance in the ether. Magicians all across the globe sensed it. A being of mystic importance had arrived from another plane of reality. I immediately began trying to trace it down to a specific place and I succeeded just last evening: an island that rose from the depths of the ocean in 1938 but was almost impossible to locate unless you knew its precise coordinates. There are many, myself amongst them, who believe that this place is the newly risen Atlantis."

The Rook looked back down at the cover, staring at the crudely drawn images. "That's him, isn't it? The man I saw in the parka? It's this…" he squinted at the magazine's banner. "Sun Koh."

"Yes," Glumm confirmed.

The Rook set the magazine down and pursed his lips. "I've heard stories of him. A few years back when I was doing some business in Europe, I heard of a Nazi superman. They said he was the embodiment of the Aryan ideal and that he led a whole team of adventurers. But then it was like he vanished...."

"That's exactly what happened! Stories in mystic circles claimed that Sun Koh was a lost prince of Atlantis, sent 11,000 years into the future to ensure that his people would survive. He arrived in 1932, just as shown in that heldromans. Then, six years after he arrived, he was gone. According to the one witness, he and his friends disappeared in a magic spell designed to send them into a world within the Earth itself."

"But now he's back? On this island that was supposedly Atlantis?"

"So it would seem."

"I need those coordinates."

Glumm hesitated, looking uncertain. "If Sun Koh is half the man I have heard he is, you will be in great danger when you face him."

"I didn't know you worried about me so much."

"My grandmother was Jewish," Glumm said, his face seemingly set in stone. "I despise everything this Reich stands for... and this Sun Koh is their champion. If he's trying to get his hands on that weapon you described from your vision... I don't want that to happen."

The Rook stared in Glumm's eyes for a moment, thinking how strange it was that a man who was as full of sin as Glumm could still have a glimmer of decency within him. "Can you tell me anything else that might help me defeat him?"

Glumm shrugged. "He is a big man, though he does not appear so at first because his body is so perfectly symmetrical. His brain is lightning-quick and he harbors no troublesome morals such as the ones you possess. I have no doubt that he will be the most dangerous man you have ever faced."

"The coordinates," The Rook said, setting his jaw. "No point in putting this off."

Glumm turned away from him, exiting the room. From over his shoulder he said, "Wait here. It will take me a moment to locate them."

The Rook watched him go, chewing on his bottom lip and wondering what he should do. Glumm was right – from what little he knew of Sun Koh, the man was not to be underestimated. Luckily, The Rook had flown to Savannah in his private aircraft, one of the two or three fastest such machines on the planet. He could reach Atlantis within a few hours... but the question was, should he go alone? He immediately thought of Leonid Kaslov, remembering what Evelyn had said about calling upon his friends for help. The last he heard from Leonid, the man was traveling in the Himalayas, seeking contact with a tribe of Yeti.

"This is your fight, son. Don't turn from it."

The Rook paused, recognizing his father's voice. The man was speaking to him from the hazy middle ground that lay between the worlds of life and death. Max glanced around but did not see his father's spectral shade. "I don't suppose you're going to clarify any of the things I saw?"

"You know I can only tell you so much. There are rules that I have to obey."

The Rook sighed, closing his eyes. "But you are telling me that I should go alone?"

"In many ways, you've been training for this moment for years, Max. Sun Koh is actually the kind of man you were designed to fight!"

"Designed?" The Rook said bitterly. "Is that what you call it? Coercing your only son into becoming a weapon… an instrument for your vengeance against the criminals of the world. Fine, Father. I'll do this on my own. But I want you to go away and stay away."

The Rook felt a brief sensation, like someone's fingertips were grazing his own, pulling away from his grasp. He momentarily regretted his words. Warren Davies had been a genuine bastard in terms of how he'd manipulated his son but the fact remained that he was Max's father. And Max had adored his father. The memory of Warren Davies being gunned down was seared into Max's consciousness and always would be.

The Rook opened his eyes to find Glumm standing nearby, watching him closely. Max wondered how long Glumm had been there and how much he had heard.

"The coordinates," Glumm said, offering a sheet of paper with a set of numbers scrawled across it. After clearing his throat, Glumm asked, "Are you unwell?"

"I'm being haunted by my dead father."

Glumm nodded, as if this were a common occurrence. Perhaps, Max mused, it was in Glumm's circles.

The Rook brushed past Glumm, offering muttered thanks. He knew that Glumm wouldn't be angry over his abrupt departure. Glumm was probably more than happy to be rid of him, after all.

Once outside, The Rook noticed that the injured band of men were on their feet now. They watched him with angry but cautious expressions. The one whose nose he'd shattered was cupping his injured area with a blood-soaked rag. The Rook spared them all only a brief glance before he stalked through the front gate and began heading toward the field where he'd landed his plane. He activated the long-range mini-radio he carried with him, dialing his home phone. When his housekeeper, Nettie, answered the call, he asked to be connected to his wife.

Evelyn came on a few seconds later. "Max? Did you find out anything?"

"I did. I'm going to be late getting back home. I'll be flying toward New Zealand."

"What on earth for?"

"I need to stop an Atlantean prince from making the world an Aryan paradise."

"Again?"

Max grinned, glad that he had someone in his life that could keep him grounded. "Very funny. Give the baby a kiss for me, okay?"

"Will do. Be careful, Max."

"Always." After an exchange of 'I love you's, The Rook disconnected. He was mentally preparing himself for a confrontation with the Heir of Atlantis, hoping that all of his training would even the playing field.

Alaska-Jim tore into the food given him, particularly enjoying the strips of meat jerky the girls had brought with them. His whiskers were dripping with saliva and his eyes were wide, giving him the look of a madman.

Imelda, sitting closest to him, was the first to verbally prod him. "You promised us answers," she reminded him.

Jim sighed, lowering his hands away from his mouth. "We managed to find this place with one of Jan's atomic planes, but Sun Koh immediately realized that there things that weren't right. There were signs of habitation here but not nearly enough to coincide with Koh's stories." Jim wiped his lips with the back of a furred sleeve. "But Sun Koh knew a spell that would transport us into the Hollow Earth. He'd come to believe that an Aryan offshoot from Atlantis had holed up in there but that they'd forgotten their way. We were going to whip them into shape and then restore Thule. And we did, too." Jim smiled at the memory. "We reminded them of the reasons why the Aryans are the greatest race of people ever to walk this world." His eyes flickered over to Akemi and for a moment, he almost looked chagrined for having unwittingly insulted her for being non-Aryan. But then he looked back at Käthe and his doubts seemed to vanish. "Once we'd won, Sun Koh offered to send us back home, saying he'd follow soon after. He did the spell again... but this time, something went wrong. Some of us were killed on the spot... Hell, I think all of them were, except for me. I ended up back here... and discovered just how awful this place really was."

Käthe glanced around. They had set up a small campsite near the well and the sky was clear. There didn't appear to be anything hellish about the island at present, though every now and again the volcano in the distance would spew out a noxious cloud of smoke. "How long have you been here, Jim? And what's so awful about this island?"

"I believe it's been two years. Honestly, I have no idea. Time begins to run together... if not for my experience in the wilds, I never would have been able to survive." He tossed aside the last of his food, seemingly having lost his appetite. "As for what makes this place so awful... well, you will see. They only come out on certain nights, usually after a heavy rainfall. They scavenge the island, looking for any birds or monkeys that might be foolish enough to fall into their grasp. I've seen boats come to these shores, too, their crews filling the bellies of the beasts here. And, of course, they'd love to sink their teeth into me. And you."

A crunch of leaves caused Akemi to spring up, sword drawn. "What sort of beasts are they?"

The answer came when seven of the creatures shambled into view. They

Akemi - The leathal Fury from Japan

were froglike things, with green skin and large, wet-looking eyes. They walked upright like men, but their webbed fingers and toes were ample evidence that they never sprang forth from a woman's womb. Pink tongues flicked out, tasting the air like they were snakes. They brandished no weapons but at the tip of each webbed finger was a sharp claw that gleamed in the moonlight. The creatures were all male, their sexual organs hanging heavily between their legs. Each of the monsters walked with stooped backs making it hard to gauge their true height, but Käthe estimated that they were slightly shorter than an average human being.

"They live in the deep waters and only come up on land to feed… and to look for human women to fornicate with." Alaska-Jim stood up and drew forth a large knife. "Ladies, perhaps you should step back and allow me to--?"

Akemi was already in action. She sprang forward, her blade whirling through the air. The katana dug deep into the neck of the nearest creature, decapitating it in one stroke. She then spun about and jabbed at another, but this one grabbed hold of the blade and gave it a good yank. Blood spurted from the creature's injured palms but its strength allowed it to divest Akemi of her weapon.

Imelda came to Akemi's aid, discharging her pistols. The bullets ripped through the monster's skull and sent it tumbling to the ground. Akemi shot her fellow Fury a look of gratitude as she plucked up her katana.

Käthe joined the fray, unrolling her whip and flicking it toward one of the monsters. It wrapped around its neck, but it fought back with amazing strength, using it to pull Käthe toward it. She resisted at first but realized she lacked the power to win a tug-of-war with the beast. Instead, she allowed herself to be yanked closer, using a spring-activated dagger strapped to the underside of her arm. It popped out into her hand and she brought it up into the underside of the creature's throat. Warm red blood gushed from the wound and the monster roared in agony, its strangled cry ending suddenly as Käthe yanked the blade to the side. The motion freed the blade from the creature's throat and also ended its life.

The clearing was now a mass of bodies as the other beasts streamed forward, eager to avenge their fallen comrades. Akemi found herself backed up against one of the stone buildings, two of the monsters swiping at her with their claws. One of them raked two long crimson lines across her upper chest, ripping through her clothing. She responded with a warrior's cry, baring her teeth and slashing back with her own weapon. She disemboweled one and then cut the other one open from groin to neck.

Alaska-Jim joined the fray at this point, moving to stand beside Käthe. The two of them used their daggers like extensions of their own bodies, carving up the amphibians with relative ease.

Imelda remained out of the main battleground, reloading twice as she emptied the chambers of her guns. Her aim was sharp – and it had to be, to avoid hitting her allies in the melee.

When The Furies and Alaska-Jim realized that there were no more of the beasts to slay, all of them stood in place, panting from exertion.

"There will be more of them," Jim muttered. "Kill one and it somehow sends a message to the others. It somehow sends them all into a frenzy. They'll stop by sunrise, though. They can't abide the light of day."

Käthe glanced at the ruins around them and decided that they didn't offer enough protection. "Gather your belongings," she told the other Furies. "We're going to resume our march upwards."

"Toward the volcano?" Jim asked.

"Unless you have a better idea?"

Jim opened his mouth to speak, but a large rock crashed into the back of his skull and his eyes rolled upward. Blood was already flowing freely down his back as he fell forward, his face landing hard in the dirt. Käthe looked up to see another half-dozen of the frog monsters moving toward them. This time, several of them brandished clubs and large stones.

"Leave everything that's not essential!" she barked, bending down to grab a pack filled with food. "Let's go!"

The Furies set a quick pace and the frog-like men were unable to keep up. Twenty minutes after they had abandoned the campsite, the women were far enough up the mountain that they no longer heard sounds of pursuit. Käthe called their march to a halt when they came to another structure, this one resembling an old-fashioned schoolhouse. She pulled free a set of binoculars from her pack and looked down the hill, while Imelda and Akemi sat on the steps of the building and caught their breath.

Far down below, she caught sight of the frog people. They were swarming around the campsite, ripping open anything they'd left behind and strewing it across the ground, even on top of their fallen people. Alaska-Jim was being ripped apart for food, a sight that nauseated Käthe. She tossed the binoculars away and sighed.

"We're going to stay up here the rest of the night," she said. "One of us will keep watch at all times."

Imelda leaned back, stretching out her long legs. "And tomorrow? What's the plan then?"

Käthe smiled at her friend. "We'll plant a flag on top of that volcano and claim Atlantis in the name of the Axis powers."

Both Imelda and Akemi laughed at that. They knew she was joking – though all three were loyal to the nations that had spawned them, they had forged closer ties with one another.

Käthe put her hands on her hips. "We're going to do what we were told to do – examine every inch of this island and then see if we can prove or disprove that it's Atlantis."

"Or die trying," Imelda added under her breath.

Käthe nodded. "Or die trying."

THE SCORCHED GOD

Sun Koh was not the sort of man to be nervous, no matter what the time or place. But his breath was somewhat quicker than normal and his attention to detail strangely off-kilter as he entered Shani's hotel room. The suite was dimly lit and there was a peculiar odor in the air. It smelled of medicine and disinfectant, not scents that he normally associated with his lover.

"Shani?" he asked, though his ears picked her up before she'd come into view. The squeaking of the wheels immediately froze the blood in his veins and he had to stop himself from looking away. He didn't want to see her like this, though he knew that he could not insult her by giving her less than his full attention.

Ashanti Garuda pushed herself toward him, navigating her way around the table in the center of the room. Her face was still as lovely as he remembered and the diamond stud in her left nostril caught the light in a most attractive manner. She wore gossamer thin robes, the duskiness of her nipples clearly visible. But Sun Koh found his gaze sliding downwards, to her legs. They ended in stubs just above where her knees should have been. A woman who had moved with such incredible grace was now a cripple, bound to a chair for her mobility.

"My Prince," she said, speaking in perfect Atlantean. "You have no idea how pleased I am to see you again."

Sun Koh knelt in front of her, taking her hands in his. "What happened to you? Who did this?"

Something halfway between a smile and a frown touched her lips. "After you vanished, I waited for you as long as I could. And then I returned to doing what I do best. Killing Englishmen. Unfortunately, one of them held a grenade in his hand. I survived, but without my legs."

"And the man you were fighting?"

"He did not survive at all."

"Good. But why are you still in this country?"

"The British have good doctors and I have the money to pay for them. I have suffered through many infections."

"I will fix you. Somehow... I will find a way to give you back your legs."

Shani laughed, a rare sound from her and one that she only allowed herself when alone with Sun Koh. "You have given me back my heart, my prince. That's a far greater gift than my legs would be."

Sun Koh leaned forward and kissed her, their tongues connecting in a most sensual manner. He lifted her out of her chair then and carried her without preamble to her bed. After laying her on her back, he stripped himself completely before doing the same to her. Throughout, her eyes smoldered with passion.

They made love for several hours before Sun Koh allowed himself release. They shuddered simultaneously and then lay gasping against one another. He remained inside of her as he breathlessly recounted all that had happened since he'd last seen her.

When they were at last lying on their backs, staring at the ceiling, it was Shani who broke the silence. "Your people need you, Sun Koh. The war is not going well."

Sun Koh turned his head to look at her. He had read up on the war that was spreading across the globe like wildfire. "The Axis Powers are winning," he said.

"Only for now. The entrance of the Americans into the battle is the beginning of the end. And Hitler is mishandling everything involving the Russians." Shani spoke with obvious distaste for the man. Sun Koh knew that she agreed with most of Germany's eugenics program… but her trust in Hitler's military strategy seemed to outweigh that.

"What would you have me do? Hitler seems to have no use for me. I was en route to Berlin when I received word that I should come see you instead."

"Yes, Hitler contacted me when you arrived. He wants me to distract you here. He even asked me what it would take for me to poison you."

Sun Koh's eyes opened wide. "But why? The man trusted me implicitly before I left!"

"He is more paranoid now. And he is afraid that people will rally around you, threatening his own control of the masses. That's why he didn't want you going to Berlin."

"But he authorized The Furies to look for me."

"No. The OFP did that. Besides, no one expected it to work. It was just a training mission for the girls and something to placate Käthe. She had been demanding this opportunity for ages."

"You know so much about the workings of The Reich."

"I may be crippled but my ears still work just as well as ever."

"Still amazing as ever," Sun Koh said, meaning every word. Shani was the closest thing he'd found to a highborn woman of his own time. "So he plans to do away with me."

"Eventually. But he knows how dangerous you are. He won't do it directly, lest you figure him out."

Sun Koh slid from the bed, his sweat-slickened body glistening. His every feature was perfection, like the chiseled depiction of an Aryan god. "I think I may not be real."

"That makes no sense."

"I mean that I was created on something called Un-Earth. I was designed to be an Aryan superman for propaganda purposes. When I was sent into the future, I was actually sent from Un-Earth to this world… but something went wrong and I ended up getting here earlier than intended. I time traveled but not the way they wanted me to! After giving it some thought, I've come to suspect that my arrival here actually led to my creation. When I vanished in 1938, someone involved with the Un-Earth program made sure I was included in the new history for that false world. When I was sent 'forward in time' on Un-Earth, I ended up in 1932 on this world. It's a causal loop."

Shani pushed herself up with her arms. She watched him intently. "Beloved, I don't understand all that you're saying… but I know that it changes nothing. You are here now and there are things you must do."

Sun Koh nodded, knowing she was right. Whatever his origins, he was dedicated to the survival and success of the Aryan race. He turned to face her, hands on his hips. Despite his nudity, he managed to maintain a regal air. "What do you suggest?"

"Go to your private sanctum and get one of your super-weapons. Use it to destroy the Allies. No matter what the Fuehrer's faults – and they are many – we cannot allow ourselves to lose this war. If the Allies are victorious, Germany will be neutered and the rise of the Aryans might become a lost goal."

Sun Koh's private sanctum was hidden away in the Arctic and was protected by a unique emerald dome that rendered it invisible from the air and impervious to radar detection. The only ones who knew of its existence were Sun Koh's aides and a small Inuit tribe that had been so cowed by Sun Koh that they would never speak of the place. The Prince of Atlantis had journeyed to the sanctum whenever he needed solitude and it was there that his most dangerous weapons – ones that were far too dangerous to share with the 20th century world – were kept.

"If I were to do that," Sun Koh said, "then I would want to be the one using the devices. I won't turn them over to Germany. Not yet."

"And you shouldn't! It is your destiny to be our savior and no one else's!"

Sun Koh made his decision and began dressing. "We should depart at once. I have no fear of Hitler's assassins but if he learns that you haven't carried out his orders, he might be able to detain us."

Shani remained where she was, though she looked away from her lover.

"What is wrong?" Sun Koh asked, sensing her troubled nature.

"I am not going with you."

"Why not?"

"Because I plan to die in the morning."

Sun Koh approached the bed and sat down beside her. "Explain yourself."

"Tomorrow an attaché from the United States is having a meeting with British and French officials. They're having the meeting here. I plan to detonate enough explosives to kill everyone in the building."

"You don't have to be here to do that. Set a detonator."

"This is how I have chosen to end my life. I have served Kali well and she has rewarded me with so much. But now it is time. You know that I am far older than I appear. I am tired and I am crippled. Give me the respect I deserve and allow me to choose the place and means of my death."

A normal man would have argued this point, proclaiming his love and desire for his partner. But Sun Koh was not a normal man. He saw the wisdom in Shani's eyes and had far too much regard for her to try and dissuade her. Though the course she had chosen would sadden and pain him, it was her decision to make. "I will miss you," he said at last and this admission meant more to her than if he'd shouted his love at the top of his lungs.

They embraced, kissing with all the passion they could bear. He pulled away from her at last and finished getting dressed. He then left her room without another word. Anything more would cheapen their last moments and neither wanted that.

Still, at the very last moment, Sun Koh turned while standing in the doorway. He exchanged a final glance with Ashanti Garuda and then he was gone, the door shutting on a very important chapter in his life.

Chapter V
From the Heavens They Fall

The Rook's airplane banked low over Atlantis and Max craned his neck, trying to catch sight of a suitable place for a landing. There was a rocky shoreline and The Rook was not surprised to spot a boat resting on the beach. He assumed that this was Sun Koh's, though he couldn't be certain. It was a foggy morning and even though the sun was shining bright, the clouds hung heavy around the island, making visibility difficult.

Not satisfied with any of the landing sites he could see, The Rook flipped a switch and activated several devices mounted on the bottom of the plane. These converted the airship into something suitable for use in the water and the new landing gear was set in place by the time he lowered the plane until it was skimming the ocean's surface. The Rook stopped the engine and dropped anchor just offshore.

Max waded ashore with no supplies. He planned to return to the plane if he needed to but if pressed, he would have admitted that he didn't expect to be on the island very long. He would either run into Sun Koh soon and the two would sort things out or he'd find out that the Atlantean was already gone and the boat belonged to someone else. In that case, The Rook would be gone in pursuit of Sun Koh as quickly as possible.

The Rook paused, reconsidering those plans. He saw three sets of footprints coming from the boat and vanishing up into the jungle. From the depressions that hadn't yet been washed away by the surf, he guessed that all three sets belonged to women. Even more curious were dozens of prints coming to and from the water itself. These prints were webbed and sank deeper into the wet sand than the women's did. The Rook knelt and examined one of them, coming to the obvious conclusion that something inhuman had come onto this island recently and then left again.

The Rook straightened up, drawing one of his pistols. He could easily spot which direction the women had gone in, for they had hacked a clean path up the incline, apparently heading toward the volcano.

Max set off after them, thinking that even if they didn't lead him to Sun Koh, they might at least have some answers… or, possibly, be in need of rescuing. For the next twenty minutes, he moved through the jungle, glad that he'd left his heavy coat back in the plane. It didn't take long for his shirt to become dripping wet with sweat and it clung to his athletic physique like a second skin. He finally came to a halt when he entered a clearing, surrounded by a number of crumbling buildings. A well lay in the center of the clearing but The Rook virtually ignored it and all the structures. He was instead interested in the strange corpses that littered the ground. At least one of them appeared to be human, though the flesh had been so torn away that it was difficult to judge. The rest of the bodies, though, were obviously what had made the web-footed prints down on the beach. The strange frog-like creatures weren't dissimilar to things he'd encountered before. These so-called Deep Ones had underwater colonies all around the world and typically made raids on land to find food or to satisfy the peculiar lusts that afflicted them.

The Rook was examining one of them when he felt something nudge against the back of his skull and the all-too familiar sound of a gun being cocked.

"Stay where you are, masked man," a female voice said in English, though Max thought he detected a slight Italian lilt to the words.

The Rook turned his head slightly and saw two more women standing nearby. Each wore slightly sexualized versions of standard military attire: one wore German, the other Japanese. It stood to rights that the Italian behind him was dressed in the same manner. "Did you ladies do this?" he asked, gesturing with his hands toward the corpses of the Deep Ones.

"Yes," Akemi said, stepping close enough for him to see the length of her blade. "And we should do the same to you."

"I agree with that," Imelda said with a laugh. "This American bastard's done more to damage the OFP than anyone else. We're laughingstocks because he keeps defeating our best agents."

"He hasn't beaten the best yet," Käthe pointed out. "He's never faced us."

The Rook smiled at that. He had a suspicion that he'd heard of these women – The Furies they were called. A group of highly trained female agents representing the various facets of the Axis powers. Supposedly, they were able to best any man on the planet.

The Rook spun about with incredible speed, knocking Imelda's hand aside. The Italian pulled the trigger, but the bullet shot straight into the ground. Before she could recover, The Rook had driven a punch into her midsection, causing her to double over. He then grabbed hold of her gun hand, pointed it up at Akemi and, placing his fingers over Imelda's and squeezing, fired it twice at the Asian beauty. Akemi dove out of the way, but one of the bullets grazed her shoulder, leaving a line of trickling blood.

Imelda yanked her hand free, muttering a string of curses in Italian. Her anger only increased when The Rook delivered a blow to her chin, striking her with an upwards thrust of his palm.

The Rook suddenly felt something wrap around his neck with painful strength. He saw that Käthe had caught him up with her whip and she gave it a yank, tightening the grip on his neck. He could barely breathe, but he tried to stay focused on what needed to be done. His hand fumbled with the hilt of his dagger, sheathed against his waist. Unfortunately, Akemi was back on her feet and had spotted his intention. She moved forward quickly, stabbing with her katana. She slid the blade into his midsection, expertly avoiding anything that would prove fatal. Max cried out in shock, feeling his belly growing warm and wet as his blood spilled from the wound.

Imelda then finished him off by slamming the butt of her pistol against the back of his head. He fell face first to the ground, wondering if he'd ever see his wife and son again.

Käthe was on him quickly, freeing his neck from her whip's embrace. She rolled him onto his back and examined his wound, giving Akemi a smile. "That's amazing how you do that."

Akemi shrugged, pulling out a small white cloth from one of her pockets. She wiped her blade clean. "All it takes is a thorough knowledge of human anatomy… and the confidence that you're not about to make a mistake."

"The only mistake being made here is to not kill him," Imelda said. "I know what the standing orders are: that if anyone captures The Rook, they're to transport him to one of the Axis powers' capitals… but all three of us know how dangerous he is. We've heard the stories. Let's kill him and just agree to tell everyone there was no way to bring him in alive."

"I have to admit, I agree with her," Akemi said. She was rubbing her wounded shoulder.

Imelda seemed surprised but pleased by Akemi's statement. She turned a hopeful face toward Käthe, thinking that with two votes on her side she might be able to sway the team's leader.

The lovely German, however, shook her head. "No. We need to find out some information first. What is he doing here? Does he know that Sun Koh has returned? Has he told anyone else if he does?" She saw the flash of anger that passed through Imelda's eyes and smiled in a placating manner. "After we question him, we can kill him."

That brought a grin back to Imelda's face. "I'll truss him up."

Käthe stepped away and took out her long-range radio communicator. She sent a signal to Captain Mueller, whose zeppelin was hiding in the clouds several miles off the island. Given the storms that seemed to cling to the rocky expanse of land, the decision had been made to keep the airship as far from it as their communications would allow.

"Yes?" Mueller sounded relieved to hear from her.

"Is something wrong, Captain?"

"An unidentified craft passed us not long ago. It didn't seem to spot us so we remained in hiding… but I was concerned that they were looking for the island."

"They were. We've captured them and would like to return to the zeppelin with him in tow. I believe that he might have information that might prove useful to us."

"Is he a soldier?"

"It's The Rook," Käthe said, looking back at the unconscious vigilante. He was more handsome than she had expected. Most of the stories she'd been told painted him as a horrible degenerate, but as she stared at his wavy hair and olive-tinged complexion, she thought he had a Mediterranean look to him and it was very appealing.

"Fraulein?" Mueller asked.

"Sorry, Captain. My mind was wandering. Could you repeat what you said?"

"I was telling you to be careful. This could mean a promotion for me and increased respect for your group."

Käthe knew she shouldn't be amazed, but she was. Here they had a man in their possession who had single-handedly become a major thorn in the collectives backsides of the Axis and all Mueller was concerned about was his promotion. "Of course, Captain," she said, keeping her tone cold and impersonal. "When will you be ready to receive us?"

"We're on our way to pick you up now. Good work. You've done something that many men have failed to do. Heil Hitler!"

"Heil Hitler," Käthe repeated emotionlessly. She turned off her communicator and pursed her lips thoughtfully. Akemi was now kneeling at The Rook's side, rummaging through his pockets. When she attempted to free his dagger from its sheath, she jerked her hand away as if she'd touched a hot stove.

"What happened?" Imelda asked, bending down to look at Akemi's fingertips. They were bright red and obviously painful.

"I don't know. That knife of his… it's not natural."

"It's the Knife of Elohim," Käthe muttered, unable to hid her disdain for the fact that the other two Furies didn't take research as seriously as she did. "It was bathed in the blood of Christ and now it deals more harm to evil creatures than is normal."

Imelda laughed aloud. "Hear that, Akemi? You're evil."

"I think it's just based off the Judeo-Christian mindset," Käthe said. "So non-Christians would be 'evil.'"

"You're no fun," Imelda said, with a roll of her eyes. She finished tying The Rook's hands and feet, testing the strength of the bonds. "He's not getting out of this."

"Look at these," Akemi said, holding up one of The Rook's modified handguns. "The barrels filled with miniature rounds, dozens of them."

Imelda took the gun and lined up the sights, firing it at a nearby tree. The trunk splintered upon impact and Imelda whistled. "They might be small, but

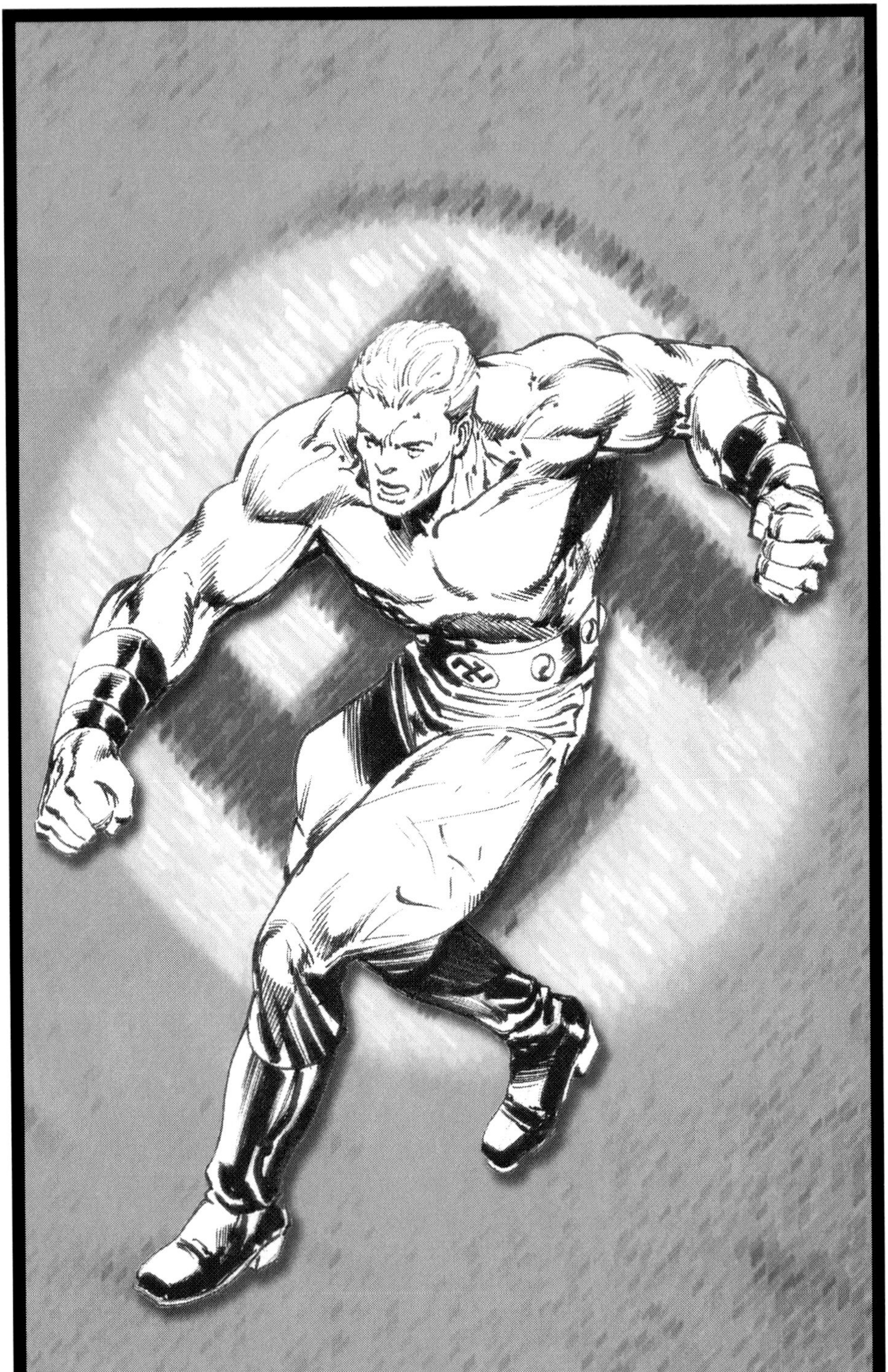

those bullets pack a punch." She stuck the pistol into her belt and claimed the other one as well.

Käthe started back down the path, heading toward the beach. "Mueller will be here for us soon. Can you two drag The Rook?"

Imelda wrapped a length of rope around her hand and began moving forward. She grunted a bit, but gravity assisted her since they were moving down an incline. "I can manage."

Akemi knew better than to try and offer her assistance. Imelda liked showing off her physical strength and would take any suggestion otherwise as an insult.

The Furies reached the beach in a short amount of time and Imelda dropped the rope, gasping for air. "He weighs more than he looks," she explained.

Käthe wasn't listening. Though she would have been loath to admit it, she was terribly worried. Most of her concern centered on Sun Koh. The man had become an ideal in her mind and that had been cemented by their lovemaking. The notion that The Rook might not be the only one to know of the Prince's return… that other forces might be massing to try and destroy Sun Koh… it filled Käthe with the kind of fear that she'd felt only a few times in her life.

Once more she looked down at The Rook. She'd find out everything that the vigilante knew, even if it meant that his suffering would become the stuff of which legends were made.

Sun Koh was not the pilot his friend Jan Mayen was, but he was nonetheless quite adept. He'd managed to convince a loyal German at the airfield to allow him to take one of their long-range flyers, calling upon the youth's overly impressionable nature. Like so many other Germans he had met since his revival, the young man had been a faithful reader of Sun Koh's exploits, or at least he had before they had ceased being published. Sun Koh now wondered if the government order to no longer publish "frivolous" adventure novels had actually been an attempt to erase the impact Sun Koh had had on the populace.

Sun Koh's plane had required refueling once along the way and he'd been forced to take up arms at the small military base at which he'd stopped. It had belonged to a foreign power, but Sun Koh was able to overpower the small squadron of men stationed there.

And now he was angling his plane in for a landing on a smooth patch of ground, deep in the frigid wastes of the Arctic. The plane settled down, kicking up large amounts of snow and ice. It skidded a bit, twisting off-course, but Sun Koh was able to bring it under control.

He wore a parka and protective goggles as he jumped to the icy ground. It was possible to blind oneself here in the Arctic, as the sun reflected off the miles of white terrain. Sun Koh remembered that he had brought Alaska-Jim with him on one of his first journeys here, when he had still been scouting for possible locations. The famed trapper and hunter had impressed upon Koh the need for adequate protection from the elements.

As Koh approached his private sanctum, he felt a momentary pang of regret. He missed his friends, having come to regard them as worthy of a place by his side in the Aryan kingdom that was still to come. Now they were all dead, including his beloved Shani. He respected her wishes and had done nothing to save her. In fact, he had not even checked the news reports to see if her mission had succeeded. In his mind, they had already parted and would not be reunited until the next life, in whatever form that might be.

The sanctum came into view as he stepped over a particularly large bank of snow. The emerald dome seemed to absorb all light, somehow rendering its surroundings so nondescript that you almost overlooked it, despite the fact that it was the only structure in sight for miles.

Upon reaching the sanctum, Sun Koh pulled off the glove covering his right hand. He pressed his open palm against the smooth surface of the sanctum, which appeared to have no windows or doors. A hum answered his touch and a moment later the dome's surface began to part, revealing a thin entranceway. It was so small that Sun Koh had to turn sideways to slip inside.

As soon as his foot touched the dome's floor, the interior lights came on. A fireplace flared to life, the crackling of the fire somewhat masked by a melodious tune that was piped through speakers mounted on the corner of each wall. The sanctum was furnished in leather, with a couch and two plush chairs. A polar bear rug lay on the floor and a well-stocked laboratory was arranged along two of the walls. The air was not musty at all, as it was kept recycled by a purification system devised by Sun Koh himself. The faint scent of roses reached the Prince's nose and he smiled, remembering that he'd added that touch to the air conditioning system in hopes that Shani would like it. Unfortunately, she would never get the chance to visit the sanctum.

Sun Koh approached the lab area, kneeling to look at the storage containers built into the wall. Not a single wasted space existed in the sanctum. Everything, including the walls and the furniture, served multiple purposes. In some places he kept his devices and tools, other things could be opened up to reveal other features that one wouldn't have assumed they'd serve. The couch doubled as a bed; the chairs could be used as long-range radios, due to the complex wiring set into the bottom of the seats; and the walls contained dozens of storage cabinets.

Sun Koh set aside a number of items that could have made a massive difference in the war effort but which didn't suit what he had planned. A small glass capsule containing enough purple dust to render most of North America sterile within a month caught his eye and he briefly considered the possibilities before moving on. He wanted something that would instill fear in the enemies of the Aryan people and that would shatter their will to fight. He wanted something big and something flashy, the sort of thing that fathers would fearfully tell to their children in future years.

He wanted the Solar Cannon.

It didn't look like a doomsday weapon, though that's what it was. Fourteen inches long and about as thick around as his forearm, the device was sealed on one end and opened in a triangular shape on the other. A crystalline oval on the top of the device served to capture solar energy and amplify it. The Solar Cannon could be hooked up to a larger device that Sun Koh had invented, allowing him to project the destructive beam hundred of miles. It could literally carve up enemy cities, demoralizing his foes by killing them with virtually no defense possible.

Sun Koh froze in place, the Solar Cannon still held tightly in his hands. Amazingly, he heard movement behind him. The door had closed after he'd entered and no one besides himself should have been able to activate the fingerprint lock system… but there was no doubt about what he was hearing.

Sun Koh slowly set the Cannon down on the floor, pretending to continue sorting through the items in the cabinet. He turned his head slightly and looked behind him, his eyes opening wide as he caught sight of the intruder.

The man standing there looking quite calm and self-assured resembled a poet or orchestral conductor. He had a great mane of black hair, a high forehead, and hollow burning eyes that were deep-set in a gaunt face. His body was long and thin, but the most noticeable characteristic he possessed was his nose, which was long and slender, ending in a sharp point. It could almost be described as a beak, the shape and design of it was so pronounced. He wore robes of deep blue and upon his feet were fur-lined slippers of the matching color. On his right hand was a ring with a large blue stone set in its face and around his neck was another blue gem, this one glittering in the firelight.

As Sun Koh stood up, turning to face this man, he kept his surprise out of his voice. "Identify yourself," he said in German. He wasn't sure what nationality this man was, for his features were that of almost any Western nation.

The man clasped his hands behind his back and replied so fluently that Sun Koh wondered if he wasn't German by birth. "My name is Arthur Grin. I watched you approach this place and knew that I had to speak to you. You have no idea how long I've waited to meet you."

"You know who I am?"

"I have no idea."

Sun Koh clenched his jaw. A part of him wanted to simply kill this man and be done with him. He was eager to undertake the task that Shani had set for him: the eradication of The Allies. But Sun Koh was no pawn to his emotions: he needed to know who this man was, where he came from and whether or not he had allies waiting outside. "I am Sun Koh, Prince of Atlantis."

"Of course you are." Grin said these words without sarcasm, but Sun Koh bristled nonetheless. The thin man inclined his head toward the sofa. "May I sit?"

"If you wish. Your clothing would not provide adequate protection from the elements so you haven't been out there long." Sun Koh watched as Grin sat down and crossed legs at the knee.

"I've been living with the local Inuit tribe for quite some time. They keep me warm and well-fed, though as you can see, I don't require much in the way of sustenance."

Sun Koh sat down in a chair facing Arthur Grin. He locked eyes with the man, knowing that usually even the most strong-willed would melt before his gaze. Grin, however, held firm and showed no sign of weakness. "You said you've been waiting to meet me."

"Oh, yes. Most assuredly. You see, I was a prisoner of the Russian,s but I managed to escape. When I came upon the Inuit tribe, I was able to… convince them… to take me in, but I could sense that they were more afraid of something else. No matter how much I threatened or cajoled them, they would not reveal to me what secret they carried. But one day I took to wandering, surveying my new home… and I found this dome. I tried to find a way inside but could not. Returning to the village, I questioned them, realizing that this was probably what they were keeping from me. Do you know what they did? They tried to pretend that they didn't know what I was talking about. Even when I marched their leaders out here and confronted them with the dome, they acted as if they couldn't see it. They tried to make me think I was going insane."

Sun Koh said nothing during all of this, though he could easily imagine it was true. The Inuit people had regarded him as some sort of terrible White God. He had made them swear secrecy about his sanctum at the penalty of their souls.

Grin continued, not in the least bit displeased by how taciturn his host was being. "But I kept at it, kept probing and knocking. I finally got a few of them to admit to knowing about the place. They told me about the White God who had forged it out of pure magic. According to them, you would return at some point and claim the dark powers you'd trapped within." Grin leaned forward, his dark eyes glittering. "And is that what you're here for? To unleash dark powers?"

"What if I am?"

Grin laughed and it was as remorseless a sound as any that Sun Koh had ever heard. "Why, then I want in, of course."

"What are you, Mr. Grin?"

"I've been called a criminal… a psychopath… and a manipulator. All of those might be true. But at my core I am a man who realizes that the world's veneer of civilization is just that: a veneer. The only way we can truly find peace is for someone with an indomitable will to seize control and force people to look in the mirror. Only by recognizing the darkness within can we truly drive it out."

Sun Koh stared at the man, wondering if he could prove useful in any way… or if he would simply prove too mad and too ambitious for his own good. Unfortunately, if Koh meant to avoid calling upon the German military to assist him, he would eventually require help in some other form. With all of his old trusted allies dead, he could use someone capable. "How did you get inside here? I know that the door closed behind me."

"I stepped in immediately after you did, then watched to see what you were doing."

"I would have sensed you."

"But you didn't."

Sun Koh's handsome face creased in a frown. Could Grin really be capable of evading his notice? Few human beings could claim that level of skill. Even Shani could not do it one hundred percent of the time and she was as capable of silent movement as anyone Sun Koh had ever met.

"I will allow you to assist me, Arthur Grin. But know this: if you betray me in any way, be it large or small… I will make you suffer in ways you cannot imagine."

Grin's eyes took on a cautious cast but he merely nodded his assent.

Sun Koh stood up. "Then let us begin. I'm planning to turn a weapon of incredible power upon the capital of the United States. Hundreds of thousands will die." Sun Koh watched Grin closely, to see if he would balk at that amount of mayhem. What he saw there was quite chilling: he saw not disgust or fear, but **anticipation.**

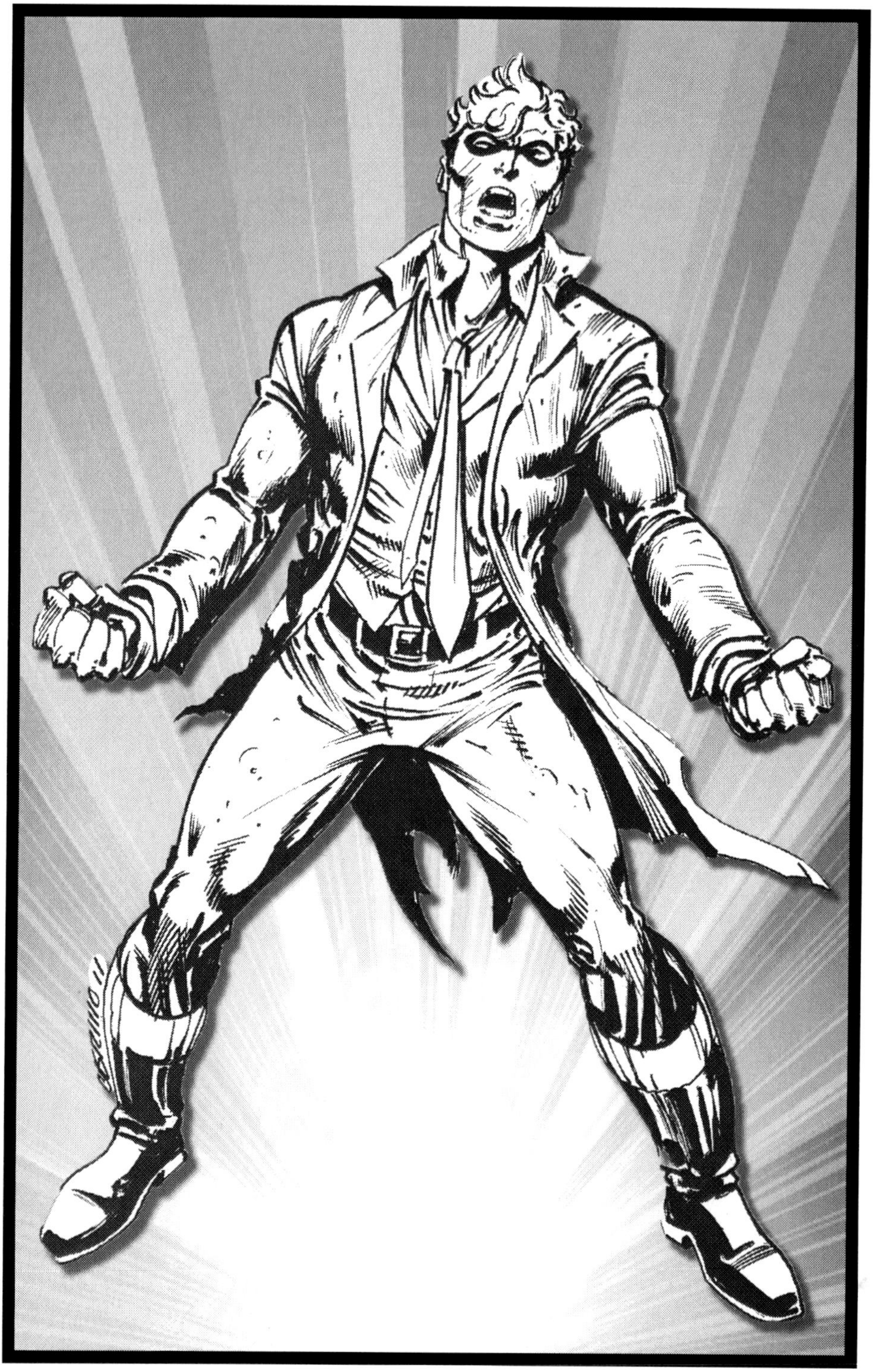

Chapter VI
Tortures, Great and Small

Max Davies was accustomed to unusual dreams. While most of his visions of the future came during his waking hours, his nocturnal excursions of the mind were typically more symbolic, reflecting those things that were troubling him.

As he sat tied to a chair, his vision blurred and his consciousness slipping in and out of reality, he dreamed of things that had never happened, could never happen... but which were nonetheless disturbing:

Men and women in fancy dress sat behind a chain link fence that ran the length of the arena. They wore Mardi Gras style masks over their faces, many of them adorned by glitter, feathers, and gaudy colors. The masks did little to hide their identities, but it was part of the game, part of the glamour. Here in the arena, you cast aside your public face and became someone new, someone more primal in his or her desires. Here you came to indulge in that most ancient of human pleasures: the sadomasochistic urges that even centuries of so-called civilization had failed to eliminate.

The Rook crouched with one hand raised behind him and the other held straight out before his well chiseled body. He moved in a semi-circle, sweat running down his lean torso. He wore only a pair of loose pants while his opponent was dressed in sandals, corduroy pants, and a vest. The man had been wearing a bead necklace when the battle had begun, but The Rook had quickly turned the jewelry into a weapon, nearly strangling the man with it before it had snapped. The beads had tumbled to the floor, becoming a perpetual hazard ever since. Twice even the nimble footed Rook had nearly slipped on the beads, which rolled about the floor at the slightest contact.

The Rook sensed that his opponent was tensing to strike and a dozen ways of incapacitating him sprang to mind. In truth, The Rook could have ended this battle long ago, but something had prevented him doing so. He realized that some part of him craved this, the excitement and violence. As his eyes briefly scanned the cheering crowd, he found himself recognizing many of those in the audience. Even with their masks in place, he knew who they were: his wife, Evelyn; their housekeeper Nettie and her nephew Joshua; Max's best friend, police chief William McKenzie; and Warren Davies, Max's dead father. They were all pumping their air with their fists, cheering him on to ever-greater acts of violence.

The attack finally came, accompanied by an animalistic roar. The Rook heard the reaction of the crowd, but he ignored them, throwing up a block that knocked the man's charge off course. The man stumbled and fell to the ground where he was unable to evade The Rook's next attack: a sharp kick with his heel to the neck. If he had so wished, The Rook could have snapped the man's neck like kindling. But Max was no deliverer of death, not if he could help it. The Rook had killed dozens, if not hundreds of men, but he never killed them when they were helpless.

The Rook relaxed, letting his arms fall by his sides. He slowly turned to acknowledge the crowd, who screamed their appreciation. Some of them demanded that the fallen man be finished but he silently refused, giving a brief shake of his head. He glanced toward the private viewing booth that overlooked the arena. There, his Sensei, the one who had trained him during his years in the Far East, sat watching impassively. The Warlike Manchu had groomed Max to be his heir, the one who would assume command of his vast criminal empire. Max had not known of the Manchu's true nature when he'd tracked the man down and asked to be taken in as a student... once he'd discovered the truth, he'd refused the honor that had been laid out for him. This had infuriated The Warlike Manchu and had begun a war of life-and-death that continued to this day. Max saw a look of resigned disgust settle on The Manchu's face.

That same look of disappointment was repeated on the faces of Max's father, wife, and friends. It hit him then, in a way that it had never done before: he was a failure to both his birth father and his surrogate one. Neither of them was satisfied with what he had turned out to be. He was neither the perfectly forged weapon against evil nor was he was dark enough to lead the Manchu's empire of crime.

And then cold water splashed into his face, forcing Max out of his dream and back into cold, hard reality. He spluttered, shaking his head in a vain attempt to clear it of the cloud of pain that ensnared it. He looked up to see The Furies watching him with expressions of amusement. The Italian held a dripping metal container in one hand. A man wearing the uniform of a Nazi zeppelin commander stood in the shadows, hands clasped behind his back. The hum of engines beneath The Rook's feet confirmed his suspicion that he was now an airborne prisoner of war.

"Welcome onboard The Valkyrie," the captain said in broken English.

"No need to butcher my native tongue. I can speak German," The Rook answered, flawlessly replying in the other man's language.

Akemi lashed out, catching The Rook with a vicious backhand. Max blinked, blood dripping from his split lip. "Remember, American, that the only reason you're currently alive is because we choose to let you live."

The Rook held Akemi's gaze, projecting such loathing that the Japanese woman took a step back. "Enjoy yourselves, ladies," he hissed between clenched teeth. "Because when I get out of here, I'm going to kick your behinds so hard you're going to sport a permanent boot print."

"Let's just kill him," Imelda said, shaking her head. "I really dislike American tough talk."

Mueller ignored her, staring intently at The Rook. He cleared his throat, drawing the hero's attention back to him. "Herr Rook. You do realize that you are one of the foremost enemies of the Reich. If I were to present you to the Fuehrer, dead or alive, I would soon be wearing so many medals that I could barely move under the weight of them."

"So why don't you do what the ugly girl says? Just kill me."

Imelda's eyes opened wide at the insult and she took a step toward him menacingly. Käthe caught her by the arm and shook her head. "Don't let him bait you," she whispered.

The Rook smirked at the exchange. Imelda was gorgeous, of course. Each of The Furies was the embodiment of male fantasy, but it was obvious at a glance that the Italian had a short fuse.

Mueller, for his part, seemed dead-set on pretending The Furies were not even present. "I don't want you dead. I want you to help me and, in return, I will help you."

Käthe looked sharply at Mueller, wondering where he was going with all this. They had talked only briefly before waking up The Rook. She had told him of her desire to question The Rook about his knowledge of Sun Koh and he had expressed an interest in finding out if The Rook knew anything about other occult objects that might appeal to The Fuehrer. She had thought that to be an acceptable line of inquiry, given the interest that The Reich had displayed in such things.

The Rook seemed equally perplexed. "What do you have in mind?"

"Are you familiar with the story of The Fourth Nail?"

"Yes."

Käthe stepped between Mueller and The Rook. She looked into the face of the zeppelin commander, keeping her voice low. "What are you doing?" she asked.

"Please move aside."

"Not without an explanation."

Mueller leaned close, his lips almost brushing Käthe's ear. "Please trust me. I promise that I will tell you everything, but I need to do this now."

Käthe pulled back, chewing her bottom lip. She didn't know Mueller very well, but she considered him to be an honorable man. She decided that she would allow this to continue – for now.

After Käthe had rejoined the other Furies, answering their questioning stares with a shrug of her shoulders, Mueller looked back at The Rook.

"Please tell me what you know," the German said.

The Rook didn't bother hiding his confusion. "According to legend, there were four nails to be used in the crucifixion of Christ. The first and second nails were for Christ's hands while the third was for his feet. The Fourth Nail was for his heart."

"But the Fourth Nail was never used," Mueller said, a faint smile on his lips.

"Right. Supposedly, a gypsy stole the nail and used it to repair his wagon. According to the story, God was pleased that the gypsy had stolen the object that would have brought instant death to his son. In return for the gypsy's unwitting service, he blessed the nail and those who held it. The possessor of the nail would be forgiven for his trespasses and would always be protected from harm."

Mueller was nodding now, pleased at what he was hearing. "And do you believe in the Nail's existence?"

"It's possible. I've certainly seen stranger things."

"Your own dagger was dipped in the blood of Jesus," Mueller pointed out. "What if I told you that I knew the location of The Fourth Nail?"

"I'd say you have too much time on your hands. Have you forgotten that God blessed the Fourth Nail? I doubt it would work for a damned Nazi."

"If it would work for a mongrel Gypsy, it would work for an Aryan," Mueller responded hotly. He composed himself quickly, his smile returning. "Regardless, I would like you to locate this item and claim it for me. In exchange, you will be allowed to go free."

The Rook noticed that the three women in the room did not seem pleased with this promise. "I don't believe you," he said. "First of all, why do you think I'd work for you at all? I like to think I'm plenty capable of getting free myself eventually and if not... I'd rather die than help a Nazi."

Mueller's lips twitched in silent amusement. "You are friends with Police Chief William McKenzie, are you not?" The Rook said nothing, though the slight shift in his features was enough to confirm that Mueller's information was correct. "He and a former agent of the OFP are currently lovers, I believe. Efforts have been made to forgive her past transgressions in exchange for her assistance to your government, but the fact remains that she is, as you would call her, a damned Nazi."

"She's turned over a new leaf."

"Yes. Well, perhaps her lover would be less inclined to believe so if he saw certain photographs that showed her in various activities that, shall we say, would diminish her modesty?"

The Rook could scarcely believe what he was hearing. "Are you trying to blackmail me into finding the Nail for you?"

"I'm trying to make a deal with you," Mueller corrected. "Find the Nail and

I do not release the photos."

"And how do I know you have them? You could be making it up."

"I can produce them for you. But I give you my word of honor that they do exist and they are quite shocking."

"Great. The blackmailer gives me his word of honor."

Mueller grunted, losing all semblance of good humor. "Think it over, Herr Rook. It may be the only thing that saves your life." Turning to Käthe, he said, "Question him as you wish but leave him in one piece in case he reconsiders my offer."

Mueller exited the room, leaving The Rook alone with three of the most beautiful and deadly women in the world.

"What the hell?" Imelda asked, looking from Käthe to Akemi. "I've never heard anything about The Reich looking for some nail."

"I think it's for him," Akemi answered. She looked pensive as she spoke. "I think we should send a message back to OFP leadership and let them know what's going on."

Käthe shook her head thoughtfully. "Not yet. Soon, if things keep going the way they are." She began to uncoil her bullwhip, snapping it loudly against the floor. "We have things to do first."

Akemi glanced back at The Rook, a flush coming to her features. "You shot me, you bastard," she said.

"To be fair," The Rook said, "The Italian girl was holding the gun."

Käthe sighed, having lost her patience. "Hit him." Her orders were somewhat imprecise, however, and both Imelda and Akemi struck him. The Italian girl punched him in the side of his face while Akemi raised a boot and drove it hard between his legs.

The Rook cried out in pain, his mind suddenly awash in pure sensation. Akemi followed her kick with a series of open-handed blows to his head and Max nearly blacked out. Imelda yanked his head back with a handful of his hair in her fingers.

"Say something smart again, American," she begged. "Say something else that I can hit you for."

The Rook spat out a bit of blood with each word. "You hit like a girl," he murmured.

Imelda drew her fist back and slammed it hard into The Rook's right eye. The blow knocked his head back so hard that he momentarily lost his bearings. He wasn't sure where he was or what was happening, but things cleared up quickly when he saw Käthe step past the other two women. She leaned over, providing him with a clear look at her ample cleavage. Under other, less painful, circumstances, he would have enjoyed the view.

"We can be much more subtle about this," she warned. "We can make your pain last for days, until you're crying like a little child. I'll personally pull out your fingernails one by one and feed them to you. Akemi knows places she can stab you that will be pure agony. And Imelda... well, Imelda would love to borrow my whip and flay you alive."

"What do you want from me?" Max asked. "You didn't act like you knew anything about The Nail...."

"I want to know why you came to the island and what you know about Sun Koh."

The Rook panted for a moment, trying to regain his sense of composure. His entire head ached and the pain in his groin was making him nauseous. "I have visions... of things that are in the future. I saw Sun Koh and I saw the three of you beating the hell out of me." He shook his head. "Guess I should have been able to avoid this one, huh? Anyway, I also saw Washington, D.C. under attack from kind of super-weapon. I think Sun Koh's related to that... and so I need to stop him."

"How did you find the island?"

The Rook hesitated, not wanting to get Glumm into any kind of trouble. But he realized that he would probably talk at some point or another – maybe if he went ahead and told them the truth, they'd lay off for a while and he could regain his strength. "I went to see a man named Glumm. He knew some of the stories about Sun Koh. He'd read some magazines featuring the guy."

"He's lying," Imelda said, but Käthe knew better. His words had the ring of truth to them. She wondered at his statement about Sun Koh using some sort of super weapon against the United States... she'd hoped he would do something of the sort, some incredible victory that would rally the Aryan world....

"So are you going to leave me alone, then?" The Rook eyed Imelda with distaste. If he were free, he'd teach her a lesson or two on manners.

Käthe straightened up and smiled sympathetically. "I'm sorry but that's not possible. If we were to leave you alone for even a few minutes, you'd probably find your way to freedom. You're too dangerous."

Imelda grinned like a predator. She was hoping that Käthe would keep her word and let them kill The Rook now that he'd answered her questions about Sun Koh. Her face fell in disappointment when Käthe gave her orders.

"Akemi, Imelda... work him over. But stop before you do any permanent damage. I want to talk to Captain Mueller before we kill him." The German woman reached out and stroked The Rook's chin. His face still hurt so much that he winced at the contact. "Such a shame," she mused aloud. "If you weren't so deadly, I'd consider keeping you as a pet." She slapped him hard, leaving a blood-red hand imprint on his cheek.

The Rook glared at her back as she turned and left the room. "I feel sorry for your kitty back home, lady," he murmured. He looked at Akemi and Imelda, who were now so close to him that their legs brushed his knees.

Akemi straddled his left leg, her pink tongue darting out to moisten her lips. "I'm sorry I hurt you," she said with a pout. "I was just angry." Her hand slipped between his thighs, cupping his genitals. "Should I kiss it to make it better?"

The Rook knew she was teasing him, hoping to weaken him somehow. Instead of replying, he jerked his head back and then forward. His forehead caught Akemi on her right temple, knocking her off his knee. She landed on her rump, reddening as Imelda began laughing.

Akemi stood up, drawing a long, slender knife from the interior of her uniform. The blade gleamed in the light and The Rook could easily imagine how sharp it was. "You will regret that, American. I'm going to make you scream."

Despite his steely nerve, The Rook found himself doing just that within moments. His shouts of agony carried all through the zeppelin.

Arthur Grin worked in almost complete silence. He had listened intently to Sun Koh's directions and then had simply gone about his assigned tasks, without any further need for instruction.

Sun Koh watched the man carefully, looking for any signs that Grin was not as loyal as he first appeared. But Grin was a conscientious worker. The Heir of Atlantis went over his Solar Cannon piece-by-piece, ensuring that the original design had been perfect. After verifying this, he took the Cannon out to the highest peak he could find and left it there, allowing the crystal to absorb the needed solar radiation.

Grin, meanwhile, was working on the long-range amplification device. It was a complicated piece of machinery, using technology that the lost civilization of Atlantis had possessed but which the modern world had long since forgotten. So much of Sun Koh's genius was wasted in this time because of the technological limitations that surrounded him. But the Solar Cannon was an exception to that rule: it would function nearly as well now as it would have in his time, the only difference being that in Sun Koh's own time, there would have been adequate defenses against such a thing.

Sun Koh checked his watch and realized it was time to retrieve the Solar Cannon from its spot on the peak. He left the sanctum and marched across the ice, ignoring the Inuit tribesmen watching him from a short distance away. They had begun arriving last night, setting up camp close enough to observe Sun Koh's comings and goings. They were obviously curious but still too fearful to actually approach him.

Sun Koh found the Solar Cannon exactly as he'd left it, though the crystal's gauge now read that it was full. Because of the ingenious power system, the Cannon could run for months off one complete charge. He was about to return to the sanctum when he heard a peculiar whining sound. It was much like the trilling of a bird though there were none in the world that sounded exactly like this. Sun Koh paused, recognizing the sound instantly but almost refusing to believe it. He reached into the pocket of his jodhpurs and pulled out a small rectangular-shaped object. It was a radio communication device that he'd created during his first stint in the 20th century. It was far from perfect, shorting out so often that Sun Koh had abandoned it for all intents and purposes. But he'd given the small devices to a few of his closest companions, each of them receiving a specific code to identify them.

Sun Koh stared at the small analog screen. It showed a three-digit number that identified the message as coming from Jan Mayen. Activating the device, Sun Koh held it up to his ear. "Who is this? How did you get this device?"

The sounds that greeted him were enough to chill the blood in his veins. They were inhuman, guttural noises that were all-too familiar. An Atlantean cult had once worshipped the fearsome forms of Father Dagon and Mother Hydra, the dark lords of the sea. It was said that some of them even went so far as to mate with the loathsome creatures, producing hybrid monstrosities. Sun Koh had accompanied his father on one hunting mission, raining death upon the beasts from their ships. Though he had not gotten too close to the beasts, he still remembered the sounds that they made and the odor of their salt-encrusted flesh. They had been dubbed Deep Ones by Sun Koh's people and were regarded as harbingers of doom.

A young girl's voice suddenly emerged from the device. She sounded out of breath and scared but reasonably calm. The noises from The Deep Ones grew quieter and Sun Koh assumed that the girl was moving further away from them. "Is this really Sun Koh?" she whispered.

"Yes."

"My name is Elsa Mayen. You knew my father."

Sun Koh paused. He knew that name though he'd only seen the girl in photographs. Jan had told him of a fling he'd had with a Jewish prostitute and how the woman had later confronted him, claiming that he was the father of the little girl she'd borne. Jan had made it clear that he had no desire to be a father to a half-blood mongrel, but he'd still sent money to take care of the girl's most basic needs. "Where are you?" Sun Koh demanded.

"I'm on Atlantis, looking for you. All I've found so far are a bunch of monsters, though."

"How did you get there?"

"In one of my father's planes." Sun Koh heard the sound of a door being slammed shut, followed quickly by the pre-flight routine that he remembered so well. The atomic plane hummed loudly, nearly drowning out Elsa Mayen's voice. "I've been tapping into Axis radio signals for the past year, doing all I can to help the cause… and when I heard reports that you'd returned, I tracked this place down. It wasn't easy."

"You need to get away from there."

"That's what I'm doing. Where are you?"

"Give me a reason to trust you, Elsa. As far as I knew, your father never taught you how to fly his planes."

"My father was ashamed of me and afraid of how you'd react to knowing that he was seeing me. He taught me how to fly and he taught me to love the Aryan part of me – and to despise the weakness that's in my blood from my mother's side. I'm a true German, my Prince! And I've waited for you and my father to return ever since you vanished!"

"Your father is dead," Sun Koh sadly replied. "He was as good a man as any I've ever known."

The girl was silent for a moment but when she spoke again, Sun Koh was impressed by her tone. "I suspected as much. I will miss him. Can I please serve you? I've offered my talents to the Fatherland but all they want is my plane, not me."

Sun Koh smiled. Given her youth – she could be no more than 16 by his counting – and the Reich's overall view of women, he could easily believe that. Though Germany used female agents such as The Furies, they were treated as lesser than their male counterparts and often ignored entirely. "I will give you coordinates where you can meet me. Can you fly to the Arctic?"

"Of course. This plane can cover many thousands of miles without refueling. It's the culmination of my father's genius – he was working on this design when he disappeared. Even you will be my impressed, my prince."

"I'm sure I will be." Sun Koh gave her precise coordinates and then signed off, a new lightness of spirit giving him hope that his mission would be successful. He had lost his old allies but gained new ones in the form of Grin and Elsa Mayen. He wondered if The Furies could be brought to his side, as well. They were smart and very capable – and the one named Käthe seemed particularly devoted to his cause.

He was still thinking these thoughts when he returned to the sanctum, where he found Arthur Grin standing beside the completed amplification device.

"You worked very quickly," Sun Koh observed.

"The design is ingenious, but once I understood the process, it was relatively simple."

Sun Koh nodded, examining the device. "It looks fine. Now we have only to test it."

"Might I suggest we use the natives as target practice?"

The Heir to Atlantis paused, looking at Grin for a moment before speaking. "You wish to kill the people who took care of you all this time?"

"Yes. I do." Grin seemed to come alive with some awful inner light. "I see a day when all civilized men will come together in knowledge and peace... but there have to be examples made. There has to be a time of fire and death before the world can be remade. Let these men who worship us as gods sacrifice themselves for the greater good."

Sun Koh wondered just how mad Grin might be. Still, the device needed testing and the Inuit peoples were a degenerate species, one of the many servant races who would serve the Aryans in the coming days. Without a word, he began attaching the Solar Cannon to the amplification device. With Grin at his side, he exited the Sanctum and pointed the barrel of the weapon toward the growing crowd of natives. Several of them took notice of the strange device that rested on Sun Koh's shoulder, looking much like a missile launcher. A loud murmuring arose from the Inuit group but Sun Koh ignored it, slowly raising the barrel until it was pointed at the skies above their heads. He activated the device, which began humming like an oncoming freight train. A beam of purple light shot from the device, vanishing into the clouds. Sun Koh continued discharging the device for nearly a full minute before he flipped a switch and lowered the weapon.

Grin alternated between watching the sky and the frightened faces of the local people. They, too, were looking upwards. Some of the more fearful members of their group had already begun moving away but most of the men stood with mouths agape, wondering what the white god named Sun Koh was doing.

A moment later they received their answer. Ionized energy coalesced in the skies above and with sudden force it came together in a blinding wall of white. The beam struck the crowd of onlookers, obliterating them in one fell swoop. There were no screams for the attack came too suddenly and their deaths were too quick.

The wall of white continued, tearing a hole deep into the frozen earth. It advanced toward the sanctum like death itself, slowly moving to eradicate everything in its path. Grin glanced at Sun Koh, who showed no fear of the oncoming wave.

The destructive beam faded as quickly as it had emerged, leaving the scent of ozone in the air. The ground where the beam had touched was a smoking ruin and the bones of the dead could be seen here and there, rising above the ash.

"I'd say that was a successful test," Grin muttered with satisfaction.

Chapter VII
The Nail

Consciousness returned slowly to Max Davies and with it came the knowledge that he was not in a good way. He hurt from head to toe and from the labored way he was breathing, he was pretty sure he had at least two, if not three, cracked ribs. He tried to look around and take in his surroundings, but one of his eyes was swollen shut and the other seemed strangely unfocused. How long had it been since he'd passed out? It felt like days.

With a start he realized that his hands and feet were free. It felt like he was lying on a cot of some kind, one with a thin sheet covering a wire frame. A rustle of fabric to his right indicated that someone was in the room with him, but he still found it difficult to lock in on them.

"I am sorry, Herr Rook," Captain Mueller said, reaching out to grasp Max's arm. He helped him up into a sitting position and then pushed a tin cup of coffee into his hands. "I knew that the women would abuse you but I had no idea the depths to which they would go. Women are ever the crueler of the sexes, are they not?"

The Rook coughed and the resulting pain nearly caused him to black out again. When he'd recovered, he clenched his teeth and said, "Still want me to go collect that nail for you?"

"I do, yes."

The Rook sipped the coffee and allowed it to warm his bones. He managed to lock his gaze on Mueller, though there seemed to be two of the man. "And you give me your word of honor that you'll destroy any copies of those photographs you might have?"

"I will."

"Then I'll do it. Just set me down where you want me to be and give me any details you have. I'll find it for you."

Mueller smiled. "You have no idea how happy that makes me. Religion is often revered by the Reich for its mystical powers, but the leadership in my country still have disdain for practical, day-to-day belief. But I have done so many awful things in the name of duty... if that nail can cleanse my spirit, then I want it." Mueller's features became grave. "I am dying, Herr Rook. The doctors say I have another six months before I will be too weak to continue my duties. And after that... I will slowly rot. What becomes of my immortal soul is now of paramount importance to me."

"My heart breaks for you," The Rook said bitterly.

"I don't ask for your compassion, only your understanding." Mueller moved to the door to the small room and knocked. When it opened, a young man was pushed inside. He was thin and delicate-featured, with the kind of emaciated look that one associated with prisoners of war. His hair was shorn close to his skull and his eyes were sunken orbs. He was barefoot and dressed in tattered gray pants and shirt. A pink triangle was sewn onto his shirt. Mueller gestured to the man. "This is Fritz. He is a homosexual. You know what that is?"

The Rook nodded, seeing the fear in Fritz's eyes.

"I know that you are promising to do what I have asked of you," Mueller continued, "But I cannot trust you to not simply run to freedom when we drop you off. If you do not return to me with The Fourth Nail in hand, I will have Fritz raped with batons and then shot in the head."

The Rook rose unsteadily to his feet. "You're a real bastard, Mueller."

"So I have been told. Consider this added security that you will keep your end of the bargain. Take a good look at him, please... and remember his face should you decide to betray me."

The Rook tried to silently project good thoughts to the poor boy but he knew that the only way Fritz would feel better was to be free of this ship. "Where is The Nail?" he asked.

Mueller's face shifted a bit. "Ah. Well, that's what makes this mission so dangerous...."

The atomic plane flew low over the Arctic landscape, Elsa Mayen's young hands moving confidently over the controls. She was attractive enough for a sixteen year old, though she was far from a classic beauty. Her blonde hair was curly and somewhat unkempt, a gift from her mother's side, and she had mismatched eyes: one green and one blue. She was also whippet-thin, with barely discernible breasts and hips. Still, her face was remarkably well structured and she had full lips, granting her more femininity than her body would have normally allowed. She wore a leather bomber jacket over a white shirt and khaki slacks, aviator goggles perched over her leather pilot's cap.

She had never been to this part of the world before but nothing could have prepared her for the devastation that greeted her. The terrain looked like it had been blown apart by some terrible attack and Elsa could pick out the shattered remains of human beings amongst the rubble.

An emerald dome stood a little past the horror, two men standing outside of it. The first was obviously Sun Koh – the man looked like he'd stepped out of a Nazi schoolbook on genetics. He was as perfect a man as anyone Elsa had ever seen. She felt a quickening in her breath as she looked down at him and a heat that spread from her loins to the rest of her body. The other man with him was tall and thin, looking like a schoolteacher or orchestra conductor.

Elsa set her plane down with the skill of a pilot three times her age. The atomic-powered aircraft came to a rest less than a hundred feet past Sun Koh's sanctum and by the time Elsa was descending to the icy terrain, the two men awaiting her were already closing in.

"From the way you handled that airship, I would have sworn that your father was at the controls," Sun Koh said. The intensity of his gaze made Elsa blush and she stammered a bit in reply.

"Thank you, my prince."

Sun Koh gestured toward Arthur Grin, introducing him without further explanation. As he boarded the plane, he took Elsa into his confidence. "We are about to embark on something that could prove very dangerous to all three of us – but if successful, should assure the Axis powers of victory."

"I'm willing to serve you in any way," Elsa responded, hoping that he didn't take her words as anything improper. Though, truth be told, she was willing to serve in a sexual capacity, as well.

Sun Koh sat down in the copilot's seat, his eyes roving over the dials and buttons. "Your father was a genius."

"He was," Elsa agreed. "I hope to honor him… I only wish I could purge the Jewish blood from my veins." She took the controls in her hand, sitting beside Sun Koh. Her face was drawn tight in self-loathing. "I swear I will be loyal to you, despite my heritage."

"The Jews are one of the servant races," Sun Koh said consolingly. "There are good Jews and bad Jews. They simply do not have the higher capacity that a true Aryan does. Because of your father, you will be able to attain things that no full-blooded Jew could ever hope for. You should be proud of that and strive to do your best. I shall never hold the race of your mother against you."

"Thank you. That… really does mean a lot to me."

Sun Koh reached out and clasped her hand tightly. "Are you ready to help pave the way for Aryan supremacy?" he asked with a knowing smile.

"Oh, yes," she laughed.

"I'm worried about Max." Evelyn Davies looked a bit sheepish as she said those words, washing them down with a shot of whiskey. She winced as the burning liquid washed down her throat but she recovered quickly, pushing her shot glass across the table for a refill.

Will McKenzie poured another drink for his friend and then gave himself another as well. One of the youngest police chiefs in the country, Will had stood beside Max and Evelyn against vampires, werewolves, and things he didn't even know what to call. It had changed his outlook on life, to be sure, turning him from a handsome and dedicated law enforcement official into someone who recognized that the world was far stranger than he could ever hope to understand. "He can handle himself. You know that."

"Sometimes I think he tries too hard to do it all by himself," Evelyn answered. They were in the kitchen of the Davies' home, which was quiet as a tomb. Little William, named after Will, was in bed, along with their housekeeper, Nettie.

Will cracked a grin. "He thinks he's protecting us."

"I know." Evelyn leaned forward and smiled. Her auburn hair was hanging loose about her shoulders and Will couldn't help but notice how lovely she was. She was beautiful, but it was an approachable sort of beauty… a healthy dash of girl-next-door was mixed in with the glamour. "I was wondering if I should call one of his friends and ask them to check on him."

"He told you he'd call and let you know he was okay?"

"Yes. And I haven't heard a peep out of him."

Will stood up and ran a hand through his dark hair. "Who were you thinking about? Kaslov?"

"Or maybe Ascott Keane," Evelyn answered. "I thought Keane might be able to figure out where he is."

Will nodded. Keane was a 'psychic detective,' one who was famous for sparring with the crimson-garbed Doctor Satan. Both Keane and Satan had crossed paths with The Rook on more than one occasion. Will found Keane somewhat unnerving and he was about to say so when a knock came at the back door. Both Will and Evelyn jumped at the unexpected sound. "You're not expecting anyone?"

"Will, it's almost 11 p.m. I don't usually have visitors this late at night." Evelyn walked toward one of the cabinets, opened it up, and reached deep inside. Her hand came back with a small handgun.

Will grinned, taking a few steps to the door. He opened it slowly, peering around the corner. When he saw the lovely woman standing there, he relaxed somewhat. It was Violet Cambridge, one of Atlanta's top private investigators. She had jet-black hair and a trim figure that filled out her dark dress in all the right places. She was also one of Will's former lovers, though their temperaments had proven too different for long-term happiness together.

Violet was smart enough that she'd eventually put two-and-two together to figure out Max's dual identity as The Rook. Evelyn had been concerned about this at first but she'd come to trust Violet, even though they had little in common.

"Hello, Will," Violet said. "How's life with the Nazi going?"

Will winced. Violet hadn't been shy about voicing her opinion of his involvement with the former Iron Maiden. He held the door open for her and took a step back to allow her in. "Things are peachy. What brings you by?"

Violet nodded at Evelyn, her ruby red lips parting in a grin as she saw the other woman's handgun. "Expecting trouble, are we?"

"Always," Evelyn admitted. She set the gun down on the kitchen counter. "Get you something to wet your whistle?"

"No thanks. I just came by to tell you that your boy might be in trouble."

Evelyn and Will exchanged glances. "What makes you say that?" Evelyn asked.

"I was paying a visit to an informer of mine – name's Glumm – and he told me that The Rook had been by recently, asking about a German superman named Sun Koh. Glumm says he's heard since through the grapevine that Sun Koh is back and has been jetting around… and get this, there was a top-secret communiqué sent back to Germany that said The Rook was in German custody."

"Must not have been very top secret if you know about it," Will pointed out.

"Glumm has resources. That's what makes him so valuable."

Evelyn let out a deep breath that she'd been holding. "If Max has been captured, I have to do something." She moved toward the phone and paused for a moment with her hand on the receiver. "I'm calling Ascott Keane."

The Rook wasn't happy about this at all. He felt slightly rejuvenated after a bath and a hearty meal, but his body still ached in a dozen different places and his midsection was tightly bound to prevent him further injuring his ribs.

But worst of all was the fact that he was about to break into the private offices of a man who, under other circumstances, would have been a close friend.

The Rook was in Manhattan, having been snuck onto the island after being transferred from the zeppelin to a private plane belonging to a Fifth Columnist. The entire affair had taken over 24 hours and made The Rook wonder just how far behind Sun Koh he truly was now.

The area of Manhattan in which he was now moving was known as The Battery, which was located on the southernmost point of the island. Battery Park lay on The Rook's right, a disreputable looking place if Max had ever seen one. Bums slept on park benches and trash littered the thick grass. Facing the park was a series of office buildings, most of them fairly recent. But the one that was The Rook's target was an ancient thing, the bronze work on the front doors green with age.

The Rook looked up to see that the stars were bright in the sky. He estimated that it was nearly ten o'clock, though he couldn't be sure. Mueller's men had taken everything that they didn't consider essential, which meant that aside from his weapons, his pockets were nearly empty. He didn't even have his long-range radio to call Evelyn.

Max hurried across the street, having watched the six-story building long enough to assure him that no one was inside. All the windows were pitch-black.

The front doors were unlocked and the lobby was clean, if somewhat barren. A directory on the wall indicated that the bottom two floors had no tenants. The fifth floor had a single occupant listed: Adventurers, Inc. The Rook glanced over at the elevator cage nearby. It was the old-fashioned kind, where the interior was visible through the grillwork. An old man in overalls sat in the cage, resting his weary bones on the single chair within. His head was tilted back and he was snoring loudly.

The Rook crept over as quietly as a mouse, retrieving a small capsule from one of his pockets. He broke it open under the man's nose, holding his own breath in the process. The old man snorted loudly and then slipped into an even deeper slumber. The Rook relaxed, resuming his own breathing. The gas capsule worked very fast, putting a full-grown man into an unconsciousness that would last for up to six hours.

After taking the elevator to the fifth floor, The Rook found himself facing a locked office. He knelt in front of the lock and expertly picked it. It was a challenging affair and took him nearly ten minutes, far longer than was usual. Before entering the office, Max took a moment to insert specialized lenses over each eye. Specially treated to enhance The Rook's night vision, the lenses were just one more example of the vigilante's mastery of the sciences.

When he stepped inside, he found himself in one of the most unusual offices he'd ever seen: it was cluttered from floor to ceiling with oddities. A bronze Chinese figurine was perched in the window, while an Oriental rug that looked like it hadn't been cleaned in years lay on the floor. Hunting riles were mounted on the wall, a diving bell was in the corner and every chair and couch was bent under the weight of books and magazines. A framed diploma from M.I.T. was on the wall nearest The Rook and beside it was a photograph of a young blond man, standing with hands on hips. This was Rush Randall and Adventurers, Inc. was his brainchild.

A child prodigy with interests ranging from physics to aviation to mountain climbing, Rush Randall had grown up to become a veritable superman. With his partners in adventure, Buzz Casey and Malcolm Dean, he had formed Adventurers, Inc. to help those in need. He had become a minor celebrity and The Rook knew that he was a potent addition to the arsenal of justice... but The Rook was crossing his fingers that their first meeting would not come tonight.

The Rook moved through the crowded room until he came to a second door, one that led to a much better ordered office. This one contained two small chairs arranged in front of a desk. A photograph of Rush Randall was on the wall behind the desk, depicting the powerfully built man holding an elephant gun and standing with one foot on the leg of a fallen bull elephant.

Max glanced about until he saw what he wanted: a small safe secreted against the corner of the back wall. Mueller had described it perfectly, having seen it shown in a photograph. *Life Magazine* had profiled Randall a few months ago and during the piece there had been an image of Randall posing in front of the open safe. The article had mentioned in passing how Randall kept the most valuable or dangerous of his acquisitions in his safe. One of the objects that could be clearly seen was an old battered nail. Though it didn't look particularly valuable in the photo, Mueller had recognized it for what it was: the spiritual equivalent of a get-out-of-jail free card.

The Rook moved to examine the safe and noted that the lock was, if anything, far more complex than the one on the front door. He broke three of his four remaining picks on the lock before he finally heard the tumblers click into place. When the door swung open, he found himself staring at quite a few unusual items. Given the time, he would have loved to spend time with each of them, puzzling out their purpose, but given that he was in a hurry to end his association with Mueller, he snatched up The Fourth Nail.

Immediately, he felt a strange energy flow through him. He felt like his minor injuries were fading away like a memory and, even more importantly, that his spirit was being lightened. Little things that he felt guilty over suddenly seemed forgotten and all the petty sins he'd committed over his lifetime didn't seem quite so important any longer.

The Rook was still basking in this peaceful feeling when the lights in the office unexpectedly came on. He stood up quickly, coming face to face with Rush Randall. The blond man stood well over six feet, wearing a light brown shirt with pockets over each side of his chest and dark slacks. Black leather boots completed his attire. The Rook uttered a curse under his breath. He must have been holding The Fourth Nail for several minutes, not hearing Randall's entrance at all.

"Mind telling me what you're doing?" Randall asked.

The Rook slipped the nail into a pocket. "You and I aren't enemies," he began but Randall cut him off.

"We are if you're stealing from me."

"My name is The Rook and…"

"I know who you are. I've seen the pictures. Now set that nail down on the desk and get the hell out of my office."

The Rook frowned, bristling a bit at the man's tone. "No."

"Then I'm going to take it," Randall said, his muscled body launching toward The Rook. He collided with the hero, slamming him against the wall, but The Rook recovered quickly, jamming the palm of his right hand up under Randall's chin. The blow snapped Randall's head back and The Rook followed with a quick punch to the man's rock hard midsection. Before Randall could respond, The Rook shoved him away, giving the vigilante a bit more room. He drew one of his pistols and pointed it at Randall, who paused in surprise.

"You're going to shoot me?" the big man asked. "It's bad enough you turn out to be a thief, now you're going to become a murderer, too?"

"All I want is the nail. When all this is over, I'll be more than glad to explain why I'm doing this… but I don't have the time right now."

Rush Randall stared at him, slumping his shoulders in defeat. "Okay. Take it if you need to." The Rook started to lower his weapon when Randall sprang forward with incredible speed. He backhanded The Rook's arm, knocking the gun from his grip. He then wrapped his fingers around The Rook's throat, applying incredible pressure. He lifted The Rook off the ground and continued squeezing, hoping to knock his opponent out.

The Rook gasped, stars beginning to appear on the edges of his vision. He thrust out one hand, pressing against Randall's face. He managed to dig his thumb into Randall's eye and the pain caused the big man to drop Max to the floor.

The Rook knew he had one chance and one chance only: he unsheathed the Knife of Elohim and stabbed Randall in the upper thigh. It was a painful attack and one that would slow even an athlete like Randall… but hardly a fatal one. While Randall cried out in pain, gripping his injured leg, The Rook sprinted past him. He didn't slow down until he was in the elevator cage, hurriedly pressing the button that would send the motorized carriage downstairs.

The Rook leaned against the back wall of the elevator and panted. He had the nail and that was the most important thing… but tonight's events were just one more thing that Mueller and The Furies would have to pay for.

Chapter VIII
Fallen Valkyrie

Käthe fought to keep her face neutral but it was difficult. Two days had been wasted on Mueller's pursuit of The Fourth Nail and the leader of The Furies was growing increasingly concerned. The Rook was being led back onto the zeppelin now, the Christian relic in his grasp, and Mueller was beside himself with pleasure.

Käthe was on the zeppelin's bridge, Akemi and Imelda standing just behind. She was facing Mueller, who seemed to have either not heard or chosen to ignore what she had just said. "Captain?" she repeated. "I'd like to know what your plans are once you have The Fourth Nail."

Mueller sighed, his expression changing to one of tired acceptance. "The Fourth Nail will cleanse me of all my sins. It will give me a clean slate. Would you have me immediately ruin that by going back on my word as a gentleman? I told him I would let him go free and I shall."

"I'm afraid we can't let you do that," Akemi said. Her hand drifted dangerously close to the katana she wore slung over her back. "We've talked it over and The Rook's going to die."

"I assumed you three would want him taken back to Berlin," Mueller said. "After all, you did send back a message telling command that he was here, didn't you?"

Käthe shrugged, not caring that he'd known about the message. It had gotten through and that had been the important thing. "All we said was that he was in our custody. Accidents happen."

"Did you happen to mention that I was bargaining with him for possession of a sacred relic?"

"Of course we did," Imelda answered. "They need to know that you're a traitorous bastard."

Mueller tightened his jaw. "I have betrayed no one."

THE SCORCHED GOD

Before any of The Furies could answer, Horst entered the bridge with The Rook close at his heels. The Rook was holding something in his left hand, wrapped tightly in a gray-colored cloth.

Horst and Mueller exchanged Hitler salutes and then Horst stepped back, clicking his heels together.

Mueller licked his lips in anticipation. "You have it?" he asked, his eyes flicking back and forth from the bundle to The Rook's face.

"Yes. Where's Fritz?"

Mueller nodded at Horst, who stepped out and returned with the youth. Fritz had a parachute strapped to him and he still looked frightened, but also hopeful. "There. You see? He has been well tended to since you left. Once you've given me the nail, you'll be provided with your own parachute and then we'll let you both jump. The wind should carry you to dry land."

"I want the parachute now."

Mueller took a deep breath but forced a smile. "You begin to insult me. I have given you my word."

The Rook's eyes flicked over to The Furies, all of whom looked like they were seconds away from giving in to their desire to attack him. "I trust you, Captain," he lied. "It's the women who make me a bit nervous."

Horst appeared again, holding a parachute out to The Rook. The vigilante took the chute and examined it, making sure that it was in good working order. He put it on expertly and then tossed the cloth-wrapped nail to Mueller.

The Nazi gasped and squeezed the nail eagerly. He unwrapped it, his eyes feasting on the rusty object. His fingers caressed it and, slowly, his expression of pleasure began to wane. "I don't understand," he whispered. "Nothing's happening."

"It was a lie," The Rook said. "Nothing more, nothing less. The nail's just a nail."

"But... Randall had it in his safe...."

"He knew it was valuable... maybe he even believed in its powers. But I held it and nothing happened." The Rook motioned for Fritz to head toward the door. "You got what you wanted, Mueller. Time for us to go."

"No," Mueller said, shaking his head. "This is a lie. A fake!" He pointed an accusing finger at The Rook. "You switched it somehow! Give me the real Nail!"

The Rook noticed that the guards in the room were drawing their guns and The Furies had their weapons in hand, too. He bolted, shoving Fritz out the door, even as bullets began to slam into the wall just over his shoulder. He reached into one of his pockets and pulled out something that he'd picked up in Randall's office: a hand grenade that had been amongst the adventurer's collection of weapons. He yanked the pin and tossed it into the center of the bridge. Several shouts let him know that the weapon had been recognized for what it was.

"C'mon, Fritz," The Rook yelled, pulling the frightened boy roughly along behind him. He was sprinting toward the airlock, hoping they could make it before the grenade went off. They almost made it, The Rook's fingers were on the door handle when the floor rattled beneath their feet and several men began to scream. In a vessel like this, fire was an incredible danger and The Rook knew there was a real chance that the entire ship could go down in flames. Yanking open the door, The Rook looked down to see ocean below. Mueller had been lying about the wind carrying them to land – there was no land anywhere in sight.

"We're trapped!" Fritz screamed, beginning to panic.

"The hell we are!" The Rook grabbed Fritz and shoved him out into open space. The boy screamed, hurtling toward the ocean below. The Rook counted to three and then leaped after him, the wind whipping through his hair. "Fritz! Open your chute!" he yelled, his voice nearly lost in the cacophony of noise as another explosion ripped through the zeppelin above them. The Rook twisted his head to see flames running along the cloth exterior of the ship, the entire body of the great vessel looking like it was about to bend in half.

Fritz suddenly shot past him, carried upwards as the wind got under his parachute. The Rook pulled his own ripcord and soon the two of them were slowly floating down to the sea. Burning bits of wreckage, along with screaming bodies of crewmen who hadn't been able to grab parachutes of their own, hurtled past them.

When they struck the water, The Rook quickly yanked out his dagger and cut both himself and Fritz free of the chutes. "Swim with me!" he shouted. "I want to get as far away from this mess as possible!"

Fritz nodded, sputtering in the water. The boy followed his rescuer, sparing only a single glance at the mighty Valkyrie, which was falling to its watery grave.

A split second before the grenade blew, Käthe turned to face her friends. "We're going down," she said in crisp German.

Akemi stared daggers at Mueller, looking like she was considering killing the man for his stupidity. If he hadn't insisted on this absurd business with The Fourth Nail, none of this would be happening. She shoved away her anger, however, knowing that the most important thing at present was survival.

All three women sprinted from the bridge, ignoring Mueller's shouts for them to stop. They were far enough away from the blast to avoid its immediate effects, though the deck rattled beneath their feet. They saw the open escape hatch and Käthe correctly assumed that The Rook and his 'damsel in distress' had jumped from there. Without bothering to tell the others what she had planned, she hurled herself out the hatch, not caring that she had no parachute. To their eternal credit, Imelda and Akemi followed suit, trusting that their leader wouldn't have led them to do this unless she thought they could survive.

They hurtled through the air, smashing into the water with enough force to

The Valkyrie Falls

rattle their bones. Imelda came up for air first, gasping and sputtering. She saw Käthe emerge from the choppy seas a few seconds later and together they waited for Akemi to do the same. When her head didn't appear within a reasonable amount of time, Imelda told Käthe to wait for her and she dove down.

While Imelda was gone, Käthe scanned the horizon. She spotted The Rook and Fritz not too far away, but just then the zeppelin overhead split in two, fire racing along the exterior of the hull. Käthe saw bodies begin to fall from the wreckage and she muttered a curse that would have brought a blush to a sailor's face.

Imelda returned, her arms wrapped tightly around Akemi's waist. The beautiful Asian girl was unconscious, blood streaming from her right nostril.

"She swallowed a lot of water," Imelda said. "And I think something may have broken when she hit the surface."

Käthe pulled open Akemi's eyes. She saw only the whites as they were rolled up into her skull. "Sling her over my shoulder and maybe we can push the water from her lungs. Keep her head elevated, though."

Imelda pushed the smaller girl over the German's shoulder and began applying rhythmic pressure to Akemi's back. After a moment, Akemi's mouth opened and a spray of seawater emerged, erupting from her nostrils at the same time. She moaned and Käthe lowered her, keeping an arm around her waist to help her stay afloat.

Akemi looked up at the sky, where the zeppelin was beginning to fall to pieces. A man's body – Horst it looked like – landed hard in the water nearby, his scalp ablaze. "I feel like closing my eyes and dying," she muttered in Japanese.

"I wouldn't do that," Käthe said, a strange smile appearing on her lips. She was looking past Imelda, at something off in the distance.

Imelda turned her head and gasped. The most unusual plane she'd ever seen was streaking through the sky, moving almost soundlessly. The ship appeared to slow as it neared them, unbelievably coming to a steady hover less than fifty feet above them. Air was being shot from beneath the ship, stirring up the water so much that the girls were squinting as sprays of seawater shot into their faces.

A rope ladder was dropped in their midst and Käthe managed to shield her face enough to see the figure who was dangling out from the airplane, gesturing for them to climb aboard. She'd seen photographs of similar planes and her heart had swelled at the sight of this one. It was Sun Koh, come to rescue her like a knight on a white steed. The idea that she was relishing being rescued embarrassed her as all The Furies prided themselves on being the equal of any man... but this was Sun Koh, the embodiment of the Aryan hero! Surely it was okay to feel the slightest bit... well, *girlish*... around such a man.

"Akemi, can you manage?" Käthe asked.

"Yes. I think so." Akemi pushed away and grabbed hold of the ladder. She began climbing, a small trickle of blood reappearing at her nose. When she was slightly less than halfway up, Imelda began ascending. Käthe went last and by the time she reached the top, allowing Sun Koh to reach out and help pull her inside, she was shivering with both exhaustion and cold.

The Heir to Atlantis wrapped a towel around her shoulders and she smiled gratefully, her teeth chattering. She saw that Imelda was drinking from a cup of coffee and that a thin man who had a professorial air about him was examining Akemi. Käthe glanced toward the cockpit, her eyes widening when she saw the slip of a girl seated at the controls.

"That is Elsa Mayen," Sun Koh said. "And this is Arthur Grin. They are allies of mine… and I'm hoping the three of you will be as well."

"Of course we are," Käthe said, accepting a cup of steaming java from the man she idolized. "We would follow you to the gates of hell."

"I hope it won't come to that," Sun Koh responded, his eyes boring into hers, reminding her of the hours of physical passion they'd shared. "But I plan to win this war for the Axis. Your Fuehrer considers me a threat to his own power and wants me dead… but I'm not going to allow that to stop me from doing what's right for our people."

Käthe blinked at his words, but she didn't try to argue them. She could believe that Hitler would fear Sun Koh's return. She'd seen signs of his paranoia before. "What do you have in mind?"

"I want to destroy Washington, D.C."

The Rook stared at the unusual plane that was now receding into the distance. He'd thought about trying to stop The Furies from boarding it somehow, but he was afraid his pistols were too waterlogged to fire and he didn't dare risk losing the Knife of Elohim by throwing it from that distance.

"Who was that?" Fritz asked. The poor thing looked like a half-drowned rat. He was too underfed to be able to swim for very long, particularly in such choppy waters.

"If I had to hazard a guess, I'd say it was a man named Sun Koh. He's the one I'm after. Have you heard of him?"

Fritz looked thoughtfully toward the floating wreckage of the Valkyrie. A few screams were coming from that direction as the dying and wounded voiced their pain. "I think so… I used to read stories about him."

"Well, he's no hero… at least not for people who don't fit his profile of the perfect Aryan."

"I can't keep going," Fritz said and The Rook turned to face him.

"I can carry you for awhile."

"You shouldn't put yourself at risk for me."

The Rook started to reassure him when he felt something strange inside his head, like a tickle. It started off so soft that he almost thought he was imagining it but then it got more intense. He must have looked as confused as he felt because Fritz was staring at him. "It's okay," he said. "I think… I think someone's coming for us. We just have to hang in here."

Fritz said nothing, obviously assuming that the masked man was simply trying to give him false hope.

The Rook reached inside his own soaking wet clothing and pulled out the actual Fourth Nail. He handed it to Fritz. "Take this. It's what Mueller wanted. It'll give you the strength you need."

Fritz took it and moaned as the energy rushed through him. He felt that his sins – both real and imagined – were being swept away. He began to cry, for the joy of being born again, beautiful in the eyes of God. "Thank you," he stammered. "Thank you so much."

The Rook treaded water, smiling to himself. "No problem. You hang on to that for awhile, okay?"

Fritz nodded and held the nail close to his chest. Off in the distance, a vessel could be seen, slowing as it closed in on their position. It looked like a deep-sea fishing ship and as it got closer, The Rook could see that the name of the vessel was painted on the side of its hull: *The Ocean Avenger*.

The tickling sensation in The Rook's brain had settled into something more familiar: the telltale mental call of an old, dear friend.

The Ocean Avenger came toward them, slowing its progress. Several sailors leaned over the railing, throwing down ropes to the two drenched figures below. The handsome face of Ascott Keane joined the sailors in peering down at The Rook. Dressed in a dark jacket and well-tailored suit, the detective looked wildly out of place on the fishing vessel.

"Ascott, I could kiss you," The Rook said, climbing onboard.

"That won't be necessary," Keane replied. "A simple thank you will more than suffice."

"How did you find me?"

"Your wife contacted me and from there… well, to put it quite simply, it was magic."

A few moments later, Fritz was bundled up in a heavy towel. He was sipping some warm chicken soup and looking as content as a fat cat, glad to be in the interior of the fishing vessel.

The Rook stood nearby, running a towel through his dripping hair. Keane was at his side, speaking in hushed tones. "I wish I could drop everything and help you but I'm in the middle of a case. It was all I could do to come and help you today… when I saw a vision that implied you might die unless I came to pull you out of the ocean, I had to put everything else on hold."

"It's okay. That's one reason why I didn't call you to begin with. I know how busy you are. Same with Leonid and the others."

Keane looked pensive, rubbing his chin with the slender fingers of his right hand. "Still, you shouldn't continue alone on this. Sun Koh is far too dangerous an enemy... and if he's allied with those Furies you told me about, he's doubly dangerous."

"I suppose I could ask Evelyn to come with me," Max said, shaking his head to indicate what he thought of that. "She's really capable... but I hate to put her at risk like that. Especially now that we have a son."

Keane nodded in understanding. He had no family himself, but he could well imagine how difficult that would make an ongoing war against crime. "I will do what I can for you. Perhaps I can give you some clue about where Sun Koh can be found... your own vision let you know that Washington, D.C. is a target, but that doesn't mean that you should just camp out there waiting for him."

"Anything you could do would be great," The Rook said. He looked around the room, noting that the crew seemed perfectly at ease being around a masked man. "Do you own this ship?"

"I do. The captain was helped by me a few years ago and as payment, he gave me a share in the ownership of his boat."

"If there's a radio, I'd like to try and get a message to Evelyn. I want to let her know that I'm hale and hearty."

"Feel free. The captain can show you where it's located." Keane placed a hand on The Rook's arm as the vigilante started to move away. "May I ask what your plans are for The Fourth Nail?"

"I'd forgotten about it in the excitement of getting rescued, actually." The Rook pulled out the nail from a pocket. He'd retrieved it from Fritz shortly after they'd been pulled from the sea. "I thought about returning it to Rush Randall... but the guy seemed like an arrogant jerk. I'm not sure he deserves it."

"If you're thinking of keeping it, you should put it someplace very secure. There will be people looking for it. I guarantee that you weren't the first to trace it to Randall's headquarters."

The Rook handed the nail to Keane, who took it with some reluctance. "Would you....?"

"If you wish. It wouldn't be the first artifact like this I've keep watch over."

"Thanks." The Rook clasped Keane on the shoulder and moved toward the captain. Keane watched him go, wondering if Max had any idea about the enormity of the responsibility he'd just placed upon him.

As night fell, Wilhelm Mueller managed to pull himself atop a scrap of metal debris from the Valkyrie. He was shivering from the cold and his eyes burned from the saltwater. He had lost his monocle on the long tumble through the sky, but it was the least of his concerns. He had lost his crew, his vessel and his chance at spiritual redemption. Now all he had left was his life... and that was not worth very much at present. A shark's fin cut through the water, circling the makeshift raft on which Mueller lay sprawled. The sharks had begun appearing hours ago, making quick work of many of the survivors. Mueller himself had stabbed one of the beasts in the eye with his dagger, losing the weapon when the shark swam away, bleeding profusely. From the churning of the water that had followed, Mueller assumed the ocean predator had become food for his brethren, which pleased him somewhat.

Stretching out on his back, Mueller looked up at the nighttime sky and wondered how long he could survive out here. Would help eventually arrive? And if it did, what was the likelihood that it would be anyone who wouldn't simply throw him into a dank cell, treating him as a prisoner of war?

The water to his left suddenly began stirring and Mueller raised his head to peer into the gloom. He assumed the sharks were on another feeding frenzy, but he wasn't sure what they could be feasting upon.

What he saw made him sit up quickly and grab his knife. It was a submarine, looking like some horrible metal-encased monster emerging from the depths. There were no markings on the ship, nothing to tell if it were an Allied or Axis vessel. Furthermore, it didn't quite look like any submarine that Mueller was familiar with. It was a little too long and a bit too curved, giving it the general shape of a French crescent roll. Why anyone would design it in such a fashion was beyond him.

The hatch on top of the submarine opened with a clang and a man dressed in a plain gray jumpsuit emerged. He was of Oriental descent and large goggles covered his eyes. "If you wish to live, you will come onboard," the man said in heavily accented but still fluent German.

"Are you part of the Japanese navy?"

The man's lips turned downward into an expression of annoyance. "I am not Japanese. I am Korean."

Mueller held his tongue. He thought all Orientals looked alike but given the choices presented him, he thought being polite might serve him better. He scrambled onto the submarine, moving like a crab until he reached the hatch. The man had disappeared within the ship by this time and Mueller threw himself into the opening, climbing down below. It stank to high heaven, as all submarines did. So much time spent in a cramped environment did terrible things to hygiene, Mueller had found.

Mueller found himself surrounded by a half dozen men, all dressed in identical gray jumpsuits that featured no ornamentation of any kind. The dim lighting did allow Mueller to note that the men appeared to be of all different ethnicities. In fact, one of the men was a Negro, which gave Mueller pause. What kind of ship would allow a black to serve on the crew?

THE SCORCHED GOD

"Welcome onboard," a booming voice said from behind Mueller. The Nazi captain turned to see a barrel-chested man watching him closely. The man had a short, bristle-like white salt-and-pepper beard. He was dressed in a dark military-style uniform, though once again it bore no signs of national allegiance. Small black gloves covered the man's hands, but Mueller thought there were something odd about the fellow's fingers, as if he were missing the small finger from each hand.

"I am Captain Wilhelm Mueller. May I ask what country you serve?"

"We serve no country," the man replied, continuing to speak in German, though Mueller could tell that it was not his native tongue. "And I know who you are. You were in command of that airship that went belly-up."

Mueller tightened his jaw. "Am I to understand that you control a rogue submarine?"

"Yes. You understand correctly. My name is Felipe Melo and you can swear allegiance to me or we will put a bullet in your brain and throw your body out to the sharks."

Mueller stared at the man in amazement. "Allegiance? What would that mean? You want me to become a member of your crew?"

"I want you to help me complete our sacred mission. It's a mission that you have an interest in as well. I want you to help me capture The Fourth Nail."

Chapter IX
Devil's Bargain

Mueller was invited to dine with Melo and his crew, an offer that he could not refuse. The food was surprisingly pleasant, if somewhat plain. The entire crew assembled in the mess hall and Mueller was seated to the captain's right.

For the first few moments of dinner, there was no talking and the only noise to be heard over the din of the engines were the scrapings of silverware against plates. It was finally Melo who broke the relative silence, sitting back and belching before addressing Mueller.

"Are you familiar with The Knights Templar?" he asked, a line of questioning that left Mueller momentarily stunned.

"I know that the group existed for nearly two centuries and was officially endorsed by the Catholic Church, until King Philip IV of France began condemning them. He rounded up many of their orders and accused them of blasphemy. Pope Clement V disbanded the Order in 1312."

Melo smiled broadly. "You are very well read, Mr. Mueller. You almost sound as if you're reciting facts from a history book."

"That's basically what I'm doing. I only know of the Templars from school textbooks."

"Well, the Templars are not dead. They continue to exist under a dozen or more names. My crew and I are affiliated with one such survivor organization. We travel the globe, collecting artifacts that can be brought together for the praise of almighty God. And if they have great monetary value, all the better." Melo added this with a grin.

"And how did you get this submarine?" Mueller asked.

"The Order has ships and planes at its disposal. I served for several years in the navy of my birth country before I was recruited into The Order. Now I live at sea, traveling around the world in search of treasure. We had men watching the residence of Rush Randall – they saw The Rook leave with the nail and they observed him return to your airship. After that, I was dispatched to follow you. When your ship went down, we laid low until the time was right to rescue you." Melo's smile faded. "Since you don't have the nail, I'm assuming that The Rook still has it?"

Mueller suddenly found himself without an appetite. He set down his fork and dabbed at the corner of his mouth with a napkin. "Yes. He betrayed me. Brought back a fake and then set off the explosion that killed my crew and destroyed my ship."

"The Rook has come to our attention more than once," Melo admitted. "He has one of the Knives of Elohim. Those blades were dipped in the blood of Christ himself. We would very much like to possess his dagger as well as the nail."

"I think I would be able to do more good if you were to let me go," Mueller said. "Once I'm back in Germany, I can call upon resources to help you. All I want is to hold the nail briefly… I'm dying, you see. I want to have my sins forgiven."

Captain Melo sipped from a glass of wine and shook his head sadly. "No. That won't do. You see, I am not a fan of Nazis. Nor is any of The Order. We regard your Hitler as a dangerous lunatic who is pushing the entire world to the brink of disaster. So, no, I don't plan to have you return to your Nazi ways, even if it did mean you would help us."

"Then, what…"

"I told you what I want. I want you to swear allegiance to me and to The Order. Then you'll become part of my crew and help me track down The Fourth Nail. When we find it, you can have your revenge on The Rook and get your salvation."

"What makes you think I can help you?"

"Because you are a desperate man, one with vengeance in his heart and nothing to lose. That is the kind of person who can be very valuable to me. And when the deeds are done, I suspect you will want to live out your days in service to Christ and to The Order."

Mueller looked away, frowning. He didn't particularly want to join what appeared to him to be a religious cult… but he didn't wish to die, either. Not yet, at least. "I'll do as you ask," he said at last. "I swear allegiance to you."

"And you renounce your Fuehrer?"

Mueller paused for a moment. "I do."

Melo held out a hand. "Then welcome to the crew, my friend. Now, finish your meal and we'll set off in search of The Rook."

Elsa Mayen tried to ignore the sounds of ecstasy coming from the rear of the plane, but it was difficult. Sun Koh had vanished with Käthe nearly an hour ago and ever since then Elsa had been forced to visualize what was occurring. Käthe had ceased moaning quite a while ago and was now making noises that were halfway between pleasure and pain; she sounded exhausted but thrilled.

Elsa, who was still a virgin, found herself growing warm at the ideas flowing through her brain. She was still at the controls of the ship, which was flying silently toward North America, but the atomic plane might as well have been on autopilot. Her right hand was buried between her thighs, pressing hard against her sex, and the scent of her arousal was filling the pilot's cabin. She had just begun to bite her lower lip in pleasure when Imelda dropped into the seat next to hers.

Elsa jumped in shock, looking both embarrassed and frightened. Imelda grinned at her, having obviously seen what she had been doing.

"How much longer?" the Italian beauty asked.

"A couple of hours at this speed."

"Really? Looked like you were going to be finished any second there."

Elsa felt her entire face turn red and she busied herself by checking a bunch of dials that didn't need reading. "Can I help you with something?"

Imelda placed a hand on Elsa's upper thigh. "I think a better question is can I help you with anything?"

Elsa reached down and pushed Imelda's hand away. "No thank you."

Imelda shrugged. If she took offense at the rejection, she wasn't showing it. She looked out the window, watching the clouds as they streamed past. "What do you think about Mr. Grin? Bit of an odd bird, if you ask me."

Elsa nodded, glad to be talking about something else besides her masturbation. "I don't care for him very much but if Sun Koh trusts him, that's good enough for me."

"You sound like Käthe," Imelda muttered. She turned to face the young girl and leaned in close, whispering her words. "I understand that he was friends with your father… but haven't you thought about whether or not it's in our best interests to follow him?"

"Of course I have. And I think it is." Elsa looked toward the rear of the plane. She saw Akemi sleeping in one of the passenger chairs and Arthur Grin was seated near her, placidly looking out the window. There was no sign of either Sun Koh or Käthe. "Don't you?"

"I'm not so sure. He's an Aryan supremacist. That means that Akemi and I aren't on his list of who makes up the master race. I have gypsy blood in me… and you're a Jew, aren't you?"

Elsa's eyes went cold. "I'm German. My father was Jan Mayen."

"And your mother?"

"What makes you think I'm a Jew?"

Imelda - the fiery-tempered Fury of Italy

"There's something about your features... I can't put my finger on it. If I'm wrong, I apologize." Imelda's lips turned up in a smile. "But I'm not wrong, am I?"

"My mother was a Jew," Elsa said, her words barely audible.

"That means there's a limit to how far you can go in Sun Koh's society. Hell, even if you were a pureblood, he thinks you should be in the kitchen, cooking his food and squeezing out his babies. That's the perfect Aryan woman, isn't it?"

"He doesn't seem to mind that Käthe is a warrior," Elsa countered.

"Sun Koh is fucking her because that's how he can control her."

Elsa blinked at the coarse language but said nothing.

Imelda continued. "He's a smart one, your Atlantean prince. He knows she's infatuated with him. And he knows you are, too. He bedded Akemi and I, too, but you could see the distance in his eyes when he touched us. We were nothing but animals to him - just warm holes for him to spend some time inside."

"I don't think he's quite like that."

"You know he is," Imelda laughed bitterly. "The entire Axis alliance is built on the unspoken knowledge that when the war is won, we're all going to turn on each other. You think Hitler is going to be okay sharing control of the world with the Italians or the Japanese?"

"So what are you saying?" Elsa asked. "If you don't want to work with Sun Koh, you can ask to be dropped off somewhere."

"I'm just saying that when the time comes... if the opportunity presents itself, we might want to take action."

Elsa stared at the older woman, wanting to make sure she understood correctly. "Are you talking about killing him?"

"If that's what it comes to. Maybe it won't. But if we can seize control of the situation and make sure it comes out better for us, we should do it."

"Have you talked to Akemi about this?"

"Not yet. She's too loyal to Käthe."

"And Käthe's loyal to Sun Koh."

Imelda nodded. "Right."

"What makes you think I won't go straight to Sun Koh and tell him what you've said?"

"Because you know I'm right. And even though you want to be a pureblooded Aryan with all your little heart, you know you never will be. It doesn't matter if your daddy left you this plane, you'll never be anything more than a tool for Sun Koh and his buddies to use. Maybe you'll get lucky and he'll sleep with you... but he'd never love you."

Elsa watched as Imelda stood up and left the cabin. She followed the Italian with her eyes, both angry and terrified by what the woman had said. She noticed that Grin was staring in her direction and she looked away, lost in confusion.

THE SCORCHED GOD

Käthe sat up, her back pressed against the wall. She could feel the humming of the ship through its surface and she liked it. Her nude body was glistening with sweat and she looked over at Sun Koh, admiring the immaculate way he was put together. He was wearing only his trousers, sitting lotus-style on the floor where they'd been having sex only moments before. The memory of the half-dozen earth-shattering orgasms he'd given her brought a dreamy smile to her face.

Sun Koh had his own eyes closed, the muscles of his body subtly twitching. It was a peculiar form of meditation and exercise, in which he concentrated on one body part after another, flexing the muscles repeatedly until they ached under the strain. In this way, he kept every part of his body in perfect shape.

Käthe looked over at the Solar Cannon, which rested on the floor beneath most of her uniform. "When the war is over," she asked, "What do you plan to do?"

The Heir of Atlantis continued his exercises, head tilted downwards as he began to flex the muscles in his neck. "You want to know if I plan to seize power from Adolph Hitler?"

"Amongst other things."

"I am obviously displeased with the way his administration has proceeded. He's dangerously close to placing his own well being over that of his race... No, I'd be willing to say that he's already done that. Trying to kill me is a sure sign that he no longer has the best interests of the Aryan people at heart."

Käthe crawled toward him, crouching behind Sun Koh. She pressed against his back. Her breasts were warm against him and he finally ceased his exercises, turning his head slightly so that he could look at her. She brought her lips close to his ear, ensuring that no one eavesdropping in the rest of the plane could hear. "I'd support you, My Prince. I'm dedicated to the cause." She ran her tongue along his earlobe and reached around with one hand to stroke him. "I think I can convince Imelda and Akemi to join us."

"I'm not sure we can trust the Oriental," Sun Koh said. He was responding to her ministrations, even though they'd spent so much time coupling.

"I trust Akemi with my life. She's in love with me, I think."

Sun Koh pursed his lips. "And the Italian?"

"She talks tough but in the end, she'd be too afraid of being alone to turn against us."

Sun Koh stood up, abruptly pulling away her. He pulled on his shirt and looked warmly at Käthe, though she noticed that the smile on his face didn't quite extend to his eyes. "You are a good Aryan woman and a true warrior. I thank you."

Käthe watched in disappointment as he left the small cabin, rejoining the others. She wondered if perhaps she had said something wrong and immediately began replaying the conversation in her mind. She found herself feeling weak again and she both loved and hated Sun Koh for putting her on such unfamiliar emotional ground.

For his part, Sun Koh had tired of their sex play and was not interested in cultivating a romance. The one woman he could regard as an equal in this time was gone and there would never be another. But Käthe was right that he had to make a definitive plan for what would occur once the Allies had been crushed. Was he prepared to seize control of the German empire? And, if so, would he seek peace with Italy and Japan… or seek their subservience?

He sat down next to Arthur Grin, disliking the knowing expression on the other man's face. "What are you thinking, Arthur?" he demanded.

"Just that you are wise to keep these Furies under your thumb. They're dangerous… you can tell that just by looking at them. But they are women, so that means they can be manipulated."

Sun Koh looked out the window, not saying anything in response. He wondered if he were doing the right thing suddenly… if he was truly a creation of the Un-Earth, perhaps that was where he should return. But he had made a promise to his beloved and that was the driving force behind his actions at present. But when it was over… would he depose Hitler? Or return to Un-Earth?

"You seem troubled, my liege."

"No. Just thinking about the future."

"Should you need counsel…."

"Thank you, Arthur, but I don't think that will be necessary." Sun Koh stood up and moved to the pilot's cabin, where Elsa was looking unusually pensive. He sat down next to her, saying nothing, and the girl seemed happy for the silence. They flew toward the United States on a mission of death, each lost in their own thoughts.

Ascott Keane sat in the middle of a pentagram carefully drawn on the floor in salt. Keane and The Rook were in the cargo hold of the fishing vessel, the dank area lit only by two lanterns, placed on opposite sides of the room.

The Rook stood nearby, watching his friend at work. He'd seen Keane perform his ritual magic before but it was always a unique experience. There was always a strange odor that accompanied this spell craft, one that smelled a bit like cinnamon.

Keane was chanting, speaking words that were mostly forgotten by the modern world. They were ones that managed to send chills down The Rook's spine, despite the fact that Max was all too familiar with the occult.

A ghostly glow began to form in the air just before Keane's face. It solidified until the image of a skull hovered there, the deep pits where the eyes should have been beginning to flash with a golden light.

"Ascott Keane," the skull said, its teeth clanking together with each word. "You are known to us. Why do you risk your soul by summoning us forth?"

The Rook straightened, feeling a growing bit of concern. He didn't realize that Keane was putting himself on the line in this way and he wasn't sure it was warranted.

Keane, however, didn't blink. Staring directly at the spirit, the occult detective said, "I'm seeking the location of a mortal... a man named Sun Koh. It's imperative that we find him, so I need to know not just where he is right now but where he will be in the near future."

"And what are you willing to trade for this information?"

"I am willing to give you one week of my life."

"No." The Rook stepped forward, being careful not to disturb the pentagram. "That's too much. I can find Sun Koh without you doing this."

Keane smiled softly. "I have made my offer." To the demon, he asked, "Do you accept?"

"It is a fair bargain. One week shall be lost from your days on this earth and the energy of that lost lifeforce shall belong to us."

Keane's face became grave. "Then tell me what I have asked: where can we find Sun Koh?"

The skull's golden glow darkened, becoming a light-tinged orange. "The Heir of Atlantis is on a plane with his allies. He plans to bring death to thousands. He will first have to set up his equipment... and he shall do so along the banks of what men call the Potomac." The skull abruptly ceased speaking, the yellow glow returning. "And now I have done as you asked. Send me back beyond the veil!"

"Not yet," Keane cautioned. "I have one last request of you: name those that Sun Koh calls his allies. We wish to know them!"

The skull made a groaning sound, as if it was pained at the further questioning. "He travels with four women, named Imelda, Akemi, Käthe and Elsa. There is a man, as well, called Arthur."

Keane nodded, digesting that information. "Thank you, o spirit. You may now depart."

The demon vanished in a wisp of smoke, leaving behind no trace of his existence.

"I wish you hadn't traded away part of your life," The Rook said.

Keane stepped from the pentagram and offered a shrug of his shoulders. "If you had a list of all the demons I've offered portions of my life to... you'd have an amazingly long list. I plan to take all necessary precautions to prolong my existence, Max, so I don't think any of those demons will get to enjoy my lifeforce anytime soon." Keane began to disperse the salt that made up the pentagram, kicking at it with the tips of his shoes. "Those names the spirit gave us – do they help you any?"

"Well, three of the girls he named make up that Furies group I told you about. The fourth one… Elsa… that's a new one. And I have no idea about who Arthur is."

Keane had opened his mouth to reply when a tremendous explosion suddenly shook the vessel. The ship dipped to one side so sharply that both Keane and The Rook had to grab the wall to keep from toppling over. A grinding sound filled the hold and, from somewhere else in the ship, they heard the unmistakable sound of rushing water coupled with the screams of the crew.

The hatch that led into the cargo hold was yanked open and the fishing boat's captain looked in, eyes wide with terror. "We have been attacked!" the captain bellowed. "A submarine has just hit us with a torpedo! We're going under!"

Chapter X
Death Trap!

Ascott Keane and The Rook were up on the deck within seconds, having sprinted up the stairs. The ship was capsizing quickly and the first thing Max saw as they reached the open air was that the crew was already readying the lifeboats. At the rate the ship was going under, they had only moments to do so.

The Rook fought his way to the railing, looking down at a partially submerged submarine. It was oddly shaped and bore no flags or colors that would identify its nationality.

"Who is it?" Keane asked, appearing at his side. The detective was clutching the railing so tightly that his knuckles were turning white.

"No clue," The Rook admitted. "But whoever it is, they're about to come out and say hello." He pulled free one of his specially modified pistols and held it below the railing, out of sight of the sub's crew. His guns were supposedly waterproof, but he'd checked them thoroughly anyway after being pulled from the sea.

Fritz scrambled past, jumping into one of the lifeboats when the opportunity presented itself. Max was glad that the kid was displaying more energy than before and he swore that if they all made it back to civilization, he'd find the young man some honest work.

A figure emerged from the hatch atop the submarine, dressed in drab gray uniform. He was of Oriental descent and had the bearing of a military man, though his uniform bore no direct signs of that. When he shouted, it was in English and quite fluent. "We will open fire on your life boats unless The Rook surrenders to us with The Fourth Nail on his person!"

Keane and The Rook exchanged glances. "Boy, you were right about people coming after that thing," Max whispered, a surprising amount of levity in his voice. Even though they were facing a far superior vessel, both he and Keane were so intimately familiar with such situations that they could laugh in the face of death.

The Rook addressed the mysterious figure, raising his voice so that he could be heard over the creaking of the dying vessel. "Who are you?"

"We are the ones who will kill everyone onboard that ship if you do not surrender to us!"

"Lovely fellow," Keane said. "You can't go with him, not with The Nail. We can't risk it falling into the wrong hands."

"Worst thing that could happen is they get saved, right?"

"And they'll be immortal, unless someone does them physical harm."

The Rook extended a gloved hand. He slid his gun back into its holster. "I have to take that chance. Hand over The Nail."

Ascott Keane looked like he might argue the point, but he looked around as the last of the lifeboats was dropped into the sea. Like The Rook, he wasn't prepared to let innocent men die. With obvious reluctance, he handed over the sacred relic. "I don't know if I'll be able to save you this time, Max."

"You won't have to, old friend. Trust me, the people on that submarine are going to wish they'd never invited me onboard."

Before Keane could respond, The Rook scrambled up on the railing and then launched himself into the open water. He landed with a splash and immediately began swimming toward the sub, pulling himself up with ease. The gray-garbed man seemed less self-assured now that The Rook was standing directly in front of him. He vanished down the hole and The Rook paused only long enough to offer Keane a jaunty wave before he dropped down after the Oriental.

The Rook's feet had just touched the deck when an all-too familiar voice spoke up. "Ah, Herr Rook. We meet again."

"Oh, no," The Rook whispered. He slowly turned to face Mueller, who was now dressed in the same drab gray that everyone else in this crew seemed to be wearing. A bearded man wearing a dark military-style suit stood beside Mueller, the unmistakable air of a commander about him.

"I can tell from your expression that you never expected to see me again," Mueller was saying, the pleasure unmistakable in his voice. "It takes more than you to kill the likes of me."

"I'll try harder next time," The Rook promised. He held The Fourth Nail aloft and a series of audible gasps filled the small chamber. "This is what all the excitement's about, eh?" Looking directly at the bearded man, he asked, "So do you want it, too? Or are you just Mueller's lackey?"

The man's jaw clenched. "I am the captain of this vessel. My name is Felipe Melo and I represent an order of Christian soldiers. That object you're treating so casually is one of the most precious things in all creation. And you're a lucky enough fool to be holding not only it, but also The Knife of Elohim. If you value your life, you'll give both of them over to us. We'll treat them with the proper amount of respect… and you can continue living your heathen existence."

"And Mueller's going to just stand back and watch me go? I don't think so. I think you're planning to get these objects and then turn me over to Mueller, so he can try to salvage his wounded pride."

Melo held up a hand before Mueller could respond. "You think yourself very clever, don't you? But the fact is, you're in our power... I don't need to make any bargains with you. I could simply take what I want. So you had best appreciate my attempts at being nice to you."

"You're so kind," The Rook answered. "But let me tell you something." He looked slowly at each person in the room, holding their eyes for a few seconds before moving to the next in line. "All of you are going to die unless you surrender your weapons. I'm going to leave each and every one of you lying on the floor in a pool of your own blood, moaning and crying like babies."

Melo's crew seemed somewhat unsettled by The Rook's bravado but neither Melo nor Mueller batted an eye. Melo reached down to the holster at his hip, unsnapping it. He drew his pistol and offered it to Mueller, who took it with obvious gratitude. "I am now offended. Mr. Mueller, feel free to put a bullet in his brain – but try not to cause too much damage to the ship."

The Rook moved so quickly that the men closest to him gasped in surprise. The Knife of Elohim appeared in The Rook's hand and the golden dagger flew through the air, the sharpened blade embedding itself in Melo's throat. Blood gushed like a fountain, staining the man's black uniform as his eyes widened. Before Melo had hit the floor, The Rook was drawing his own pistols, dropping into a crouch and spinning, blowing out the bellies and knees of the men around him.

Mueller, momentarily stunned by the sudden shift in events, tried to draw a bead on The Rook, but the vigilante threw himself forward, rolling in a ball until he came up on his knees directly in front of the Nazi. He pulled the triggers of both guns, ripping open Mueller's belly and sending the man flying backwards. He crashed into a control panel, sending up sparks.

Mueller panted, one of his hands going to his stomach. It came away dripping with blood. "You bastard," Mueller whispered. "How in the hell did you manage to do this?"

The Rook strode toward him, smoke curling from the barrels of his pistols. "You should have been glad that you survived the fall of The Valkyrie, Mueller. You could have gone on your way and enjoyed the rest of your miserable life. But you had to come after me again – and I never give second chances."

Mueller raised his gun with a shaking hand. Before he could pull the trigger, The Rook swung a leg up and kicked it away. It clanked off the hull and landed nearby.

The Rook put away his own guns and began pulling off the glove that covered his right hand. On his middle finger he wore a ring adorned by a blood-red gem. The gem's surface was marked by the image of a rook in flight. It had been forged in the heart of a powerful demon, a messenger to the old gods who existed before humanity crawled from the sea. "I'm going to kill you, Mueller, but not before I mark you."

Mueller shook his head, feeling weak from the loss of blood. He knew what was coming, had read about it in the reports that had come back on The Rook. The vigilante had a habit of pressing his ring against the foreheads of his enemies. Somehow, the ring's mystical origins allowed it to brand the flesh of evildoers, leaving the imprint of a rook on their bodies forever.

The Rook grabbed Mueller's hair and yanked his head back. He brought the ring close enough that Mueller could feel the air sizzle around it. He then shoved it hard against the Nazi's skull, causing Mueller to cry out in agony as his skin burned. Almost too quietly to hear, The Rook whispered his mantra, one that had become feared by all who faced him: "When the good is swallowed by the dark, there The Rook will plant his mark!"

Ten minutes later, The Rook had successfully canvassed the rest of the submarine, ensuring that none of the crew had escaped his notice. The injured and dying had been branded, one by one, and then dispatched to the next stage of their existence with a single bullet to each skull. Max didn't relish killing, in fact he'd taken an oath against it more than once, but he also realized that sometimes death was the only way to truly end someone's threat.

The Rook had gone through Captain Melo's papers, enough so that he now knew that the mysterious Order was a worldwide organization that was willing to kill for its religious beliefs.

It also reaffirmed a decision that he'd come to shortly after killing Mueller. The Knife of Elohim was a weapon that had proved its worth in his personal arsenal again and again… but The Fourth Nail was a problem. By its very nature, it was something that men would covet… and he was already tired of protecting it.

The Rook found the launching area where the sub's torpedoes were sent out on their errands of destruction. He carefully strapped The Fourth Nail to the side of one of the torpedoes and then launched it at the wreckage of the fishing ship, which by now was settling to the ocean floor. The resulting explosion was unlikely to destroy The Nail, but it would definitely make it harder for anyone to ever find again.

Max then set about using the periscope to check for Keane and the other survivors. Strangely, he didn't see them, which could only mean that Melo had given orders for the submarine to proceed at high speed away from the area. Given enough time, Max was sure that he would be able to navigate his way back to them… but he wasn't sure how much time he actually had. Sun Koh was on the loose, heading toward the Potomac. From there, he would launch his assault on the nation's capital….

The Rook had contacts in law enforcement, most notably the mysterious Mr. Benson who had played such a large role in smoothing over Max's own problems with the law. But would anyone believe him if he told them that he'd had a vision of death and destruction raining down on the city?

Deciding that the best way to help was to get there himself, The Rook changed the submarine's course, plotting a direction that would hopefully take him somewhere close to where he needed to be. He would use the radio to contact any ships in the area, sending them toward Keane and the others. Piloting a submarine wasn't something that The Rook was trained for, but his expansive knowledge meant that he was able to recognize the basics of it all and get it to work, though it wasn't easy running the entire vessel on his own.

When things seemed under control and he was able to finally relax, Max found himself drifting into a deep slumber. Given all that had happened in recent days, it had only been adrenaline that had kept him on his feet. He slept in the pilot's chair, head tilted backward… and he dreamed.

The thin barrier that resided between the worlds of the living and the dead was a fog-enshrouded place. There was no landscape to speak of, only clouds of white and gray that extended as far as the eye could see. The air here was slightly damp and smelled like fresh earth after a heavy rain.

Max Davies was as familiar with this awful purgatory as any human being in the world. It was here that he sometimes came when his father wanted to speak face-to-face, as opposed to the way Warren Davies usually preferred: sending horribly painful visions that compelled his son to do what he wanted of him.

Warren Davies appeared through the mist, wearing the suit he'd worn on the day he'd died. There were dried stains on the front of his shirt, as if the blood that had once flown from his wounds had marred him even in death. Max suspected that his father could have changed his appearance if he'd so desired… but he knew the impact that seeing him like this would have on his son.

"Max," Warren said, loving warmth coming through in the way he said his son's name. "You're doing well so far… but you have to pick up the pace. Sun Koh isn't waiting on you."

The Rook clenched his hands into fists, feeling once more like a little boy being berated by the man he idolized. Warren Davies had been a hero to everyone, including his son. He'd stood up to the criminal forces that had threatened his city and in the end it had gotten him killed. But even in life, Warren had been a stern father, always pushing Max to be the very best. And now that Max knew that his father had continued pushing and prodding, even from the grave, it made matters all the worse. "It's not like I'm sitting around doing nothing. There's been the little matter of The Furies and The Fourth Nail."

Warren moved closer but stopped just short of his son, as if he was afraid of any contact. Max felt the same trepidation. If his father were to embrace him, he wasn't sure how he would react — would he shove him angrily away? Or would he break down in tears? Either way, Max was too proud to want to find out. "I'm not condemning you, son. Things have a way of cropping up. I know that. But those visions of yours... they're for real. Sun Koh plans to destroy the nation's capital and then he's going to drive a stake right through the heart of the Allied forces."

"Do you have anything to tell me that might actually help... or are you just going to try and scare me into moving faster?"

Warren Davies didn't seem to take any offense from his son's tone. "The people that Sun Koh has surrounded himself with... they're not nearly as loyal as the ones he used to travel with. This group is filled with divisions and there's the potential for them to turn on one another. Use that, son! It may be the only thing that can stop Sun Koh from succeeding."

The Rook looked away, wondering about his father's words. He'd sensed some tension within The Furies whenever Sun Koh's name had come up... the German woman seemed devoted to him, the Japanese less so and the Italian didn't seem particularly inclined to follow him. And then, of course, The Rook knew nothing about the mysterious Elsa or Arthur.

"Thanks," he said at last. "I'll try and keep that in mind."

"Son?" The Rook looked his father in the eyes and Max was surprised to see something close to fear in the dead man's eyes. "You've never fought a man like Sun Koh. He was designed... he was built... out of psychic energy. He's specifically your opposite number. You're as an American ideal as they come. You were trained to be what you are but anyone could have done it, if they'd have the nerve and determination. Sun Koh receives all of his gifts through genetics. His heritage and his racial characteristics define him. That's the Nazi philosophy. When you two clash, it's going to reverberate amongst people on both sides. It's a war of ideologies, not just of men."

"That's an awful lot of pressure to put on me," The Rook said with a hint of a smile.

Warren Davies returned the grin and then, with obvious hesitation, reached out and gripped Max's shoulder. "I won't see you again until this is over, one way or another. Take care."

And then Warren Davies was gone, leaving The Rook alone in the void. He stood there, collecting his thoughts, until he felt himself slowly drifting back toward the world of the living.

Elsa Mayen had proven her worth to Sun Koh by the time they set down on the shores of the Potomac. Not only had she managed to evade detection by the myriad air defense systems in place around the American capital, but she'd also made amazing time while doing so. A large portion of the credit had to go to Elsa's father for having devised such an incredible aircraft, but Elsa had piloted it so well that one would have been hard pressed to believe she hadn't been the plane's creator.

After setting down, the group had stretched their legs outside the plane, setting up a small campsite near the water. The Furies were quite adept at this, having a lot of experience in dealing with the wilderness. Sun Koh allowed them to handle the bulk of the work, choosing to stay close to Elsa as she ran through a series of post-flight diagnostics. Elsa was nervous in his presence, but eventually grew used to him and began to ignore him as she went about her work. In fact, she didn't even notice when Sun Koh finally moved away to locate Käthe.

Elsa was wiping a bit of grease off her face when she heard movement behind her. Without turning, she assumed it was still Sun Koh. "Do you need the flashlight, Herr Koh?" she asked, knowing that it was becoming pitch black outside the sphere of light she'd set up so she could work.

"For a girl so slight and so young, you're quite a morsel."

Elsa froze in place, immediately recognizing that those words did not emerge from the lips of Sun Koh. She slowly turned her head to see Arthur Grin standing there, his lips twisted into a terrible leer. Elsa wasn't sure how to respond given that she was mostly unfamiliar with men hitting on her. She managed a mumbled "Thank you" and set to putting away her tools.

"Are you a virgin?"

Grin's question made Elsa jump. "Why would you ask something like that?" she gasped, unconsciously wrapping her arms around her upper body. "We don't know each other."

"I'd like to know you," Grin said, moving closer. His eyes seemed like deep pits of unending darkness and Elsa found the lack of passion there even more frightening than his words. She sensed the danger she was in, but felt like a deer caught in the headlights of an approaching vehicle. She couldn't avert her gaze from his and she began to tremble all over. "I'd like to be your first," he added in a lower tone. "When I was with the Inuit people, I made use of their women, but it was unsatisfying. There's something about being the first to plow those fields that is so intoxicating. Virgin territory, so to speak." He laughed then, though there was not a trace of humor in it.

Elsa suddenly bolted, trying to step around him, but Grin caught her up in his steely grip and shoved her to the ground. Though he didn't weigh very much, he felt like a sack of potatoes on top of the small girl. She struggled, but Grin caught her with a painful backhand that brought blood to her lower lip. He placed one hand around her throat and squeezed.

"You make a sound and I'll kill you," he said calmly. "Do you understand?"

Elsa nodded, tears filling her eyes. She suddenly wished her father were here and the thought of him made her feel ashamed. Maybe her tormentors had been right – she was no true heir to Jan Mayen. She was just a little girl playing dress-up....

Grin relaxed his grip on her neck, sensing the defeat in her spirit. He sat up and began tugging her pants down, revealing the soft downy fluff of her pubic patch. His eyes drank in her nudity and he quickly pushed his own trousers down, revealing his desire to her frightened eyes.

"Please," she whispered. "Don't do this."

Grin paused, his eyes traveling the length of her body. They settled on her face, watching as a tear ran from the corner of her eye. He leaned forward, tongue extended, and swept it from her face. He groaned at the salty taste and roughly shoved her legs apart. He placed himself at her entrance and shoved, causing her to scream in agonized despair. She was dry and her vaginal walls ripped terribly as he forced himself deeper.

Grin was grunting into Elsa's ear and so he didn't hear the approach of footsteps behind him. He cried out in surprise when he felt someone grab him by the collar and yank him to his feet. He slid out of Elsa with a sickening sound and Elsa immediately rolled onto her side, moving into a fetal position.

Grin gasped as he felt something sharp come to rest at the base of his erect penis. He turned his head to see that Imelda held him by the scruff of his neck, while Akemi brandished her katana dangerously close to his manhood.

"Looks like we interrupted something," Akemi said with a sneer. She leaned close to Grin and bared her teeth. "What's the matter, Arthur? Are you afraid to deal with a grown woman? Is that why you prefer little girls?" With every word, she pressed a little harder with the edge of her blade until Grin felt the skin break and a warm trickle of blood roll over his scrotum.

"She wanted it," Grin whispered calmly. "You saw her. She wasn't screaming or fighting."

Imelda reached up and took a firm grip on Grin's hair, yanking hard. "Is that true, Elsa? Did you want to rut with this pig?"

Elsa sat up slowly, wiping her nose with the back of a hand. Her eyes were red and angry, matching the vitriol in her shaky voice. "He's a liar," she hissed. "I didn't ask for that."

Akemi's eyes glittered. "Seems like you misinterpreted her desires. Are you going to apologize?"

Grin shrugged his shoulders as much as possible. "Of course. Elsa... I'm sorry."

The girl sniffled, looking away. It was at this moment that Sun Koh and Käthe walked into the scene. They found everyone bathed in flashlight, Grin's erection having wilted under the pressure of the blade.

"What is going on?" Sun Koh demanded, using the tones of a born leader.

Imelda gestured with her chin toward Elsa. "Our pilot was raped by Mr. Grin."

Sun Koh moved swiftly to Elsa's side, kneeling to examine her. She flinched at his touch, obviously ashamed, but he soothed her with kind words. When he saw the blood around her vaginal opening, he turned angry eyes toward Grin. "Arthur, explain this."

"The girl had been looking at me earlier. I thought she was interested. When I approached her, she seemed tentative, but I assumed it was because of her youth. She did not cry out when I began touching her."

Sun Koh gestured toward Elsa's lip, which was swollen and bloody. "And this?"

"She asked me to hit her. I was shocked, to say the least, to find one so young who was so… well, forgive me for saying so… slutty. She said she liked it rough."

Sun Koh stood up slowly. He approached Grin, their eyes locked on one another's. "I have killed many men in the pursuit of my goals. Bloodshed and violence are things I have grown accustomed to. But forcing yourself on a girl, one who is just past being a child… I cannot stomach that and I cannot allow it to exist in the Aryan paradise that I plan to create. Akemi, please remove the offending member."

Grin moved so quickly that not even the two Furies holding him could react. He slammed his head backwards, catching Imelda on the forehead. She released her grip on his hair and neck, allowing him to catch Akemi with a sharp blow to the chin. Her blade slid along the underside of his penis, drawing a deep cut but not severing it.

Grin spun away from them, well aware of Käthe's presence. He struck her in the chest with the flat of his right foot, driving her back. Then he whirled about to face Sun Koh, dropping into a martial arts fighting stance.

The Man of Destiny had remained unmoved during all this. If anything, the expression on his face had darkened, reflecting his displeasure at being betrayed. He had taken Arthur Grin into his confidence and now he was facing the man in open combat.

It called Sun Koh's decision making into question and that did not please the Heir of Atlantis.

"I'm going to take over this expedition," Grin was saying. "That gun of yours can help me bring peace to this world."

"You talk of peace after raping a woman?" Sun Koh asked.

"I was giving her a blessing, allowing her to lay with a real man for her first sexual experience. She should be thanking me."

Sun Koh danced forward, his body moving with flawless grace. He seized Grin by the wrist and yanked him forward. He slammed an elbow into the back of Grin's head and then flipped him through the air, sending the man tumbling onto his back. Sun Koh then kicked Grin on the side of the head, causing the fallen man to cry out in pain. But Grin was not defeated just yet. He snatched out with his hand and grabbed hold of Sun Koh's leg. He sat up as he drove his other fist into the Aryan's kneecap. Sun Koh grimaced as pain flared through his leg. He yanked himself free, but found that putting all of his weight on that limb was now impossible.

Grin did an impressive flip to get to his feet, spitting out some blood before rushing toward Sun Koh. He caught the Atlantean with quick jabs on each side of his face before Sun Koh drove a punch into Grin's midsection. Sun Koh then grabbed hold of Grin's penis with one powerful hand. The intense pain was enough to give Grin pause and he winced, unable to respond physically.

"You escaped the blade," Sun Koh whispered, "but you cannot escape my justice. Let this be a lesson to any who betray me!" The Man of Destiny yanked with all his incredible strength, stretching the already bloodied flesh. He kept pulling until Grin's penis came loose with a hideous rending sound, blood spraying the ground and Sun Koh's jodhpurs.

Grin fell back, shock already setting in. He fell to his knees, his groin a ruined mess. Sun Koh tossed the man's sexual organ to the ground. He caught Akemi's eye and gestured her closer. "Kill him," he ordered.

The Japanese woman needed no further encouragement. She raised her katana and brought it across in a swiping motion, cleaving through flesh and bone. Grin's head flew into the air, spinning end over end before landing at Elsa's feet. The girl didn't scream at the gory sight, however. Instead, she began to laugh. It was not a pleasant sound, as it contained more than a trace of madness.

Käthe came toward the girl, helping her to her feet. "Let's go get you cleaned up," she whispered, wrapping an arm around Elsa's shoulders. "It's going to be okay."

"I know it will be," Elsa said, a manic grin on her face. "He's dead. Chopped his head off!"

Käthe exchanged a worried glance with Sun Koh before leading the younger girl away. "Akemi and Imelda… help me, won't you?"

The Furies followed their leader, Imelda tentatively feeling her head and wincing. Grin's attack had left her dazed but mostly unharmed.

When the girls were gone back to camp, Sun Koh relaxed the breath he'd been holding. Arthur Grin's betrayal had wounded Sun Koh on a personal level and left him with the unusual feeling that perhaps he had not made the wisest of decisions. But he also knew that with the correct handling of the situation, this might draw the women tighter to him. They were all pleased with how he handled the matter. He could see that in their expressions. He only hoped that Elsa Mayen would be able to pull herself together.

Sun Koh turned to face the lights in the distance. Somewhere, not far away in the grand scheme of things, the President of the United States was readying himself for bed. The President had no idea that death was readying itself for a visit.

Chapter XI
Pieces of the Puzzle

Mr. Benson was a most unusual man. He was neither particularly tall nor wide but he possessed a rugged strength that spoke of many physical pursuits. His hair was white and close-cropped. His eyes were pale gray, though there was the occasional flash of blue, as if chips of ice lurked beneath the surface. His face was the most peculiar aspect of his appearance, however. It was so dead and white that he looked like he'd just crawled from a fresh grave.

His clothing stood in marked contrast to those he passed on his way through the halls of the Pentagon. While most men there wore either carefully tailored dark suits or military uniforms, Benson wore a gray jumpsuit that appeared to be completely without pockets. This was quite an illusion, however, as the interior of the suit was lined with a number of storage areas, each pocket containing useful devices or weapons.

Benson nodded now and then at men he passed and he was acutely aware that few of those were willing to stop and talk to him. There was an air of gravity about Benson, a singularity of purpose that made others uneasy. They all knew his story, of course: of how his wife and daughter had been snatched away from him, throwing Benson's features into paralysis and sending him down a one-way trip to Hell. Benson had forged in the crucible of his pain, becoming something both more and less than human. He had spent years hunting the predators of the innocent before moving to Washington, D.C. Now he helped the government deal not only with Fifth Columnists and gangsters but with those enemies who sought nothing less than world domination.

When he approached his office, a young woman stood up and moved around the desk that rested in front of his door. She was as slim and dainty looking as a Dresden doll, but Benson knew she possessed the fiery heart of a warrior. "Chief, there's someone here to see you," she said.

Benson cast a quick glance around but saw no one waiting in the two chairs reserved for such purpose.

"I went ahead and let him inside. I hope that's okay."

Benson's eyes were the only part of his face capable of showing surprise and they did just that. No one was ever allowed into his office when he wasn't there, not even the lovely woman standing in front of him. "I take it that I know this person?"

"Yes. He's an old friend… from Atlanta."

Benson stared at her for a moment and then nodded, reaching out with a steady hand to open his office. He stepped inside and closed the door behind him, his eyes scanning the office. Though most people would have seen nothing in the shadows, Benson immediately spotted Max Davies standing in the corner. Max stepped forward. He looked tired but otherwise unharmed. He had left his mask and weapons outside, not wanting to try and sneak them into the Pentagon. In fact, the only reason he'd gotten in at all had been that he'd directly namedropped Benson.

"Mr. Davies," Benson said, moving around the desk to sit down in a plush chair. The top of the desk was incredibly well ordered with only a few small stacks of folders set on the corner. "I'm surprised you didn't simply call me."

"I was in the area and thought I'd drop in to say hello." Max sat down across from Benson, leaning forward. "Can I speak freely?"

Benson nodded. "There are no recording devices in this office. I've made sure of that."

"I wasn't sure if you'd be in Washington. I did call your New York office first and one of your agents told me that you were here."

"I'm spending most of my time in Washington, at least for the duration of the war."

"I need your help."

"You know I'm always prepared to assist you."

"Are you familiar with Sun Koh?"

"Yes. He's an Aryan superman who vanished several years ago. Rumors suggest that he's returned but that the Reich isn't happy about it. We've picked up reports that indicate he's been marked for assassination by no less than Hitler himself."

Max didn't bother trying to hide his confusion. "Why in the world would Hitler want Sun Koh dead?"

"Because he views Sun Koh as a threat to him. Sun Koh is everything that Hitler is not these days: he's handsome, he's the epitome of everything that an Aryan is supposed to be… and most importantly, he isn't tainted by the growing doubts of those around him. Sun Koh has yet to lose – while Hitler's victories are coming slower than before and with more loose ends. If Sun Koh wanted to challenge Hitler for leadership of Germany, he'd have a good chance of swaying the populace."

Max took a moment to digest that before he continued, using the words he'd rehearsed on the way over. "Sun Koh is here, in America. He's hidden somewhere along the Potomac River and he's got a super-weapon that he's planning to use against Washington. He's going to kill thousands of people."

"How do you know this?"

Max hesitated. "I had a vision. My dead father sometimes sends me glimpses of the future... I saw what was going to happen."

Benson regarded Max coolly, his eyes searching the other man's face. "You know that I can't officially authorize anything based on that."

"But you believe me, don't you?"

"I have never experienced the supernatural, though many of my enemies have claimed to possess such powers. Always, it ended up being lies or deception, rather than true occult powers."

"I'm not lying."

"I didn't say you were. I simply said that I have never experienced the supernatural myself." Benson stood up and moved to the window, which overlooked a staff parking lot. "As I said, I cannot officially authorize anything... however, unofficially, I can give you what assistance I can." Benson turned his head slightly to look at Max. "What would you need?"

"I don't know where along the Potomac he's hiding, but he arrived by plane. An atomic plane, one invented by his old assistant Jan Mayen. It's supposedly invisible to radar, but they couldn't hide it once it was on the ground. I'd like to take my own plane and fly it along the river's length, looking for him. Once I find him, I'm prepared to deal with him and his allies personally. But his weapon – it generates a beam of light that destroys everything it touches. Just to be safe... I think you should evacuate the city, particularly the areas nearest the White House and the monuments."

"That's asking quite a lot."

"You know you can trust me, Benson. You helped get the police off my back and I'll always appreciate that. Since then, I've been able to help a hell of a lot more people than I would have otherwise. So believe me when I say that I know how hard this is: you'd be putting your faith in a man who just told you his dead father told him this information. But I could have come here and lied. I could have told you that I'd found this out from an informant or that I'd personally heard Sun Koh describe his plans. I chose not to do that because I didn't want to lie to you, even if it meant you might not believe me."

Benson looked back outside and finally gave a curt nod. "I'll speak to the President myself. I think I can convince him to evacuate the White House and close the monuments and museums for a few days. The press can simply be told that we've uncovered a plot by Fifth Columnists. There's simply no way I can do more than that – the panic that would ensue if we evacuated the entire city would be immeasurable. How long do you think you'll need?"

"Two or three days should be more than enough." Max stood up and approached Benson. He offered a hand in thanks, suspecting that Benson wouldn't take it. The man seemed to eschew physical contact. To his great surprise, Max felt Benson clasp his hand, squeezing it in a firm grip.

"You're a good man, Max Davies," Benson said. "Too many men in your position, with your wealth, would focus on personal happiness to the extent that they wouldn't apply themselves to helping make the world a better place. Most men don't apply themselves to bettering their surroundings until they've suffered a terrible loss, one that makes them view things differently."

Max swallowed, knowing some of Benson's back-story. "Thank you. That means a lot to me."

Benson dropped his hand and moved toward his desk, picking up the handset of his phone. "Miss Grey. Get me the President, please."

Max gave a wave as he exited the office, grateful beyond words. Sometimes it paid to have friends in high places.

Evelyn unlocked the doorway to her husband's private lair and, after making sure no one was watching, she descended the steps into The Rook's Nest. The name was a bit overly dramatic for a secret hideout hidden in a storm cellar, she had always thought. Then again, given the wide variety of equipment stored inside, it probably did deserve a better name than "the basement."

The Rook's Nest was where Max did his tinkering on gadgets, his scientific experiments and updated his files on criminals both great and small. There were details here that could sink political aspirations and ruin marriages, amongst other, even darker, things.

Evelyn had been somewhat soothed by a brief call from Max, who had told her all was well and that he was almost finished with his business. She'd known he was lying from the start. He had that vague quality to his speech that he always gained when he was concerned about worrying her. It was insulting, she mused, that he continued to sometimes treat her like she was too fragile to handle the truth.

Of course, if he had been totally upfront about his troubles, he'd probably have assumed that Evelyn would go off and do something foolish in an attempt to aid him.

Which, of course, was exactly what she was going to do.

Evelyn walked past a mannequin that wore her own adventuring clothes. She had a small domino mask similar to Max's and a set of padded clothes that helped her resist the blows and small-arms fire that inevitably came her way when she helped her husband on his nocturnal adventures. She had found it an interesting way of bonding with him early in their relationship and she'd definitely gotten a rush out of it from time to time. But she'd also realized how foolhardy it was to put her life on the line again and again. It was only a matter of time before someone snuffed out her candle, so to speak. She wasn't like Max – he'd trained for this almost his entire life. Being a flexible young girl who watched what she ate didn't really prepare her for dodging bullets.

Evelyn sat down in front of Max's filing cabinet, unlocking it with one of only two keys in the world that would do so. The locks were rigged with acid, so that if anyone attempted to pick them or otherwise force them open, the contents of the cabinet would be dissolved before they could be read. The other key was, of course, in Max's own possession.

Inside she found folder after folder detailing the many criminals that The Rook had encountered over the years. Many of them were amongst the worst the world had ever produced: The Warlike Manchu, Doctor Satan, Jacob Trench, Rasputin and Prof. Lycos. Those were just a small taste of the madmen that The Rook had faced and Evelyn had been at his side for most of them.

A much smaller, though still quite detailed, set of papers lay beyond those. These listed other mystery men and vigilantes that The Rook considered allies in his war on crime. Men and women like Leonid Kaslov, Ascott Keane, The Domino Lady and The Black Bat were included in these pages, which listed not only their contact information but also their observed strengths and weaknesses. That was something that Max naturally did – looking at human beings and sizing them up, breaking them down into strengths and weaknesses. At first, Evelyn had been slightly disturbed to discover that about her husband but in the end, she knew that it was simply how he saw the world, always preparing for potential threats.

Evelyn ignored all of those, instead choosing a small manila folder that lay flat in the back of the cabinet. It was completely unmarked and was sealed with packaging tape. She felt along the tape and quickly realized that she would never be able to tear it open with just her fingernails. She looked around and spotted a small cutting knife and quickly used it to slice open the envelope. She emptied the contents of the folder into her right hand, her eyes glittering when a single object dropped heavily into her palm.

It was a crucifix, dating back to the 13th century. Made of iron, it was quite heavy when worn. A plain chain link necklace was fitted through the crucifix. The Rook had picked it up a few years back, lifting it from a criminal aptly dubbed The Mad Monk. It was part of a paired set, the other piece being a much smaller version that Max now sometimes wore in one of his coat pockets. It wasn't that Max was particularly religious – it was simply that the mystical qualities of the crucifix sets were too powerful to ignore. Whoever held the larger of the two could be teleported to the side of the person carrying the smaller. The Mad Monk had used them to keep track of his mistress, whom he frequently accused of straying. Max had given the larger of the two crucifixes to Evelyn as a way of placating her, so that she could always find him in an emergency. But she didn't carry it around with her because of its weight… and because the device carried a taint of its own, making it a bit dangerous.

Anyone who used the crucifix had to pass through another plane of reality, one that was not the kindest of realms. Evelyn had never been through it herself but Max had done so, as part of his testing of the artifact. Evelyn knew that Max was not in mortal danger at this moment… but she also knew that he was going forward alone, without Keane or Kaslov to back him up.

There was no way in heaven or hell that she was going to let the love of her life do such a thing.

Evelyn closed the filing cabinet, locking it up tight. She then donned her adventuring gear, placing the mask on at the last moment. She always felt a bit silly wearing the thing, but she tried to tell herself that it was just another role for her to play. During her acting career, she'd handled every part conceivable, save for action-adventure hero. So these excursions were an excuse to indulge in a new genre for her.

Picking up the crucifix, she studied its heavy weight for a moment before closing her eyes and concentrating, visualizing her husband. A sudden gust of wind picked up her auburn hair and sent it flying, causing her to open her eyes. What she saw in her surroundings was enough to cause her to gasp in shock.

Gone was The Rook's Nest… in its place, she was now standing in the middle of a large lake of blood. Off in the distance she could see land and what appeared to be a herd of skinned elk dipping their crimson heads to sip from the bloody waters. A black crow flew overhead, its beady eyes seeming to examine Evelyn as it passed.

There was no clear direction for her to go in and Evelyn tried to remember what Max had said about the place: *The dimension belongs to a blood god named D'lham,* he had told her. *He isn't evil, per se, but he does require sacrifices from his followers. They have to regularly provide blood and flesh that he uses to build up his kingdom. When I was there, I had to swim to shore and cut my wrist. After making my offering, D'lahm himself appeared and let me pass. For a second there, I thought he wasn't going to… and that second was an awful one.* Evelyn remembered the look in Max's eyes as he recounted his experience… it had contained something that was almost never found in there: fear.

Evelyn began swimming to shore, angling her progress so that she wouldn't end up too close to the animal herd. Several of them were standing still, their heads raised so that they could better see her. She tried to ignore the revulsion she felt about her surroundings, but it was hard. The blood felt thick and syrupy and several times she thought she felt something moving against her legs. She shuddered to imagine what sort of fish could live in this environment. When she reached land, she pulled herself up and out of the water with a grunt, laying on her back on the rocky ground. She stared up into the sky, which, like everything else in this realm, was a reddish color. Thick, brownish-tinged clouds were hanging low in the sky and Evelyn had a clear vision of crimson rain falling from their bloated interiors. She hoped to be gone before that happened.

After fishing out a small knife from one of her pockets, Evelyn moved into a crouching position and extended her left arm. She placed the blade against her wrist and was about to press downwards when a silky male voice stopped her.

"Such a shame to mar such beautiful flesh."

Evelyn turned her head, spotting an entity that could only be D'lahm. The demon was over seven feet tall and crimson-skinned with a small brown beard and large obsidian horns that protruded from the front of his skull. His legs bent backwards and ended in hooves, a forked tail swishing behind them. He was completely nude and his sex organ hung low and heavy between his thighs.

"I'm… just going to make an offering so I can pass through," Evelyn said, finding her voice after a moment of surprise.

D'lahm turned his head slightly, examining her. "Why are you here? You are no occultist. I do not smell their powders or protective spells about you."

"I'm trying to get to my husband. I think he needs my help." Evelyn held up the crucifix. "I have this and it's supposed to take me to him."

D'lahm stared at the artifact and something came over his face, though Evelyn wasn't sure if the sight repelled or attracted him. "Yes, it does open a portal through my realm. An odd thing, isn't it? A Christian symbol that takes you into a realm where that God has no power?"

"I hadn't really given it much thought," Evelyn admitted.

"The men who created those trinkets were my followers, though they wore the mantles of Christians to avoid detection," D'lahm explained.

"I see. So may I pass through?"

"I must have my payment."

"That's what I was trying to do when you interrupted me."

"I can take payment in other ways, in ways that will not require you to spill a single drop of blood."

Involuntarily, Evelyn's eyes drifted quickly down to the demon's penis, which swayed a bit as he shifted his weight. She looked away quickly. "I'm a married woman," she pointed out coolly.

D'lahm threw back his head and laughed so loudly that it seemed to echo throughout the land, sending the herd bounding away in fear. When he had regained control of himself, he stared at Evelyn with obvious amusement. "You think highly of yourself, don't you, girl? If I wanted sex, I have hundreds of desirable women who would gladly do anything that I asked of them. No, I have other wishes for you. Amongst my servants on Earth are the vampires, a group that you have had dealings with."

"Unfortunately," Evelyn muttered. She felt strangely insulted by D'lahm's dismissal of her, though she was glad that he wasn't looking to force himself upon her.

"You are bound by threads that you do not realize," D'lahm said, his voice growing quiet. "In the days to come, you will be reunited with one of my servants. As a gift to him, I would like to weaken the barriers that hold your memories in check, so that you might remember fully who and what you are."

"I don't understand," Evelyn said.

"You will… in time. All I need is for you to agree to allow me to place a spell upon you, one that will ensure that you remember all that you should… when the time is right."

"All you want is to… give me my memories back?"

"Yes. Don't fear – I will not tamper with your mind in any other way. And you will not remember anything differently at this point. Only should you cross paths with my champion will you remember those things that have been lost."

Evelyn remained confused, but she didn't see the harm in allowing someone to help her remember something. "Fine. But then I want to be allowed passage through your realm."

"Agreed." D'lahm reached out and ran a hand through the air above her head. He whispered something that Evelyn couldn't make out and then he stepped, gesturing toward a fiery doorway that had appeared in the air. "Step through… and know that you are welcome to return."

Evelyn stared at the doorway, amazed that it had been so simple[3]. She moved quickly, afraid that D'lahm would change his mind. She jumped through the opening, afraid that the flames would singe her on the way through, but aside from brief warmth against her skin, she felt nothing.

The doorway closed tightly behind her, leaving D'lahm with a knowing smile upon his face.

---

3) This bargain comes into play in "Dead of Night" (The Rook Volume Four)

Chapter XII
Death in the Skies!

"**E**lsa? How are you?"

Elsa Mayen was in the river, her clothes left behind in the grass. She had been in the water for nearly an hour now and she was beginning to shiver terribly. Käthe and Akemi had been watching her for the past several minutes and after much discussion they'd decided they needed to do something. The rape of the previous night had obviously had a terrible effect on Elsa as the girl had not slept a wink. She'd simply sat in the midst of the camp, hugging her knees against her chest.

"Elsa?" Käthe repeated. The German woman sighed and began kicking off her leather boots. She tossed aside her cap and gloves as well before rolling up the legs of her pants.

"Are you going in after her?" Akemi asked.

"Somebody needs to."

"Imelda says she doesn't trust her to fly us safely."

"The girl was raped. She's traumatized, but she's strong. She'll bounce back."

Akemi watched as her friend dipped her legs into the water, slowly wading out to Elsa's side. She admired many things about Käthe, but it was her incredible ability to believe in the strength of her friends that was most impressive. Käthe could somehow make you stronger simply by showing you that she knew you could do it. That was one of the things that made Käthe such an incredible leader.

Elsa didn't seem to notice Käthe's presence until the blonde woman touched her shoulder. The girl then jumped, her head whipping about. She relaxed immediately, but her eyes remained wide and frightened.

"Elsa… it's time to get dressed. Sun Koh's going to want to get a little closer to the city."

"What happened to his body?"

"Grin? We burned it."

"I think it should have been left in the woods, for the animals."

Käthe nodded, putting an arm around Elsa's shoulders and drawing her close. "You're freezing. Let's get you dressed."

"Have you ever been raped?"

The question made Käthe pause. "No. I've had men try to force themselves on me but they never succeeded. I was trained to fight early on. Most men who tried that with me ended up regretting it."

"Can you teach me?"

Käthe smiled. "Yes. Would you like to become one of The Furies?"

Elsa looked quite solemn as she responded. "I can't."

"Why not?"

"Because then there would be two Germans. Imelda would want another Italian added to keep things fair."

Käthe blinked and then laughed long and hard. Elsa joined in after a few seconds and Akemi watched them both in amazement from the shore. "You seem to be doing okay," Käthe said at last. "Why aren't you sleeping? Why soak yourself for an hour out here?"

Elsa shrugged her slim shoulders. "I want to wash his stink off me. I can still smell him. And sleeping... I didn't want to sleep. I wanted to think about things. About how I should have reacted... and how Sun Koh punished him."

"I'm glad Sun did that," Käthe said. "Grin deserved even worse."

"Me too." Elsa leaned close and whispered, "It sounds so gross but after watching that, I wanted Sun Koh to lay with me. To make me a real woman, not like what Grin did to me. Isn't that awful? I'd just been raped and there I was, thinking about sex. I must be a whore."

"No... You were just wishing the first time had been different. Every girl thinks that way. Besides, Sun has a way of making women feel differently than they normally would."

They stepped onto the grass and Akemi helped Elsa get dressed, while Käthe rolled down her pants legs and slipped on her boots.

"Are you going to be okay?" Akemi asked in German.

"Yes. I think so," Elsa replied.

Käthe sauntered over, a smile on her face. "She's going to join us. We're going to train her to be a Fury."

Akemi glanced at Elsa. "That's true?"

"I'd like to be, yes. Do you have to get permission from your superiors?"

"They might like for me to... but no, I don't think so. Sun Koh told me that by remaining with him, we might become temporary enemies of the state. Hitler himself has targeted him for assassination. We might as well start making our own decisions."

Akemi put her hands on her hips and sighed. "Imelda isn't going to like that. She won't care about Elsa joining – I think she'd be fine with that – but she's not going to like becoming a traitor, even if we have Germany's best interests at heart."

"Once Sun is in charge, things will go back to the way they should be," Käthe pointed out, though she didn't sound all that convinced herself.

"Maybe… but I know Imelda views her loyalty as being to her government, not yours. She's not prepared to be an outcast so we can foster a revolution in Germany."

Käthe was about to answer when Elsa grabbed her arm. "What's wrong?"

Elsa was staring skyward. "Don't you hear that? A plane is coming."

"I don't hear anything."

"Neither do I," Akemi said.

"I do. It's a plane with silencers on its engines, just like on my dad's aircraft." Elsa finished pulling on her shirt and then she bolted toward their camp. She ran past a surprised Imelda, who was busy cleaning her guns, and bounded onto her plane. A moment later, the engines began to whirr to life and Imelda stood up as Käthe and Akemi entered the camp. Elsa leaned out the open door, waving at Käthe. "I'll be right back!"

"Where are you going?" Käthe shouted.

"There's only two men in the world who built engines like that: my father and The Rook."

Käthe looked around but still saw nothing in the skies above. "Don't go anywhere," she urged. "We need to find Sun!"

Elsa backed away, shaking her head. "I can handle this! I'll prove I'm ready for The Furies! I can take him in the air – that's my element!" Elsa pulled the door shut, just as Sun Koh stepped into the campsite, the Solar Cannon held in his hands.

"Where is she going?" Sun asked. He listened with growing alarm as Käthe filled him in on what had happened. There was nothing he could do to stop Elsa from taxiing forward and taking off into the air. He thought briefly about using the Solar Cannon to bring her down, but he didn't want to risk injuring her or destroying the plane.

"She's going to get herself killed," Imelda said.

Sun said nothing in response, though he did silently mutter an Atlantean prayer. The Rook was a dangerous foe, but Elsa had been trained well by her father… Sun would have to hope that would be enough.

The Rook flew through the clouds, careful to keep out of sight. His aircraft was painted black and was without markings, the few insignia normally on the exterior of the plane having been painted over. With the plane's silencing equipment operating at full power, The Rook was virtually undetectable to anyone below. Unfortunately, so far he'd spotted no signs of habitation save for a small group of fishermen camping a couple of miles outside of D.C.

Max wondered how the pilot had managed to avoid detection when entering American airspace. They had to be amongst the best pilots in the world to have managed it, even with a sophisticated atomic plane at their disposal.

It was at that exact moment that Elsa Mayen's atomic plane cut through the clouds and moved into view. It was moving to intersect with The Rook's flight path and for a brief moment, The Rook was so shocked that he wasn't sure what to do. He hadn't anticipated encountering the plane in the air – he'd been positive that Sun Koh would be down below, setting up his doomsday device. But there it was: a plane so sleek and beautiful that The Rook had to admire its design. Even from here, he could see some similarities to his own plane and this brought a new level of concern to him. If the pilot was as good as he suspected and that plane as powerful as it seemed, he was in for quite an aerial dogfight.

The atomic plane's guns suddenly spat out a fiery attack, the bullets strafing the underside of The Rook's own vessel. He sent the plane into a quick turn, avoiding the worst of the attack, but Elsa Mayen matched him, angling her own plane so that her guns continued to hold him in their sights. It was only The Rook's incredible skill that kept him one step ahead of her.

The Rook's plane vanished into a thick cloudbank, but Elsa Mayen was quick on its tail and Max realized that the atomic plane was even faster than his own incredible craft. The Rook pulled back on the controls, sending the nose of his plane higher. He hoped to come down in an arc, ending up behind his quarry but Elsa was too smart for that. She spun about, bringing the two planes nose-to-nose for a second before The Rook sent his ship downwards, just avoiding a midair collision. It was quite obvious that Mayen was wiling to crash her own plane if it meant bringing down The Rook.

The two planes circled each other, like prizefighters squaring off in the middle of the ring. This time it was The Rook who struck first, pressing a lever that caused flaps to open on the underside of his aircraft. Something that looked like a torpedo appeared held aloft by metal clamps. It was an air-to-air missile of The Rook's devising, designed to be ultra-lightweight, but quite deadly. A tiny propulsion unit on the back of the rocket flared to life and The Rook allowed the metal clamps to release, allowing the missile to fly toward its target. Elsa was stunned by the sight and made a futile attempt to avoid being struck. The missile tore off the backside of her plane, shearing it off like a knife slicing through butter.

The Rook watched as his enemy's plane broke in two, but his eyes widened considerably when he saw a strange fiery glow emanating from the shattered rear of the craft. He realized he was staring at the shattered atomic reactor that powered the unusual craft… and though The Rook didn't claim to be an expert in the burgeoning field related to atomic power, he knew that both the Allies and the Axis were working on bombs of considerable power using this as its chief element.

A human figure – shaped like a young boy or a particularly slim girl – ejected from the front half of the aircraft, a white parachute expanding out above them a moment later. The Rook saw the pilot staring back at the ruined aircraft and though he was too far away to read the expression on the person's face, he thought he detected horror and sadness in the posture.

The Rook pushed his plane toward the falling power core, wondering what he should do. If it crashed to the earth below, it could set off an explosion that could rattle windows in D.C., if not worse. He'd heard stories that such power sources could contaminate the ground and water for years to come. Realizing that he couldn't allow that to happen, he armed the second and final missile that his aircraft carried. He took careful aim and fired the missile, knowing that he was risking his life with this maneuver. He was going to detonate the bomb in midair, hopefully lessening its impact on the area below. That meant that The Rook could be caught in the explosion, however, and the aircraft was going to be little protection.

The missile slammed into the power core and the resultant flare was enough to light up the sky for hundreds of miles around. The impact slammed into The Rook's plane, rattling everything so hard that Max's teeth chattered. He closed his eyes and looked away, holding tightly onto the controls in the hopes of riding out the explosive fury. He thought he heard the plane groaning in pain and for a moment he could visualize what could be happening around him: the metal curving under the heat, melting in places, the windows suddenly bursting inwards, showing him in glass and flame. But after what felt like an eternity, the shaking lessened and Max opened his eyes to find that his plane was emerging from a cloud of fire and smoke to blue skies on the other side. He laughed aloud, having cheated death once again.

"Well, that was scary as hell."

Max's expression froze and he spun about in his pilot's seat. Evelyn was standing there in mask and adventuring clothes, a look of confusion writ on her pretty face. "How did you...?"

Evelyn held up the heavy crucifix she wore around her neck. "Emergency device, remember?"

"You nearly joined me in the grave," The Rook answered tartly and Evelyn was momentarily taken aback by his anger. "If we both die, who's going to take care of little William?"

Evelyn frowned and moved closer. "Both of us could die in a car wreck, Max... or be struck by lightning. Things happen." Evelyn kissed him on the head and smiled. "Don't be mad. I came to help."

Max sighed and nodded. "Sorry. I'm glad to have you here... but you showed up right when I was nearly blown up."

"And you think I should be home with the baby."

"No. It's not that, despite what I said. I just... I worry, that's all. About you and about our son. It was hard enough on me growing up without a father. I can't imagine having no parents at all."

"If something did happen to us, McKenzie would look after little William. You know that."

Max smiled as Evelyn settled into the seat next to him. "That was some great flying back there, huh?"

"Yes, it was."

The aircraft's radio squawked to life and a familiar voice came over the speaker. "Do you mind telling me what just happened?"

The Rook picked up the mike. "Sorry, Benson. There was a small atomic detonation over the Potomac. I tried to do it high enough where it would do less damage… but there's bound to be some. You might want to get somebody out here to monitor the water and soil in the days to come."

"I will do that. Is Sun Koh dead?"

"I don't think so." The Rook felt Evelyn touch his shoulder. She pointed down below and Max followed her gaze, noting that down below were a small campsite and an area of grass that showed that it had been used as a take-off and landing strip. "But I'm about to find out. Rook out."

"Ready to face the devil?" The Rook asked his wife.

"As long as you're at my side? Always."

Elsa Mayen's fall was carrying her straight into the maelstrom. She'd tried to angle her descent to carry her away from the explosion, but it seemed that she was being inexorably drawn toward it. She could feel the heat already and the air seemed to ripple before her eyes. She wished that she had known the touch of another man besides Arthur Grin… but that was not to be. She would never be a Fury. She would never lie moaning beneath Sun Koh. She would never become a **true and proper Aryan princess.**

And worst of all, she would never live up to her father's legacy.

She began to cry, then, and that was the worst shame of all.

Her father's voice seemed to call to her as she felt her body tumble into the flames of death. He was calling her name, asking her to join him in the pits of Hell.

Chapter XIII
Death Comes Quickly

The camp was empty but recently occupied. The embers still burned in the fire and a few odds and ends had been left behind in the party's haste to move out. Evelyn found several hair clips and other evidence of female habitation while Max noticed footprints that belonged to a heavy male wearing boots.

"They couldn't have gone far," Evelyn pointed out. "You don't think they might have been onboard that plane that attacked you?"

"I don't think so. Only one person ejected from it. They're probably out there right now, watching us."

The Rook drew one of his pistols and gestured for Evelyn to do the same. She reached down to her right pants leg and hiked it up, revealing a small handgun strapped to her calf. She unholstered it and checked to make sure it contained a full clip.

"What are they waiting for?" Evelyn wondered aloud. "If they can see us, they can shoot us."

"Only one of them is a marksman. The other two Furies prefer melee weapons. And Koh… I'm sure he's a master shot, but from all I've read he prefers close quarters as well."

Evelyn was about to say something when a fierce warrior's cry caused both her and The Rook to spin around. Akemi exploded through the air, leaping out from several trees. She held a katana in her hands, slicing at the air. She landed in a crouch and then, with a snarl, was upon them. She feinted with the weapon, driving The Rook and Evelyn back several steps. From the opposite side of the camp came Käthe. The German was cracking her whip loudly, a deadly expression on her face. The third and final of The Furies, Imelda, moved forward, a powerful hunting rifle in her hands.

It was Käthe who spoke first. "Not many men escape our grasp, Herr Rook. We salute you. And we offer you thanks for allowing us the opportunity to avenge our earlier failure. This time, you will die... we will make sure of it."

The Rook didn't have a chance to respond. Imelda fired her rifle and the shell ripped through The Rook's left shoulder, exiting out the other side. He bellowed in pain but was too well trained to not strike back immediately. He fell forward, spinning into a roll. He came up right in front of Akemi and fired, the bullet catching her in the belly. The Rook's specially designed shells were incredibly powerful and the hole that appeared in the Japanese woman's midsection was considerable.

"Akemi!" Käthe shouted. She saw her friend stagger back, a look of profound confusion on her face... and then Akemi toppled over, her right hip falling onto the blade of her sword. It cut deep and prevented her from falling completely. She remained several inches off the ground, blood and gore spilling to the ground.

For a moment there was absolute silence in the campsite. The Furies had faced defeat before but never like this: the three women were like sisters, having lived and trained together for years. They had shared joys, sorrows, loves and more... and now their trio was sundered. Making it even worse was the fact that Akemi had been killed by a man... all three women had struggled to prove themselves the equal of any male in the world. They had delighted in humiliating and killing their male enemies... and now one of them had dispatched "Red Beauty" with a single shot from his gun.

This strange period, when everyone simply stared at Akemi's bleeding form, ended quickly enough. Imelda saw Evelyn raise her pistol toward her and she squeezed the rifle's trigger again. Once again, her aim was true and Evelyn cried out as her fingers exploded in pain. She dropped her gun and held her bleeding hand against her, quickly counting to make sure she hadn't lost any digits.

The Rook had no time to aid his wife. Käthe struck quickly, seeking revenge for Akemi's pain. Her bullwhip wrapped around The Rook's throat and the Nazi was pleased to hear Max gasp in pain. He pointed his gun at her, but Käthe sprinted forward, yanking the vigilante toward her. She drove her free hand into his face, her fist connecting solidly with the bridge of his nose. He lost his balance and fell to one knee, unable to defend himself as Käthe slammed a knee into the side of his head.

"If she dies, I'm going to make sure that everyone you care about suffers." Käthe looked over at Akemi, seeing the icy stillness that had fallen about her friend. "I'll start with this girl you're with... and then I'll find out if you have any other lovers or children. And I'll kill them. Do you understand me?"

"I understand," The Rook gasped, "that you're insane. Sun Koh is a murderer."

"He is an Aryan hero," she answered, slamming another fist into his head. "And you... you are nothing but a coward. If you were half the man that Sun is, you wouldn't hide behind a mask. You'd stand tall and proud, encouraging others of your race to raise up arms!"

The Rook stared at her with venom in his eyes. "I hide my identity to protect those I love... and to prove a point. Under this mask, I could be almost anyone.

That's symbolic... I fight not for just **one** skin color or country. I fight for the **human race**."

The German woman scowled at him, amazed that anyone could spout such nonsense. She twisted the whip, binding it tighter around The Rook's throat. She saw tiny droplets of blood oozing around the strap.

Käthe looked over at Imelda, who was approaching the moaning woman with caution. "Knock her out," Käthe commanded. "But don't kill her yet."

Imelda nodded. "Who are you?" she asked Evelyn in English. "His mistress?"

Evelyn continued moaning until Imelda was within a few feet. Then she lunged forward, throwing her weight against the Italian's legs. The sudden impact sent Imelda falling backwards and she landed with a thud on the grass. Evelyn, trying to ignore the pain in her wounded hand, sprang upon her enemy's chest and snatched the rifle away before Imelda could secure her grip on it. Imelda looked up in surprise to see the rifle's barrel pointed directly between her eyes.

"Any last words, cow?" Evelyn asked.

"Don't do this," Imelda whispered. Her eyes flickered over where Käthe was standing with her back to them. The German was still beating and kicking The Rook, unleashing all of her fury upon him. Imelda looked back at Evelyn. "We are both women. We are sisters in a man's world. We..."

"I said last words, not last soliloquy." Evelyn pulled the trigger and Imelda's once beautiful face exploded in a shower of blood, brain, and bone.

Käthe froze at the sound, thinking that Imelda had refused her orders. She turned, readying her rebuke, and suddenly felt her insides begin to churn. Another Fury was dead, another friend and comrade had been lost.

Käthe reached down and unsnapped the holster at her hip. She drew out her own Mauser and took careful aim at Evelyn. The masked woman was standing up now and had turned to face Käthe. The rifle was pointed at the ground, but Käthe knew it could be directed upwards very quickly.

"Step away from him," Evelyn said. "Or you're going to join your friends."

"There is no negotiation," Käthe said, tears stinging her eyes. She fired twice, the bullets slamming into Evelyn's chest. Evelyn swayed on her feet for a moment before landing beside Imelda.

"You bitch!" The Rook said, suddenly yanking on the whip himself. Käthe's grip on it had loosed as she dealt with Evelyn, allowing Max to both regain his breath and take control of the situation. Käthe landed on her rump beside him and Max threw both hands around her head. He was surprised that she didn't struggle in the end. It was as if she knew what was coming and accepted it. The only words she said were "I loved him," and then she was dead, her life ended as The Rook twisted her head with incredible strength.

The Rook sagged back and then forced himself to his feet. He felt dizzy, both from the loss of blood and from the multiple blows he'd taken to the head. He crouched beside Evelyn and nudged her. "You okay?" he asked.

Evelyn sat up, looking surprisingly well for having taken two bullets. She pulled open her shirt, revealing the padding she wore beneath. The slugs were there, embedded in the fabric. "You're a genius, Max. I just wish my gloves offered the same protection." She held up a bloody hand and winced in pain. "Feels horrible."

"Looks just as bad," Max deadpanned.

"Oh my god," Evelyn said. "Look."

Max turned and saw something straight from his nightmares: A powerful beam of solar energy was headed toward Washington, D.C. It was the scene he'd witnessed before and he'd failed to stop it. Sun Koh was about to rain death down upon the nation's capital.

The Man of Destiny knew that his Furies were dying, but he could not save them. He had to put his priorities in order and the most important thing – the thing he had promised his beloved he would do – was to drive a stake through the heart of The Allies.

As soon as he'd witnessed the detonation in the air, he'd known what was going to happen. Talented young Elsa Mayen was dead and The Furies would have to delay The Rook so that Sun Koh could begin the final phase of his plan. Ever since Käthe had told Sun Koh that the American vigilante was searching for him, the Heir to Atlantis had begun studying all that he could find on The Rook. He had tapped the minds of all three of The Furies, plus Grin, and had pieced together what he believed was an accurate portrayal of his enemy. Like himself, The Rook was a master of multiple disciplines, foremost amongst them being all manner of hand-to-hand combat and mechanical engineering. He believed that The Rook was, in so many ways, his opposite number… it would be fitting that such a man would rise up now, when Sun Koh's victory was so close at hand. Sun firmly believed that a man could be judged not just by the quality of his friends, but also by the skills of his enemies. Great men eventually found great opponents for it was in the defeating of such foes that true growth was attained.

And so Sun had asked Käthe and the others to deal with The Rook. They had seemed excited by the task and he knew that all three considered the fact that The Rook was still alive as a personal slight to their prowess. Perhaps, he mused, they would find a way to defeat him. They had, after all, captured The Rook once before… but somehow, Sun didn't believe that likely. Götterdämmerung had come and there was no turning back – The Rook would know this and would come fully prepared to fight his way to Sun Koh.

The Solar Cannon had fired its first deadly burst into the air and Sun Koh had felt a sense of great elation. The Rook was going to be too late…. Washington was going to burn. Even if The Rook had somehow managed to warn the residents of the great city – and that seemed very likely, since The Rook had inexplicably managed to trace them to this location – there would be no time for everyone to be evacuated. Thousands were going to die and The White House would smolder in ruins.

After Sun Koh had attached the cannon to the amplification device, he threw the switch that caused it to hum to life. The Solar Cannon's ray then shot high into the air, ionizing the upper atmosphere until a solid sheet of white light came crashing back down. It tore into Pennsylvania Avenue, ripping up asphalt and steel, destroying cars that had been left behind on the city streets and eradicating fences and yards. Benson had been good to his word about rushing people away from the major tourist spots. Right now, men, women, and children were huddled together in various shelters, having been told of a possible Fifth Columnist attack on the heart of Washington, D.C. Not everyone had been pushed to the shelters and the screams of the dying could be heard, even over the crashing din of the solar attack.

Sun Koh made sure that the Solar Cannon was locked in place and he pushed hard on a switch that would ensure that it continued to fire even though no one was directing it. He stepped back from the Solar Cannon and flexed his mighty muscles, rolling his head around in a circle. "They were good women," he said aloud, speaking in fluent English. "When the war was over, I would have found them good men for breeding purposes... if I had not chosen that honor for myself. Even the Oriental and the Gypsy could have added strong bodies to the Aryan cause. I shall make sure that they are never forgotten."

The Rook stood nearby, a pistol in each hand. "Turn off that machine. Now."

Sun turned to face The Rook, a coolly confident smile on his lips. "No. I shall not do that."

The Rook pointed both guns at the Solar Cannon and fired. The explosive shells ricocheted off the Cannon, flying in all directions. Sparks flew wherever they touched the weapon but aside from a few scratches, they did nothing to damage the machine.

"Did you really think I'd build an inferior device? There is only way to stop the Solar Cannon." He gestured toward the controls located at the back of the unit. "You have to go through me."

The Rook pointed the smoking barrels of his guns at Sun Koh. "Then that's what I'll do."

"You won't shoot me."

"What makes you think that?" The Rook asked, cocking both pistols.

"Because both you and I need to settle this. We need to know who is truly the stronger and more deadly."

"I'm not going to let people die while we thump our chests. Turn off the Solar Cannon or I'll see if you're as bulletproof as that weapon of yours."

Sun Koh's smile faltered a tiny bit and he shrugged his shoulders. "Perhaps I misjudged you. I think you mean what you say... but something has kept you from shooting me, so I think my words have some truth to them." Koh reached over and turned off the Solar Cannon, stopping the deadly beam that had destroyed nearly half a city block, reducing it to rubble. "I will reactivate it once you are dead," the Aryan superman declared.

The Rook lowered his guns and holstered them, quickly discarding the long coat he usually wore. This left him in his shirt, tie, and slacks. He pulled off the gloves that covered each hand and tossed them to the ground. He would have kept his promise, shooting Sun Koh in cold blood if he'd had to. But he was glad it had gone this way… just as Sun had said, there was a part of him that relished this.

The Rook had faced "opposite numbers" before but never quite like this. Even though The Warlike Manchu had found a man whose back-story mirrored Max's own and had trained him to be the murderous Shinigami, The Rook had never truly felt that he'd encountered his true reflection. And The Warlike Manchu deserved a special sort of hate on Max's part… but they were as different as they were alike.

But Sun Koh… as his father had pointed out, there was something deeper at work here. It was truly the clash not just of two men but also of two ideologies: the power of the self-made man versus the theory of eugenics. Which was, in the end, the correct path to follow?

"No weapons," Sun Koh said, reaching behind his back to retrieve a dagger he'd kept in the waistband of his pants. He held up the blade and then flung it aside. The Rook nodded and undid the set of holsters that held his guns. They, along with The Knife of Elohim, were set in the grass.

"One of us is going to die," The Rook said. "Are you sure you don't want to rethink this? You're brilliant… there's so much we could accomplish together. We could end this war and find a way to build a lasting peace."

"You're to be commended for making me such an offer… but you know as well as I that any alliance between us would be doomed from the start. We are fundamentally different and there is no enduring union that can be forged. Let us dispense with falsehoods. You and I both know that we have waited for this from the moment we heard of the other. You have chased me halfway round this globe. And now we shall see who is the greater man."

The Rook sighed, dropping into a fighting stance. Sun Koh mimicked the pose exactly and both men gave the other a silent nod, reflecting that they appreciated the skill and grace the other possessed. Then, without preamble, they rushed toward one another. Birds took off from nearby trees and the ground itself seemed to shake. Two of the deadliest men ever birthed in this or any other world were now locked in mortal combat.

The Rook caught Sun on the side of the head with an open-fisted blow and almost simultaneously the Aryan jammed an elbow into The Rook's ribcage. Both men were silent as they exchanged more blows: The Rook ran a fist under Sun's chin and followed with a backhand that sent spittle and a bit of blood spraying from the Atlantean's mouth. Sun was just as precise with his own attacks: he hit

- 116 -

The Rook with the strongest blow to the midsection that The Rook had ever felt, making Max wonder for several breathless seconds if the force of the impact had actually stopped his heart. Then the blood began flowing again, pounding in his ears. Sun had also kicked with the heel of his boot, catching The Rook in the left knee, causing it to buckle long enough for Sun to shove The Rook onto his back. The advantage was short-lived, however, as The Rook managed to spring back up with a gymnastic move that would have wowed any Olympic judge in history.

The Rook then barely ducked out of the way of another powerful roundhouse from Sun Koh and he reached up to grab the slightly larger man's arm. He used Sun's own momentum to carry him forward, flipping him hard to the ground. The vigilante then slammed his foot down, hoping to crush Koh's windpipe. But the Atlantean threw up his hands in time, catching The Rook's foot and giving it a terrible twist. The snapping of bone echoed in the clearing and The Rook cried out for the first time since the battle had begun. He pulled free of Koh's grip, but found piercing pain shooting through his entire leg whenever he tried to put weight on it. Sun rose almost leisurely, well aware of how badly hurt his enemy now was.

"Do you wish to yield? I will make your death quick and painless if you do."

The Rook resisted the urge to spit in the other man's face. "I thought we were dropping the lies," Max responded. "If I did give up, you'd make an example out of me... my death would be something the Nazis back home would be talking about for years."

Sun nodded, spreading his hands out wide in an apologetic gesture. "You are right, my friend. I suppose I felt obligated to play the part. Still," he said, gesturing to The Rook's injured foot, "you are no match for me now."

"Even with one leg, I can still beat you."

Sun appeared impressed by The Rook's resolve. "I would expect nothing less of you," he said with obvious respect. "Even though you were on the wrong side, we will remember your name in the days to come as well. You are a symbol of our ultimate nemesis."

The Rook gritted his teeth as Sun Koh came at him again, moving so fast that he seemed almost a blur. The Rook managed to block a blow to his head but quickly realized his error: the headshot was simply meant to disguise Sun's true intent. Even as The Rook threw his arms up in protection, Sun was whipping his leg behind his foe's, taking him off his feet. Max landed hard on his side and he was grateful that his injured ankle ended up on top of the other foot and not the other way around.

Sun threw himself toward The Rook, slamming his knee into The Rook's ankle. The pain that shot through Max's body was enough to cause him to temporarily black out. Even though it only lasted a few seconds, it was enough to put him into dire straits. When he regained his focus, he saw that Sun was now crouching on his chest, knees holding his shoulders to the ground. Sun reached out and gripped the sides of The Rook's head. Max had a sudden vision of

Käthe's final moment, when her own neck had been snapped.

"She said she loved you," The Rook blurted out.

Sun paused. "What are you saying?"

Max kept his eyes fixed on Sun Koh's face, but was sure that he recognized where he'd landed. He couldn't risk looking to make sure but if he was right, he might have found his salvation. "The blonde. The German. She said she loved you right before she died."

"Her name was Käthe. She was a good woman. The Aryan ideal."

"That didn't save her life," The Rook pointed out. "She was the vision of your Fuehrer's perfect race, wasn't she? Blonde, blue-eyed, physically fit but in the end, she died just like any other woman would: with the memory of her lover foremost in her mind."

"What are you getting at? Are you simply stalling for time?"

"Just thought it was interesting." The Rook stretched out his hand while he was talking, his fingers moving through the grass. "Did you love her, too?"

Sun hesitated, seemingly unable to resist answering. He seemed strangely troubled by the discussion of Käthe's death. Max assumed it was because he'd cared for the girl... but the truth was that Sun was simply tired of death. He had seen too many good men and women die in his name and it was beginning to create chinks in the armor of his self-assurance. "There was only one woman I ever loved... and she is gone."

The Rook's fingers curled around the hilt of The Knife of Elohim and he suddenly brought the blade up high, jamming it into Sun Koh's neck. Blood spurted in a thick gush and the Atlantean fell off his enemy, his face twisted in agony. The blade burned those of evil intent and right now it was causing the flesh around the wound to sizzle and turn black. As Max scrambled to his feet, gasping in pain, Sun Koh reached up and yanked the blade free, hurling it away.

"You cheated," Sun muttered, holding one hand against his neck. The blood was flowing copiously and Max knew he'd hit something vital. "No weapons," Sun reminded him. With each word, more blood was pumped out from his throat and specks of the crimson fluid appeared on his lips.

"I prefer to think of it as good old-fashioned ingenuity." The Rook reached out and caught Sun Koh by the collar of his shirt. He dragged the Aryan toward the bank of the river, forcing the man to his knees. Each step was agony for Max, but he knew how close he was to ending it and this drove him forward with renewed energy. "It's still not too late, Sun. I really did mean what I said earlier. We could help each other. Will you consider it?"

The Heir to Atlantis looked at him and gave a curt shake of his head. He said something, but his words were lost in the garble of blood that came pouring forth with the effort to speak. Max thought he was saying something about finding his friends again but he wasn't sure... and in the end, it didn't matter.

The Rook shoved Sun Koh's head into the water. He held him down firmly, holding on despite the thrashing that ensued. The struggle was very brief, however, as Sun had lost too much blood to maintain his strength.

After about five minutes, The Rook pulled Sun free of the water. The man's eyes were wide open but glassy and there were no signs of life about him. The Rook hobbled over to pick up his weapons and then returned to the corpse. In his line of work, he'd seen people revived from worse than this… and so he took the further precaution of putting a bullet into Sun's head.

When that deed was done, The Rook closed his eyes, intending to take a moment to catch his strength. Before he knew it, he had slipped into unconsciousness, his body tumbling over onto Sun's. They lay like that, one atop the other, until Evelyn finally came looking for them.

Chapter XIV
All Hail the King

"I'm comin'! No need to get your horses all slathered up!" The housekeeper at the Davies Plantation was an old woman named Nettie, whose skin was so leathery that it looked like parchment stretched taut over her bones. Despite her age, her eyes burned with a keen intelligence – had she been born in another place and time, this Negro woman could have achieved wonderful things. As it was, she was a beloved member of the household and as dear to both Max and Evelyn as their own mothers.

Another knock came from the front door and Nettie uttered an oath that would have shocked her preacher. As it was, she opened the door with a lovely smile on her face, giving no clue as to the annoyance she was feeling. "What can I do for you today?" she asked sweetly.

The grim expression on the face that awaited her momentarily caused her to gasp aloud. She'd met Benson before, but every time she looked into the fiery depths of his eyes, she was reminded of her own mortality. "I'm here to see your employer."

"Mr. Davies? He's not feeling very well."

"He's well enough to see me. Please tell him that I'm here."

Nettie stepped back and allowed Benson in, showing him to the study. Normally, she would have offered a guest some iced tea but in this case, she just wanted to be away from the man as quickly as possible.

Benson sat ramrod straight in his chair, his eyes never moving from the fixed spot he stared at: he was looking at a painting on the wall, showing Max, his wife and their son, only months after little William's birth. If the image sparked any memory of Benson's own lost family, his eyes betrayed nothing.

When Max entered the room, he was alone and dressed in a button-down white shirt and slacks. He moved as though his entire body ached but what caught Benson's attention the most was the weariness he saw in the other man's eyes.

"Your housekeeper said you were unwell. I apologize for disturbing you."

"I'm sure you wouldn't be here if it weren't important."

"That's true. Your heroism has been noted at the highest levels. If not for you, the death toll could have been much greater and the entire affair could have derailed the Allied war effort. The President wishes me to personally extend his thanks."

Max sat down and smiled. "And what else?"

Benson's eyes flashed. "Where is the Solar Cannon?"

"Oh, that."

"Yes. That."

"I don't think anyone should have something like that. It's too dangerous."

"That's not really for you to decide."

"Actually, it is. I was the one there with it and I knew your men were coming. I had to decide if I was okay with that… and I wasn't."

"We're at war, Max. A weapon like the Solar Cannon could help us win it sooner."

Max leaned forward, lowering his voice. He was one of the few on the planet who was not intimidated by Benson's gaze. "A lot of people would die horribly. I know about the bombs that we're developing and I'm not sure how I feel about those either… but I do know that I saw this thing at work and it was awful. I trust you, Benson… I really do. But I don't trust everyone you work for. The Axis powers have to be defeated but it doesn't mean we have to use the tools of the devil to do it."

"You could lose a lot of that goodwill on Capitol Hill saying things like that, Max."

"I'll take that chance."

Benson nodded, looking away. "Might I ask what you did with the body?"

Max smiled a little. When the authorities had arrived, he'd shown them where The Furies had fallen, but he'd hidden Sun Koh's body before they'd arrived. "I didn't want to see it stuffed and mounted in the Smithsonian."

"He was a murderer. That fate would be exactly what he'd deserve."

"I don't deny it. But there was something noble about him… even at the end, I kept wishing things had been different. That he'd have been willing to listen to me. Outside of Leonid Kaslov, I've never met someone as brave and intelligent as this Sun Koh was."

"You sound quite taken with him."

Max shifted his body and Benson recognized indecision in the other man. "I just think he had a destiny and there wasn't anything that would let him change course from that. It makes me wonder if we're all just pawns in someone else's story. I wish he'd had the chance to be the hero he could have been rather than the villain that his hatred made him become."

"We aren't characters in Sun Koh's heldromans, Max. We're all free people with the ability to decide our own fates."

"I burned his body, along with the Solar Cannon, here on this property." Max spread his hands wide. "So you can arrest me if you want. But I did what I felt was right. For the record, though, I think you're right."

"What do you mean?"

"Real life doesn't have tidy endings, not the way those magazine tales do. Sun Koh's final story would have had a very different climax if this had been a work of fiction. Not all of us get the ending we deserve, I suppose."

Benson, who knew something about unfinished business, could only silently agree. He rose from his chair and offered a hand to Max. "You did a good job. Congratulations and thank you."

Max accepted the handshake. "Are you going to get into any hot water over what I've done?"

"No. The army brass will move on to some other concern soon enough. As I said, there's a war going on. No one has the time to dwell on recent events."

Max stopped Benson from leaving, placing a hand on the man's arm. "Thanks for the help. And for trusting me in the first place."

Käthe stepped into Sun Koh's private chamber, finding her lord and master seated at his desk, signing another of his many proclamations. The war had long since ended, beginning the rather tedious process of building an enduring empire amongst all the conquered lands. It was an arduous task but if anyone could pull it off, it was going to be King Sun Koh.

"Are you going to keep them waiting all day?" Käthe teased, standing at attention near his desk. "Your Queen wishes me to inform you that soon she will lose patience."

Sun looked up and smiled. Käthe was pregnant with their second child and she was proving to be one of his best consorts, capable of aiding him in day-to-day running of the empire and also strong enough to provide him with many good, strong heirs. "I'm surprised she didn't come to get me herself."

"She wanted me to remind you that the last time she did that, the two of you ended up making love on your desktop and you were even more late than you are now."

Sun Koh laughed and stood up. He wore a dark suit, the sleeve of which was adorned by a Swastika. All over Europe, various symbols of his power were being erected – the Swastika was only one of those. He had also brought back a number of Atlantean designs and motifs, reminding the Aryan people of their heritage.

Together they strode down the corridors of power. Once, Adolph Hitler had ruled from here, but his corpse was now piled in a mass grave, along with those who had remained loyal to him. Most people had recognized the power of Sun Koh, especially after he had destroyed Washington, D.C. and personally slain The

Rook. But there had been a few holdouts, particularly those who knew their own power base was going to be weakened under the new regime.

Käthe led her Fuehrer to a balcony from which he would be addressing the people of Berlin. Thousands were crammed into the area beneath chanting his name. His cabinet of advisors greeted him with smiles and nods. They were all here, the men and women he loved, and they in turn adored him: The Furies, Ashanti Garuda, Alaska-Jim, Sturmvögel, Jan Mayen and his daughter Elsa, Rolf Karsten and Ludwig Minx. Only Arthur Grin was absent, having been dispatched to quell an uprising in Greece.

Sun Koh stopped long enough to kiss Ashanti on the lips and then he moved to the edge of the balcony, leaning out over the railing. The sea of Aryan faces below went wild, chanting even louder and pumping their fists into the air.

They loved him, their Prince of Atlantis, their Aryan King. In the tongue of the ancient Aryan peoples from whom he'd sprung, Sun Koh addressed the crowd. "Sons and daughters of the master race, I salute you! Our victories have been won on the field of battle with honor and blood. And now an era of Aryan peace is upon us!"

The cheers were so loud that they drowned out what Sun Koh was about to say, but the King of the Aryans did not mind. This was heaven and he was glad to be here.

Sun Koh had won and his heart was filled to excess with happiness.

THE END

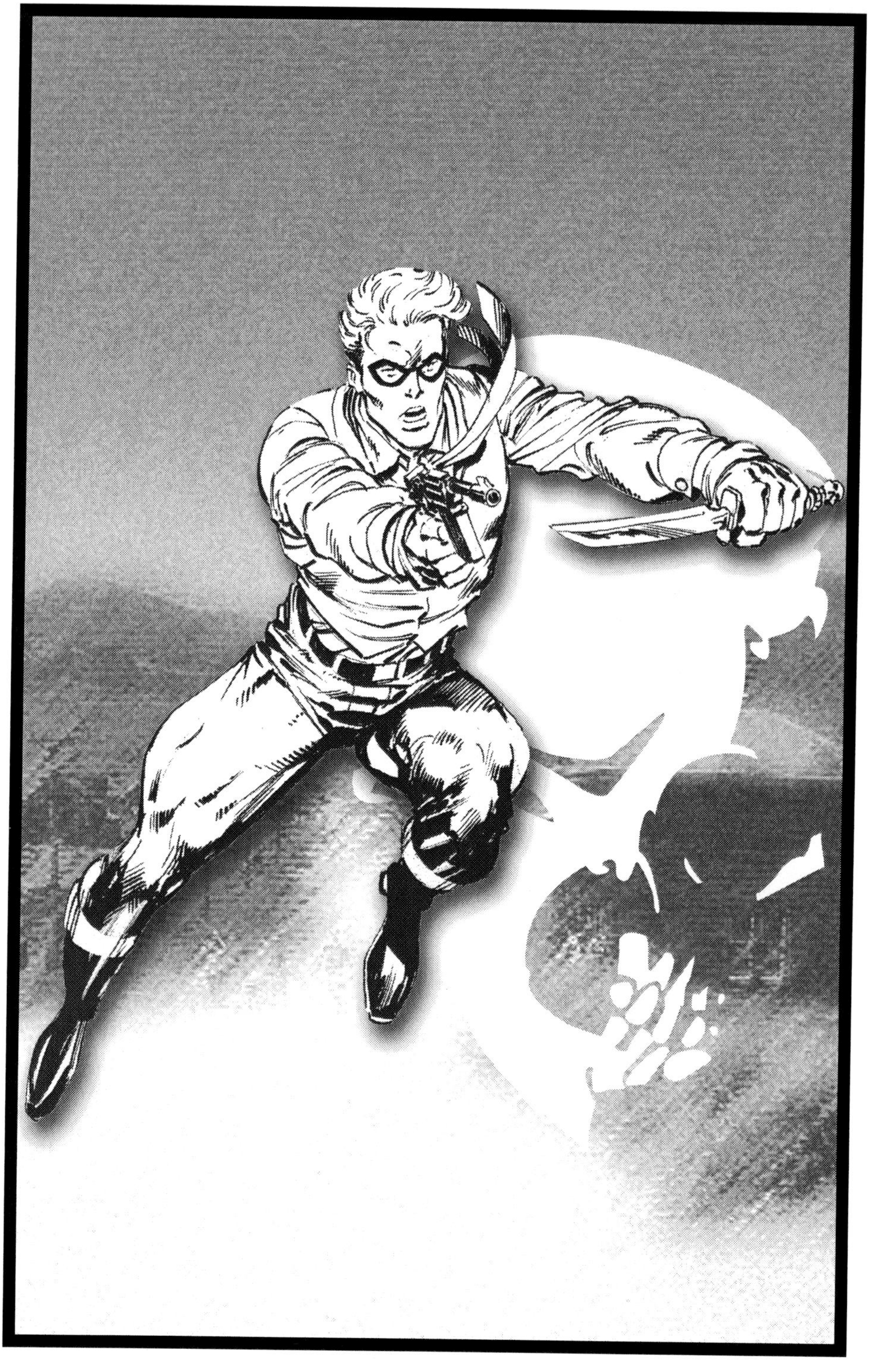

SINS OF THE PAST

An Adventure Starring the Rook
Written by Barry Reese

Chapter I
A Stranger in Town

He rode up from the desert, a weather-beaten sheepskin lined coat wrapped over his powerful frame. His clothing was covered with dirt and he smelled of sweat and horse, the result of a long, hard ride up the Southwestern corner of the state. His dark hair had a slight wave to it and his olive complexion hinted at Mediterranean ancestry. But it was his face – strong and well-defined – that caught the attention of the men and women he passed as he entered town. There was a dangerous cast to his eyes, as if this was a man who had seen his fair share of death… up close and personal.

His chestnut colored horse ambled through town, making a beeline for Mabel's Bed and Breakfast, the only decent place to stay in the town of Eagle Eye. There were a few rooms for rent above the bar but most of those were snatched up by the drunks who couldn't find their way home in the evening.

The stranger dismounted in front of the Bed and Breakfast, tying his horse to the hitching post. A stiff wind was creating little dust devils about his boots, further obscuring their black surface. They were the kind of boots worn by the military, but there was something in the man's manner that suggested he wasn't cavalry. He was something else entirely.

Once inside, the stranger removed his hat and pulled open his coat, revealing

THE SINS OF THE PAST

a pair of odd-looking pistols. The desk clerk who leaned across the counter, watching the new arrival with undisguised interest, thought to himself that he'd never seen the likes of them before. The gun chambers seemed fatter than usual and the clerk wondered at what sort of bullets could be stored in such things. From where he was standing it looked like each gun held several hundred miniature rounds.

Curious now, the clerk took in the rest of the picture, examining the man's dusty boots, rugged dungarees and a flannel shirt. The clothing was all very nice, despite the worn nature of their appearance, making the clerk wonder if the stranger was from the big city. In the stranger's right hand was clutched a clasped box about the size of a small shoe box. It was carved of wood and looked very old.

"Can I help you?" the clerk asked. As the stranger approached, the clerk made sure to show off the hand-made name tag he wore. It read 'Rusty' in big block letters. "Need a place to stay, I reckon?"

"Yes. Thank you." The stranger's voice sounded strangely disbelieving and Rusty straightened, wondering if he was going to be like the last city fellers who came through... always laughing and pointing at the 'hicks' in Eagle Eye.

"Where from?" Rusty asked, pulling a ledger out from under the desk. He pushed it toward the stranger, who deftly picked up a pen and signed his name in a flourish.

"Atlanta."

Rusty nodded, taking a gander at the ledger as he did so. "Well, that'll be four bits, Mr. Davies."

"Just call me Max," the stranger replied, pushing several shiny coins at Rusty. The clerk stared at them for a moment, lifting them up and examining them closely. "Those are United States currency," the man said, seeking to soothe Rusty's doubts.

"They look funny," Rusty muttered. He deposited them in a drawer with a last glance at Max and snorted. He set a key on the counter top. "Nice set o'guns, Mister."

"Thanks. I modified them myself."

"Mind if I ask what you do for a living?"

"I'm self employed. Where's my room?"

"Upstairs, third floor. Room 6. There's a small dining area right around the corner from here. That's where you'll find Mabel. She bakes the best apple pie you've ever tasted."

"I'll have to give it a try," Max said. He dropped the key in the pocket of his shirt and leaned forward, subtly pushing the box he held toward Rusty. "Do you know where I could find a man named Joe Gentry?"

Rusty nodded, smiling a bit. When he did, he revealed several missing teeth and several more that looked in poor shape. "Sure. Joe hangs out at the saloon. He's there most every afternoon and evenin'."

"Thanks." Max glanced past Rusty and noted the yellowed calendar that hung on the wall. It was nothing fancy, just a large sheet of white paper on which a series of squares had been drawn in pencil. A number of the day squares had been crossed through with a large X. "Rusty, can I ask you something you might find a little strange?"

"I've heard just about everythin' in this job," Rusty answered with a laugh. "What do you need to know?"

"What year is this?" Max asked, his face serious.

Despite his bluster, the question caught Rusty off guard. He sputtered for a moment before answering. "Why, it's 1884. Why on Earth did you ask a question like that?"

Max said nothing, instead choosing to incline his head in thanks. He headed up the stairs, box still in hand. The clerk's answer had confirmed his suspicions… there was something terribly wrong in the town of Eagle Eye – while everyone seemed to believe themselves still in the 19th century, the truth was that it was currently October 1943… and a World War was raging outside the confines of this anomalous little town.

Chapter II
The Rook Goes Hunting

Max Davies washed off and took a few moments to rest his tired bones before heading back downstairs. Though he was surprisingly vital for his age, he was 43 years old and the hard ride into town had left him weary. He'd flown a private plane as far as he could but the engine had begun sputtering nearly a hundred miles outside of Eagle Eye, confirming the rumors he'd heard about the area. Modern technology seemed to be adversely affected by something in the area... and that was just the beginning of the problems Max was now confronting.

Eagle Eye itself had once been a thriving town, the very epitome of the rugged Wild West that had become a staple in popular fiction. But in 1884, things had gone horribly wrong... every man, woman and child had vanished, leaving behind all their belongings and homes. The place had become a ghost town, forgotten by all but the most ardent of history buffs.

Two weeks ago, the strange little box that Max now possessed ended up in Atlanta. Its owner told of a bizarre town into which he'd wandered with some friends. They'd run afoul of the locals and all but one of the group had been killed... the man who'd fled ended up passing on the evidence of his journeys to Max.

Truth be told, the transfer of the box hadn't been done willingly. Max was known in the darker shadows of Atlanta as a masked vigilante, one who called himself the Rook. Under that guise, he had done his best to clean up the city over the last decade... and his exploits had sometimes spanned not just the nation but the entire globe. When he'd heard rumors about the box and its contents, he'd gone in search of its owner... and found a man who should have been in his mid thirties, but who instead looked like he was over 90... and aging fast.

The Rook had forced the truth from the man, who had seemed unwilling to part with his treasure: a box containing a number of gold coins, all dating back to the 19th century. Max had carefully handled the box after procuring it from the man, who had literally crumbled to dust before his eyes. At first he had feared that any contact with the box might be enough to activate whatever curse lay upon it… but now he had changed his views on the matter. He believed that it wasn't the acquisition of the box that had brought death upon this man… it had been something else related to his time in Eagle Eye.

All of that had brought Max to the place that should not exist, a town that existed outside of time.

Max sauntered into the saloon after having a brief but delicious meal in Mabel's restaurant. True to Rusty's word, the apple pie had been delicious.

The saloon was a noisy, boisterous place. Two women were doing a high-kicking dance on a stage nearby, their movements accompanied by the steady rhythm of a piano player. Max still held the box of coins at his side and he scanned the crowd for a man who matched the description he'd gotten from Rusty after dinner. He spotted Joe Gentry toward the back of the bar, a shapely brunette perched on his knee. She was playfully pushing him away from her neck, which he'd been attempting to kiss. Max had a feeling that this particular scene had played itself out many times before.

Gentry was in his early fifties and grizzled to the extreme. His skin was leathery from exposure to the sun and his prickly beard looked unkempt. He wore a scarf about his neck and a hat was perched roguishly atop his head.

Max approached their table, stopping just a few feet away. The girl noticed him first, looking up at him with interest. Gentry followed her gaze and frowned as he did so. "You want somethin', mister?" he demanded in a gruff voice.

"I want to ask you a few questions about Harry Pinsler. He came through here a few weeks back with some friends of his and—"

"What about him?" Gentry asked, roughly pushing the girl away from him. She let out a huff and stalked away, smoothing down her dress. She cast an angry glare at Max, obviously blaming him for the loss of hard-earned money this evening.

"You and your friends gunned down the men who were with him," Max stated without emotion.

"Yeah and we'd do it again, too. They were good fer nothin' city fellas. Laughed at us like we were hicks. Are you a good fer nothin' city fella?"

"He stole this from you, I believe," Max answered, refusing to be baited into a conflict with Gentry. He had no doubt he could take the man in a fair fight but nothing about Gentry made him believe there'd be anything fair about the conflict.

Gentry's eyes widened when he saw the box. Max set it down just in front of him, but the grizzled cowboy didn't make any move to take it. "He didn't steal it from me. He stole it from… someone else."

"Who? Who did he steal it from?"

"Why do you want to know?" Gentry seemed to recover his footing and leaned back in his chair, taking out a rolled cigarette. He lit it after striking a match to his boot. "Seems to me if you know what happened to him, you'd know that this isn't something you should be stickin' your nose into...."

Max reached and turned over Gentry's table, spilling his drink on the floor and knocking the box to the very edge, where it hung precariously. The entire room grew quiet as everyone turned to stare at the scene unfolding in the corner. Several of the men quickly began placing bets on who would survive the confrontation. Max drew one of his pistols and pointed it straight at Gentry's chest. "I don't have time to play games with you. Every second I'm in this godforsaken place puts me at risk. So I'm going to ask you one last time: who does this chest belong to?"

"Better put down that gun, boy," someone said from behind Max. Gentry laughed and nodded but Max's only reply was to sigh in annoyance.

The Rook dropped down and spun, kicking out a foot and using it to sweep the legs out from under Gentry's friend. A tall man went down on the ground, losing his grip on a handgun he'd been brandishing at Max's back. The Rook quickly rose to a standing position and fired two bullets into the man's leg. As the wounded man began to moan in pain, he turned back to Gentry. "Are you going to answer me or do you want to join your friend on the floor?"

Gentry stared at him coldly for a moment before breaking into a hearty laugh. He stood, holding his hands upright. "I'll be more than glad to take you to him, stranger. But I gotta warn you… you might wish that you'd just turned tail and left."

"I'm willing to take my chances." Max gestured for Gentry to head toward the door and he followed the other man at a close pace, ignoring the faces of those who were watching them. Max couldn't help but notice that many of the men and women seemed to have knowing smiles on their faces.

Chapter III
Acts of the Devil

"So were you a friend of his?" Gentry wanted to know. He was leading Max through the dusty streets of Eagle Eye, sauntering along with his cigarette dangling from the corner of his mouth. Every now and again he'd glance over his shoulder at Max, obviously making sure that the gun was still pointed at him.

"Pinsler? No. I only met him once. It was right before he died. His skin turned to dust and he fell to pieces."

Gentry didn't look surprised, confirming Max's suspicions that he knew about the curse. "I'm not the most educated of men, mind you, but I know that this here town is under some sort of spell. A very bad thing occurred here... and when it did, all of us kind of went to sleep. It's the strangest thing... but I have a feeling we do just about the same thing every night and every day. Until Pinsler and his boys showed up... and then things kind of changed. And now there's you...."

"I'm here to make sure that whatever killed Pinsler doesn't harm anyone else," Max explained. He saw Gentry come to a stop just outside a small stable. "What's in there?"

"The answer to your questions," Gentry replied with a laugh. "Want me to go first?"

Max nodded and followed Gentry into the darkened room. He narrowed his eyes and peered into the gloom, watching as Gentry found an overturned lantern. After setting it upright and making sure the oil inside hadn't spilled out, Gentry lit the lamp and illuminated the room.

There was a small carriage covered with cobwebs in the room. Inside the carriage was a number of crates and boxes, many of which had been broken open, revealing a massive amount of money and bars of gold.

Max couldn't hide his astonishment... why was all of this wealth here? Why wasn't it in a bank? "Who does all this belong to?" he asked, gesturing toward the fortune before them.

"A man named Clarence Waller came through town. He was a Negro preacher." Gentry said these last words with disbelief, as if the very thought strained credulity. "Said he wanted to start up a school for Negro children, was gonna teach 'em about God. He said we all worshipped the same God... like *our* God would ever let a man like *him* be a preacher." Gentry spat a wad of phlegm on the floor.

"Where did he get all this money?" Max inquired, feeling the hairs on the back of his neck begin to stand on end. There was a definite presence here... a palpable sense of rage that charged the air.

"He said he'd been a slave when he was a boy, back before the War. His daddy had been a house slave or somethin'... and when the man who used to own 'em died, he left a bunch of money to Waller."

Max approached the carriage, his eyes traveling over the length of it. It was a fine piece of work, obviously well-wrought. Max found himself reaching out to touch the carriage's surface... and the contact was electric. He jerked his hand away, images flashing before his eyes.

He saw a youthful-looking black man lying on the ground, blood spilling from his mouth. He'd been shot three times, each bullet passing through his chest. As Clarence Waller tried to crawl away, a group of men crowded about, laughing not only at his pitiful expression but also at their sudden, newfound wealth.

Clarence had closed his eyes, trying to find it within himself to pray for survival and to forgive the men who had done this to him... but in that awful moment he could find no solace in God. He found only hate... raging, pain-fueled hate. Through blood-splattered lips, he'd whispered "This town'll never be rid of me. Not ever. Every man, woman and child who ever steps foot in this place will know what you did... and they'll suffer for it."

While Max staggered under the onslaught of his visions, Gentry laughed and shook his head. He balled the fingers of his right hand into a fist and drove it hard into the side of Max's skull. The blow knocked the vigilante off his feet. Max landed facedown on the floor, the small domino-style mask he wore as the Rook slipping free from his shirt pocket.

Gentry stooped and picked up the mask, twirling it around on his fingers. "What in tarnation is this? You like dressin' up, stranger?"

Max gritted his teeth and quickly slipped a hand into one of his pockets. He drew forth a knife whose blade shone with a golden light, stabbing out with it in an attempt to bring his opponent to an equal footing with him. Max caught Gentry behind the ankles, driving him to the floor. Max sprang up, driving a knee into Gentry's back. "Don't call me stranger... call me the Rook," he hissed. He reached down and plucked the mask from Gentry's grasp. A second later, the mask was affixed to Max's face and something subtle had changed in his demeanor. An aura of power seemed to emanate from the Rook and he gripped

Gentry by the hair, painfully yanking the man's head back.

"You're a racist little bastard," Max hissed in Gentry's ear. "You killed an honest man and laughed as he lay bleeding."

"What's it to you?" Gentry whined.

"My father was killed by someone like you… he was gunned down right in front of me. I swore then and there that I'd punish the guilty if I ever got the chance."

Gentry's eyes widened as Max shook a glove off his left hand. A red signet ring came into view, a ruby stone emblazoned with the image of a bird in flight shining in the light. Max shoved the ring against Gentry's forehead, causing the flesh to sizzle and smoke to waft into the air. The pain was enormous and Gentry screamed, the Rook's symbol etched onto his skin forevermore.

Gentry collapsed, having gone into shock and Max stepped off of him. He replaced his glove, hiding his signet ring. It had come to him through harrowing means and he hid the ring both for secrecy and for his own peace of mind.

Max suddenly paused, for an odd scent began to make his nostrils flare. It smelled of death, as if a casket had been thrown open, revealing something rotten.

"*Every man, women and child who ever steps foot in this place will know what you did… and they'll suffer for it,*" the voice of Clarence Waller said.

The Rook turned around slowly, his eyes widening slightly. A spectral figure hovered in front of him… it was the body of Clarence Waller, but it was semi-transparent and composed of some sort of ethereal smoke.

"Clarence… you've made these people suffer enough." The Rook put away his weapons, knowing they would do no good against a spirit like this. "Let it end."

"*They killed me… and I was just trying to do God's work!*"

"It was wrong what they did," Max agreed. "But your curse has removed them from the natural order of things. This entire town exists outside of time now… and anybody who wanders in can't leave without dying. The man who came here a few weeks ago… he didn't do anything to you. Neither did I. And neither did most of the people in this town. They're innocents."

The spirit of Clarence Waller began to wail and the reverberations of his torment rattled the walls throughout Eagle Eye.

The Rook stood his ground, realizing that this was not going to be easy….

Chapter IV
Souls in Torment

A powerful blow, charged with spiritual energy, sent the Rook flying through the air. He was thrown clear of the carriage house, landing on the dusty streets outside. For a moment his vision was blurred by pain, but as it cleared he realized that he was not alone… all about him were the shambling forms of Eagle Eyes' residents, their flesh now hanging in tatters from their skeletal remains.

Gentry himself was walking from the carriage house, though the skin on his face was now drawn tight to the bone, like a mummy's. The burned mark on his forehead could still be seen, however, showing that even in death the Rook's message held true.

Gentry's thin lips pulled back in a leer. "He's not gonna let you go, stranger. He won't let any of us go and he ain't gonna let you go, neither."

The Rook struggled to his feet, realizing that everyone in this town was being tied to the mortal plane through the spiritual force of Clarence Waller. He drew his pistols as the undead creatures approached and broke into a run, seeking shelter as he pumped hot lead at his foes. The bullets ripped through rotting flesh and bone, causing those they struck to dance about from the force of impact. None of them fell, however, as they were immune to the sort of pain that mortal men and women felt. Men, women, and even children continued to approach the Rook, eager to make him one of them.

The Rook spied several barrels standing next to the saloon and he leapt atop one of them, using it as a springboard to launch himself at the roof. He snagged the rooftop with his fingers and managed to pull himself up to safety, though the undead continued to mill about below.

Max had dealt with angry spirits before… but in most cases it was simply a matter of finding some way to appease the spirit so that it would release its hold on the world. With regards to this one, though… Max wasn't quite sure what the solution would be.

"Come down and join us," someone shouted from below, eliciting a round of laughter from their compatriots. The Rook felt certain it had been Rusty who had spoken up.

The Rook walked to the edge of the roof and looked around. He spotted a wagon parked just down the street from the Sheriff's office. The vehicle was loaded with mining equipment, including boxes of dynamite. Max idly wondered if blowing up the town might be enough to exorcise the spirits from the surrounding land. Before he could act on the impulse, the Rook heard footsteps from behind him. He turned, coming face to face with what appeared to be the corporeal form of Clarence Waller. The preacher wore a dark shirt and pants, a large white cross hung about his neck.

"Clarence... listen to me. My name's Max Davies. I came here to find out what was going on... and I'd do anything to help you. But there's nothing to be done. You're dead. The men and women who laughed while you were dying are dead, too. Let it go. Move on."

"That's easy for you to say," Clarence answered. The Rook was a bit surprised, especially after seeing the rage the spirit had manifested earlier. He was pleased to see that Clarence was still capable of rational thought. "I've done a lot of terrible things, Mr. Davies. I don't imagine there's any room for me in Heaven... and I don't really look forward to Hell."

The spectral being raised both hands and held them toward Max. A blue-tinged lightning shot from the dead man's palms, knocking the Rook up against the edge of the roof. He teetered on the brink for a moment but managed to hold his balance.

Max tried to blink away the pain, knowing that if he did slip and fall, he'd surely die. Even if he survived the drop itself, there were the shambling undead down below.

Clarence looked pained but he moved toward Max, even as tears ran down his cheeks. "I don't enjoy doing this, Mr. Davies. I really don't. But there's nothing I can do to get back all that I lost... and it just makes me so *angry*."

Again the lightning flashed and Max cried out as the energy struck him. He swayed once more and all around him the world seemed to flicker. The town shifted back and forth in time, returning to its proper place in history and then crashing back into the present.

Panting, the Rook looked up into the sky, which was beginning to darken as night began to loom. He tried to summon every ounce of his willpower, knowing that if he didn't defuse this situation, he didn't stand a chance. Clarence was simply too powerful for an ordinary man with a gun and a knife to handle. "If you could, Clarence... you'd stop all this? You'd let this town fade into the past?"

Clarence closed his eyes and Max looked back at him, seeing the sort of calmness that would have made the young man a wonderful preacher. "It just makes me so *angry*, like I said. I know it's wrong but I can't help it... I only wanted to do the right thing and they killed me for it! They—"

Max suddenly snapped his fingers, a smile appearing on his face. His body ached terribly, but his sudden enthusiasm gave him the strength to approach Clarence. "I have an idea. You came here because you wanted to build a church. You never got the chance to use that money the way you wanted to… but the money is still there. I can build that church for you. You'll have accomplished what you wanted to do all this time. And maybe that will remove some of the taint from your soul."

Clarence blinked, the darkness that had fouled his face suddenly lifting. "You would do that for me?"

"I would… but you'd have to stop the curse you've put on this place. I'd need to be able to leave, with the money." The Rook offered Clarence a hand. "I know you have no reason to trust me… but I'm telling you the truth. I won't steal your money. I'll do everything you want me to do with it."

Clarence stared at him for a moment before taking Max's hand, every moment of pain passing quickly through his mind's eye one more time. Max thought he saw a glimmer of the old anger swelling up again… and then it faded, as quickly as it had first arisen.

Down in the streets, the bodies of the townspeople swayed and then collapsed, their remains crumbling into dust. A gentle wind then picked up what was left of them and spread it across the abandoned town, in which only one spirit remained.

Max Davies, the Rook.

"I'm going to do you proud," Max whispered, staring at the place where Clarence had recently stood. "Ashes to ashes, dust to dust."

The Rook began to climb down from the rooftop, his joints still carrying a terrible ache. He would keep his promise to Clarence Waller, a good man who had met his end in the wild west. "It might have taken awhile," he whispered to himself. "But eventually you'll help bring about good things in this area, Clarence. I'm going to see to it."

The town around him began to fade, even as a lone tumbleweed rolled across the dusty streets. There were no signs left of this being a living town. There were only ghosts to be found here now and they were thankfully silent.

THE END

Darkness, Spreading Its Wings of Black

An Adventure Starring
Lazarus Gray & The Rook

Written by Barry Reese

Chapter I
Birds of a Feather

Maurice Chapman opened a small white container and pushed a rubber-gloved finger into the white material it contained. He then smeared the grease under his nose, wincing slightly. He offered the container to the two people who were in the autopsy room with him: the dainty, beautiful Samantha Grace and her employer, the tall and thin Lazarus Gray. "You'll want some of this," Maurice said when neither of his guests took the container.

"We'll be fine," Gray answered, his mismatched eyes focused on the body that was hidden beneath a white sheet. The corpse's feet extended past the sheet and he could see that her toes had been painted red, probably a week or so before the murder. The paint was chipped in places and in need of a touch-up. The scent of medicinal products and cleansers was almost overwhelming, but it didn't come close to matching the odor of putrification that arose from the dead body.

Chapman resisted the urge to press the matter. He was sixty-two years old, born and raised in the cesspool that was Sovereign City. He'd seen burly cops enter his lab and turn away vomiting at the things he showed them. He knew false bravado when he saw it – and neither of these two were displaying it. Lazarus

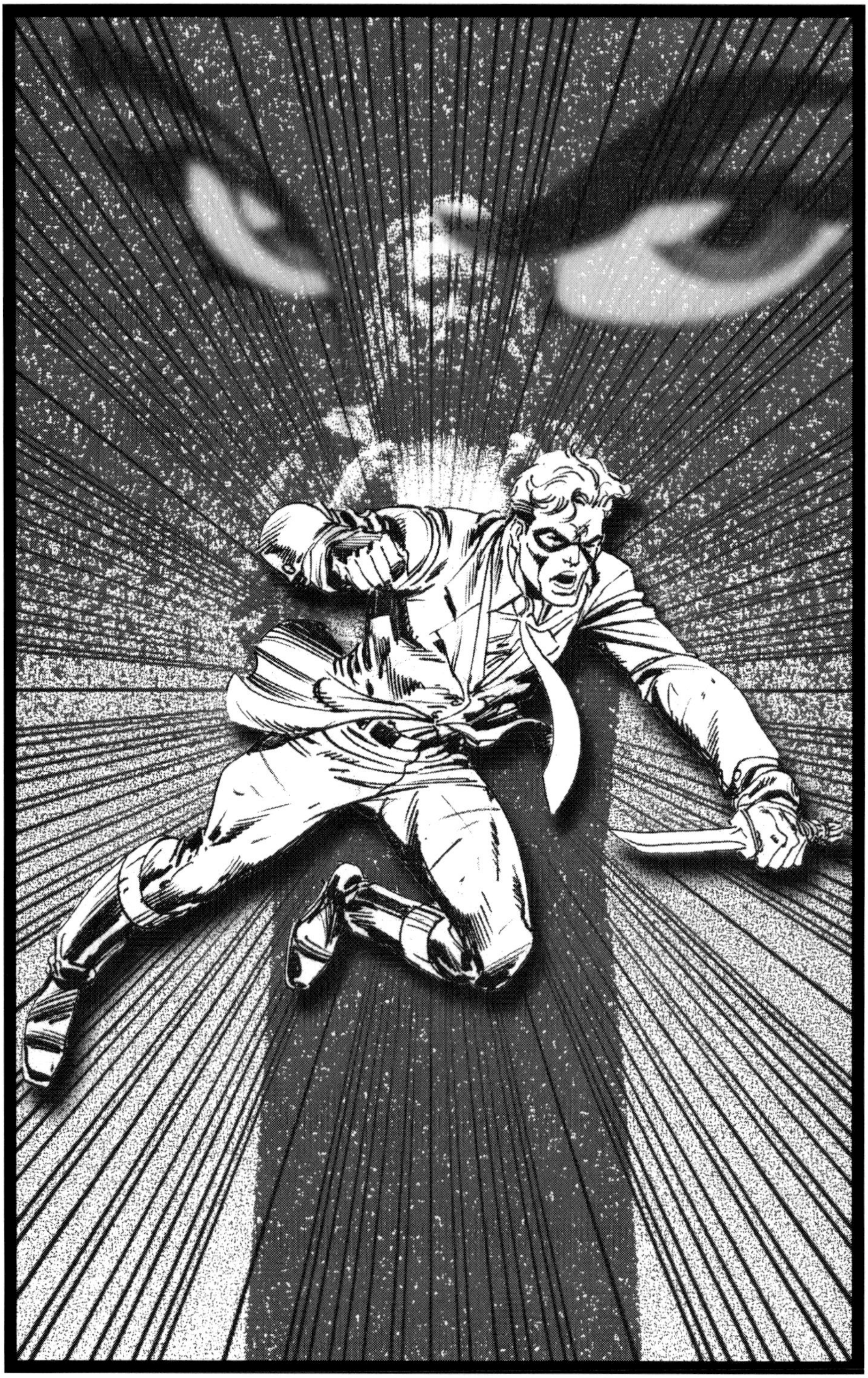

Gray looked like a man who had seen enough death to no longer be disturbed by it. Chapman studied him for a moment, having read about the man in the newspapers but never having met him before. The head of Assistance Unlimited's hair was more gray than brown, making him look older than he was, though a close examination of his features revealed that he was in his late twenties. He was tall and slender, though with a rangy musculature that indicated he could more than hold himself in a fight.

The girl was another matter entirely and it was only because Chapman had known the girl during her youth that he knew she was more than she appeared. A stunning blonde whose parents were wealthy philanthropists, Samantha had grown up with every opportunity possible. She could speak five languages fluently, was a champion swimmer, and was a veritable encyclopedia on topics as varied as fashion, European history, and the socio-political climate of the Orient. Chapman would normally have balked at having a female in his lab, especially when he was about to show off a corpse in this state – but Samantha Grace was no mere slip of a girl, despite how she might look at first glance.

Chapman set the container aside and pulled the sheet away, revealing a body that had been horribly mutilated. The nude form was neatly bisected at the waist and the face had been slashed from the corners of the mouth to the ears, giving her a macabre parody of a smile. The dead woman's black hair was matted and still bore traces of leaves and insect casings. Her body was that of a fit young woman and was admirably formed, but the unhealthy condition of the body was consistent with being exposed to the elements for several days before discovery.

"The victim was 24 years of age," Chapman began. "Her body was found in a vacant lot on the west side of South Page Avenue midway between West 42nd Street and Robeson Avenue."

Samantha exchanged a quick glance with Lazarus. "That's not far from our headquarters." She was obviously troubled to think that a woman could have been brutally assaulted so close to where she and her friends slept every night.

Gray nodded silently, urging Chapman to continue with a quick motion of his hand.

"The body was discovered by a local resident named Betty King who was walking with her four year old son earlier this morning. If you'll notice, the wounds are very clean. They were done with surgical instruments and the body was drained of blood. There are signs that the corpse was washed, probably in an attempt to remove traces of evidence. Furthermore, the body was posed with the left arm draped across the breasts and the right hand covering the pubis region."

"As if she were covering her nudity," Samantha observed and Chapman murmured an agreement. "So she wasn't killed at the scene? Someone dumped her there?"

Chapman spread his hands. "I'm no detective but in my opinion, that would be the case."

"Who was she?" Lazarus asked. Chapman found himself staring at the man's eyes: one was a dull brown and the other a glittering emerald.

"Her name was Claudia Schuller. A packet was sewn to the skin between her shoulder blades and it contained the items you see over there." Chapman gestured toward a nearby table upon which a number of papers had been arranged.

Gray moved toward them, slowly touching each one. Claudia's birth certificate was the first thing he lifted, but he also brushed his fingers across business cards, photographs, names written on pieces of paper, and an address book with the name Max Davies embossed on the cover.

"Has anyone contacted Mr. Davies?"

"Of course we have. We don't just sit around waiting on you to solve all the crimes for us."

Lazarus turned his head to see that Inspector Cord of the Sovereign PD had entered the room. He was a whippet-thin man who had one eye that seemed to be perpetually narrowed. His disdain for Assistance Unlimited – and its founder, in particular – was well known. "Inspector. Just the man I was hoping to see."

"I doubt that." Cord reached up and removed his hat, bowing slightly to Samantha. "Afternoon, Miss."

Samantha gave him a cool smile in reply.

"You were saying that your men had contacted Mr. Davies?" Lazarus prompted.

"Oh, yes." Cord took out a cigarette and lit it, though he knew that Gray hated the smell. He moved closer to Gray, blowing out a long cloud of smoke that enveloped the taller man. "He's here in Sovereign, on business he says. Apparently, his father – Warren Davies, now dead – was a newspaperman back in Boston. One of the papers he owned at one time was The Sovereign Gazette. The younger Davies still has some stock in the paper, though he's a minority holder. Says he met Miss Schuller for the first time about a week ago at a dinner party thrown by the Gazette's current majority owner, Theodore Groseclose. Supposedly, they went out together for drinks two nights later and that was the last time he saw her. Coincidentally, it's the last time anybody's reported seeing her."

Samantha looked at Chapman. "How long ago did she die?"

"I'd estimate it was about five days ago, given the rate of decomposition."

Lazarus knew what his aide was getting at and so did Inspector Cord. Five days ago would have been the same night she'd had dinner with Max Davies. "Where is Mr. Davies now?" Gray asked, confident he already knew the answer.

"He's coming in for questioning right now. I think we've got him dead to rights." Cord took a long drag on his cigarette, a look of confidence on his face. "Last man seen with her and there's his address book right there."

"Then who sewed this packet onto her back?" Gray asked, his words carefully neutral but his eyes betraying his dislike for the other man.

"What do you mean? He did, of course. Davies."

"Why would he include his own address book? And these business cards:

Robert Phillips, Chairman of the city's Building Association; Merle Hansome, Attorney; Theodore Groseclose... all of them should be questioned but I don't think any of them are the killer." Lazarus looked back at the corpse of Claudia Schuller. He tried to imagine her in life, young and beautiful. It was difficult with her reduced to a bisected piece of meat. "Whoever did this horrible act wanted us to know these men's names. The question is: why?"

Cord looked like he'd bitten into something sour. "You're over thinking things, Gray. In order to kill like this, a man has to be insane. Once you establish that, none of his actions should be taken as a surprise. I've seen killers throw themselves into our grasp, explaining every gruesome detail of their acts. That's probably what happened here. Davies wants to be caught." Cord lowered his voice, doing a stage whisper that was easily overheard by Samantha. "Besides, this isn't the first time that Davies has come to the attention of the law."

Gray looked at him steadily, waiting for Cord to continue. When it became obvious that Gray wasn't going to say anything, Cord took several more puffs on his cigarette before uttering a sigh.

"Back in Boston, there were accusations that he might be related to a murderous vigilante known as The Rook. Nothing could ever be proven but get this: he's put his home up for sale. Rumor has it he's planning to head out west or maybe down south. Why would an innocent man flee the town he'd grown up in? Maybe because he's not so innocent?"

Gray turned away from Cord and caught Samantha's eye. Without a word to Cord and just a brief thanks to Chapman, the duo exited the room.

"Where to, Chief?" Samantha asked, the clicking of her heels on the tiled floor seeming very loud. Gray noticed she was wearing a new scent today and he found the perfume to be quite pleasing. He wasn't blind to her interest in him but for many reasons, he didn't think it wise to encourage it.

"We're going to speak to Max Davies."

Samantha smiled softly. "You're planning to get to him before Cord does, aren't you?"

A rare grin seemed to dance upon Gray's lips, but it vanished so quickly that Samantha wasn't sure if she had actually seen it. "No sense in allowing the Inspector to ruin a perfectly good investigation."

Max Davies was thirty-five years old, though he could have passed for a man ten years younger. He was stunningly handsome with wavy black hair and a slightly Olive complexion, which made Samantha think that he had Mediterranean ancestry. He wore a black suit, white shirt and red tie, looking like he'd stepped off the cover of a European fashion magazine.

Having booked the penthouse at Sovereign City's most expensive hotel,

Davies was reclining in relative luxury when Lazarus and Samantha arrived to speak with him. The room looked barely lived in, despite the fact he'd been staying there for over a week.

Davies was sitting now, his legs crossed before him. He held a small glass of scotch in one hand though Gray was positive the man was merely swirling it about in his glass for effect. Twice he'd brought it to his lips without actually taking a sip.

"You two just caught me," Davies was saying, gesturing for both of his guests to take a seat. "I was just walking out the door."

"We appreciate you taking the time to speak to us," Samantha said, smoothing her skirt over her long legs. She noticed that Max's eyes dipped down to watch the gesture and she smiled. Though she was the equal of any man when it came to a fight, she wasn't above using her beauty to her advantage. After all, it was one more weapon in her arsenal.

"How could I refuse an invitation from someone so attractive?" Max smoothly replied. With a twinkle in his eye, he added, "And might I say, Miss Grace, that you're quite a looker as well."

Samantha stared at him for a moment before the joke hit her. She looked over at Lazarus and saw that he wasn't quite as charmed as she was.

"Mr. Davies, perhaps you don't understand the severity of this situation," Lazarus said, his voice betraying absolutely no emotion. "You're the last person known to have seen Claudia Schuller alive. And an address book bearing your name was found on her person."

"Along with the business cards of other men, isn't that right?"

"How did you know that?" Lazarus asked, his eyes narrowing.

"Inspector Cord told me when he phoned earlier."

Samantha could see Lazarus visibly composing himself. He didn't care much for Cord's methods, which bordered on the incompetent at times. "You're still considered the prime suspect. Could you tell us the nature of your relationship with Miss Schuller?"

"She was at a party I attended. Apparently, she works in the newspaper secretarial pool. She was alone at the soiree and so was I. We struck up a conversation and I invited her to have dinner with me. She agreed to do and a couple of nights later, we went out and ate at O'Malley's. Afterward, we came back here."

"And then?"

Max glanced quickly at Samantha, who was the very picture of decorum. "Miss Schuller remained here for several hours and left my residence just past midnight."

"Did the two of you have sexual relations?" Lazarus asked.

"No. Not if you mean intercourse, anyway."

Samantha felt a flush rise to her cheeks and she smoothed out her skirt once more.

"And everything that happened here was consensual?" Lazarus didn't seem shocked by Max's intimations and Samantha remembered that in his old life, the one he'd had before arriving in Sovereign City, Lazarus had lived in Europe and traveled a great deal. He'd been exposed to things that weren't openly discussed in polite company.

As Max answered in the affirmative, Samantha found herself studying her employer. Not quite two years ago, Lazarus Gray had literally washed up on the shores of the city with no memory of who he really was. In his possession had been a small medallion depicting a nude male figure with the head of a lion. The words 'Lazarus Gray' had been printed below the image and he'd taken the name as his own. It wasn't until after founding Assistance Unlimited, a group dedicated to helping those in need, regardless of their ability to pay, that Lazarus had learned the truth: that once he'd been Richard Davenport, a member of a ruthless International organization known as The Illuminati. He'd turned against them and had nearly lost his life in the process. Now, he fought against his old allies, standing up to the forces of darkness with only his three aides at his side: Samantha, the young Korean Eun Jiwon, and former confidence man Morgan Watts.

Max set down his glass and leaned forward, clasping his hands between his knees. "I assure you, Mr. Gray, that I'm not the kind of man who would have done those things to a woman. To anyone, really." Something passed over the man's face that caught Samantha's attention – it was like a veil had fallen over his eyes. "I saw my father gunned down by criminals when I was eight years old. He was a good man and he taught me to stand up for those in need. I've tried to do that all my life. The kind of killer who did this… that's the kind of man who should be brought to justice."

Lazarus said nothing in response for a long moment, though it was obvious that his mind was running through everything that Max had just said. "I believe you, Mr. Davies. But it doesn't change the fact that a young woman is dead and that someone, for whatever reason, wanted your name thrown into the mix. Do you have any idea how your address book came to be with her body?"

"No. Someone obviously broke into my hotel room at some point but I never saw any sign of it and when I asked the clerk downstairs, he assured me that no one other than the cleaning staff had been here in my absence."

Samantha spoke up, voicing a thought that had come to her repeatedly since they'd left the morgue. "Maybe they just wanted to waste everyone's time, forcing the police down fruitless paths, while the real killer escapes town."

"That's possible," said Max, standing up and quickly crossing to a small briefcase that lay on a nearby table. He opened it as he continued to talk. "But unlikely. The killer's still here in Sovereign."

Gray watched as Max returned with several newspaper clippings in his grasp. Gray took them and his eyes quickly scanned the words, drinking in their meaning. "This wasn't the first murder," Gray murmured.

Max nodded, noting the look of surprise on Samantha's face. "Three years ago, a prostitute was found with her hands and feet removed. The body had been bled dry and washed. Six months later, a fourteen year old runaway girl was found, beheaded and with one leg missing. Again – surgical cuts, the body was dry and had been washed. Last fall, a third one was found: a Chinese immigrant who made a living washing clothes for others. Her breasts had been surgically removed but the other aspects matched perfectly: the body had not a drop of blood left in it and the murder occurred elsewhere with the body having been cleaned afterward."

Samantha shook her head in amazement. "That doesn't make sense. Why didn't Cord mention that?"

"Because he doesn't know," Lazarus answered. "Miss Schuller is the first victim who would be considered of any importance. Prostitutes and immigrants aren't high priorities. There aren't many family members to press for an investigation. They're simply forgotten."

Max nodded. "That's right. It's actually the real reason why I'm here. I sometimes comb through old crime reports, looking for story ideas that I can feed to the editors of the papers I still have a stake in. I came here to talk to Mr. Groseclose about these murders and to see if the Gazette could look into them."

Lazarus took a deep breath before speaking. "May I take these clippings with me?"

"Feel free."

Lazarus collected them and nodded to Samantha. She understood the gesture and stood up. They were leaving, as Lazarus had evidently gotten everything he thought he needed from Max Davies.

Lazarus placed a hand on Max's shoulder. "I'm sorry to say that you'll still be expected to visit the police station and file a formal statement. I think you should heed my advice: don't mention these clippings or the other murders. To a man like Cord, your knowledge of such things might only increase the likelihood of your involvement."

"You believe me, though?"

"Yes. I do. You're much more than you appear to be, I'm sure of that... but you're not the man we're looking for."

Samantha wondered at those words, but said nothing until they were outside in the car. "I'm not sure I believe all that," she said at last.

Lazarus started the car and began smoothly gliding it down the perpetually rain-slicked streets of the city. "You mean that he came here in response to the murders?"

"Well, yes. I mean, it seems terribly convenient, doesn't it? He comes here because he knows women are being murdered. They're all vagabonds or street people so nobody cares about them. Then he meets a girl who doesn't fit that pattern – but sure enough, the killer takes an interest in her anyway."

Lazarus glanced toward her and that faint hint of a smile that he sometimes got reasserted itself before vanishing, like a thin wisp of smoke. "I'd wager that we only saw the real Max Davies at the end of that conversation. The moment he shared with us the details about those other murders, his demeanor changed. Before that, the bored playboy routine, the overly flirtatious act — it was just that. An act."

"So you think he might be the killer?"

"Oh, no. I don't think that at all. I think he's someone with genuine concern about these women but for some reason, he doesn't want the world to know it. I'll look into his background when I get the chance but for now, I don't think we should waste our time focusing on him."

"What about the other men whose names were found with her body?"

"As we were leaving the station, I stopped to call the Assistance Unlimited HQ. Eun and Morgan have been looking into the other men who have been implicated in this."

Samantha nodded, looking out the passenger side window. She saw one gray-colored building after another. It looked like the entire city was slowly falling under a haze of decay. "That poor girl. No one should die like that. And to think that more women have died over the years, with no one missing them… It makes me wonder if we can ever really save this place. My grandparents used to tell me that Sovereign wasn't always like this but nowadays it's hard to believe that. There's something rotten at the core of the city, Lazarus. It's breeding murder, corruption and despair."

Samantha felt her employer's hand settle on hers. He gave it a firm squeeze and when he spoke, there was unusual emotion in his words. "You're right. The heart of Sovereign is spoiled. That's why we've got to find the source of the evil and carve it out."

Chapter II
Men of Power

The death of Claudia Schuller was front-page news on every paper in the city. The Gazette ran two photos, one depicting Claudia on the day of her high school graduation and the other a grainy crime scene image with a body draped by a police blanket. The grisly details were listed in explicit detail, bringing fresh pain to the victim's family and friends.

Speculation was rife. Though the names of the men implicated were not revealed in the papers, rumors linked virtually every prominent businessman in the city with the young woman. Stories circulated that she had been of loose morals and had traded her beauty for monetary gifts from the men.

"Read about de slain beauty! Police officials baffled as investigation continues! All de details included here! Will the killer strike again?"

A newsboy's cry caught the attention of two men who were riding down Main Street in a taxi. One of the men – an elderly, gray-haired gentleman in a tweed suit – turned to his young companion and asked, "What's this about a murder, Smithson? I didn't hear anything about such a thing when we were coming in on the train yesterday."

"Young Miss Claudia Schuller was brutally murdered a few days ago," Smithson answered. He was a handsome man with dark hair and eyes. "The papers are abuzz with the news. It was quite awful, from what I've heard."

"I haven't read any of today's papers," remarked the elderly man. "Such a violent city," he added with a shake of his head.

Smithson waited for the question that he knew was inevitably going to come.

"Schuller, you say? Didn't we meet her at the party thrown by Groseclose? Attractive young thing from his secretarial pool?"

Smithson nodded, his face drawn grave with concern. "We did, Mr. Melvin. She was quite generous in her praise of your revitalization efforts in the city's East Side."

Donald Melvin bit his lower lip, his eyes taking on a faraway state. "Awful. To be cut down in the prime of life like that. She could have made some man very happy, you know."

Smithson said nothing, hoping that this turn of conversation wouldn't ruin his employer's mood. The meeting they were going to was an important one and Melvin sometimes lapsed into gloomy periods that impacted his decisions. Amalgamated Industries was Melvin's pride and joy and it was currently involved in the removal of dozens of unsightly tenement buildings, replacing them with tremendous structures that towered over the landscape. In decades to come, people would point to Melvin's work as a key part in the revitalization of Sovereign City.

Smithson and Melvin stepped from their cab and entered the lobby of The Amici Hotel, a massive building that occupied an entire block. One of the few new hotels to have opened since the Stock Market Crash of '29, The Amici prided itself on an aristocratic atmosphere.

Within the gorgeous lobby, Smithson made an inquiry at the front desk and then informed Melvin that their meeting was being held on the twenty-fourth floor.

After traveling upward in an elevator, the two men stepped into a conference room where a small group was waiting for them. One by one, Smithson introduced Melvin to the men, even though in most cases, introductions were not truly necessary. It was a formality and one that the older men seemed to enjoy, as if it confirmed their importance in things.

Theodore Groseclose, publisher and chief editor of the Sovereign Gazette, was the first to shake Melvin's hand. Groseclose was a tall, gray-haired man in a dark suit. He looked a bit unnerved and Melvin rightly assumed it was because of the death of the man's secretary.

Also present was Robert Phillips, Chairman of the city's Building Association. He was a bear-like man with a thick, bristled beard and piercing eyes.

The final man to whom Melvin was introduced was Merle Hansome, a wiry fellow with thinning hair and a nervous habit of licking his upper lip. One of the most prominent attorneys in the city, Hansome was very good at his job, despite not having the demeanor to put anyone at ease.

Phillips cleared his throat as everyone took a seat. He had a commanding presence and was obviously used to being in charge. "Let's get this under way, shall we? You've looked over the papers we sent your way?"

Melvin nodded, waiting for Smithson to take out a pad and paper before continuing. "I have. Fifty million dollars is quite an investment. If I'm going to do as you ask, I have to receive certain assurances."

Groseclose leaned forward, clasping his hands together on top of the table.

DARKNESS, SPREADING ITS WINGS OF BLACK

"You know I'll do what I can for you, Mr. Melvin. I've kept all the news stories about what you're doing in a positive light. It's going to be a little bit tougher with this new deal, but I can swing it."

Smithson dutifully took notes while the men conversed. He was skilled enough in his craft that he could let his mind wander while his pencil spun across the page, distilling the conversation into shorthand. The three other men had approached Melvin with the idea of spearheading a plan to purchase the grounds on which a hospital for the poor now resided. The sick people who currently received treatment for their infirmities were going to be kicked to the curb if the plan bore fruit, but none of these men considered that worthy of stopping their plans. The men, women, and children who frequented the place were too poor to afford treatment at standard facilities, probably resulting in dozens of deaths.

But if things went to plan, a high-rise apartment building would pop up in its place. The bottom floors would contain expensive offices while the upper rooms were rented or sold to the lucky few who could afford them. It was all part of a long-term revitalization project and one that had sparked grumbling amongst those who had been displaced. Thankfully, Hansome had made sure that all the legalities were covered, while Phillips took care of all the required permits. Groseclose then handled the media side of things, ensuring that the general populace didn't focus too much on the negative.

Hansome stood up and began pacing, bringing the discussion to an abrupt halt.

"What the devil's the matter with you?" Phillips demanded.

"Aren't we going to talk about the murder?" the lawyer asked, his pink tongue darting out to wet his upper lip. "I mean, it's the elephant in the room, if you ask me."

Melvin blinked in surprise. "What are you talking about?"

"Schuller!" Hansome ejaculated. "Are you so dense that you don't realize what danger we're all in? That girl was cut to pieces and all of our names are associated with her! I heard from a source at the police department that Assistance Unlimited is working on the case, too!"

"I barely knew the girl," Melvin said, shrugging his shoulders. "I don't fear an inquiry and neither should any of you. None of you killed her, did you?"

"Of course not," Hansome muttered, though he cast a wary glance around the room. "But this could still derail our plans... the scandal!"

"There won't be any scandal," Groseclose said reassuringly. "Didn't you notice that I made sure none of our names ended up in the paper today? I have enough favors owed to me by the other publishers in this town to make sure we're not linked in any rival accounts, either."

"Word will still get around," Hansome protested.

Melvin loudly exhaled. "I don't see what all the fuss is about. So what if we all knew her? And so what if there are questions to be asked? The law will prove us innocent, mark my words."

Smithson cleared his throat and all eyes fell upon him. The handsome secretary rarely said anything during these meetings, preferring to share his views with his employer in private. "Miss Schuller was an attractive young woman but she was rather promiscuous. The rumors about that are already circulating, I believe. I think it goes without saying that several of the men in this room may have had… delicate relations… with her?" The silence that fell was answer enough - only Melvin seemed shocked by the suggestion and he was obviously about to say so when Smithson continued. "I think that Mr. Melvin is correct in saying that none of you have anything to fear. But just in case, perhaps Mr. Groseclose could have one of his journalists look into her background. Throw a bit of doubt upon her character, as it were."

Groseclose looked uncomfortable. "She wasn't a bad person. Not at all. I'd hate to make it appear that she was."

"It was just a suggestion. I think that if people assumed that she was a bit of a tart, then they'd be less likely to focus their attentions on all of you."

"Could be just the opposite," Phillips muttered. "A pretty young girl, illicit sex, and a grisly murder… no, the more details they get, the more the people will chatter away. But I'm not worried about the police or the press – I have an alibi for the night she was murdered."

Smithson looked around the room. "Who here doesn't have an alibi, if I might ask?"

Groseclose lit a cigar. "Of course, I saw all of you at the party earlier in the evening. After that, I retired to my bed. My butler brought me some warm milk at half past midnight."

"So it would have been possible for you to have left and done the deed," Smithson pointed out.

Groseclose looked offended at the suggestion but said nothing. He'd already heard that same accusation from the Korean who worked for Assistance Unlimited. The young immigrant had pushed Groseclose hard on the matter, but the newspaperman didn't plan to share that with anyone in this room. They were business partners but certainly not friends.

Hansome licked his lip again, a nervous habit that left his mouth perpetually chapped. "I don't have one. I went to a movie and then to a bar for a drink. I didn't return home until very late. I'm not sure I could find any of the men who might have seen me."

Smithson tried not to smile. Hansome's homosexuality was a poorly kept secret amongst the group. It made sense that he wouldn't want to call upon any of his male companions to verify his story. Plus, given the fact that Schuller apparently wasn't sexually assaulted might make Hansome all the more suspect if his secret came to light. Some would say that he would have struck at Schuller out of some deep-seated resentment of women.

"I think it's all a lot of poppycock," Melvin said. "We're all good men. To think that any one of us could ever assault a woman… it's preposterous!"

DARKNESS, SPREADING ITS WINGS OF BLACK

Phillips nodded in agreement. "To get us back on track here… Are you in for more money or not, Melvin? This new project could become the centerpiece for the revitalization effort and make us all very rich men in the process." Phillips chuckled. "Or, in Melvin's case, richer."

Melvin smiled in reply. "I am very excited about this, gentlemen. Very excited, indeed."

Night fell quickly in Sovereign City and the few residents who might be called innocents hurried for the relative safety of their homes, leaving the streets to those with darker intent.

A moving patch of darkness passed along the sidewalk beneath the glare of a street lamp. The long streak of darkness ended in a perfect silhouette. The man who cast this shadow was tall and well-built with an olive-complexion and wavy dark hair. He wore a long overcoat, a suit and tie but it was the adornment on his face that set him apart from every other man in the city: he wore a tiny domino-style mask over his eyes and on the bridge of his nose rested a tiny beak-like protrusion. This was The Rook, a being whom the underworld had come to greatly fear in recent years. Having left bullet-ridden bodies in his wake throughout the Northeast, The Rook was like a one-man police force, bringing the guilty to their final judgment, even when the Law could not touch them.

Just up ahead lay the private residence of Merle Hansome. It was a modest home, but it was light-years beyond the residences that were being torn down to make way for Melvin's new high-rises. The Rook calmly approached the wrought-iron fence that surrounded the property and expertly scaled the barrier, dropping easily down to the grass on the other side. He approached the front door and lightly tried the knob. It was locked, which drove him around back. The rear entrance opened easily and The Rook felt a small smile form on his lips. Even in a roach's den like Sovereign, there were men who felt themselves safe and sound in their own home. It was all like a fallacy, of course, but it made The Rook's job that much easier.

Very few people in the world knew that Max Davies led a double life and even fewer still understood why he did it. An armchair psychiatrist would have zeroed in on the events that occurred when Max was eight years old and while those would have helped filled in the gaps, they would not have told the entire tale. Max's father, Warren Davies, had run a newspaper campaign against mobsters who threatened to take over the city. When he refused to knuckle under the pressure they were putting on him, Warren found himself the target of a hired assassin. He was gunned down in front of his son and Max had the memory of his father's final bloodstained memories imprinted into his memory.

But it was what happened later that truly set Max Davies down the path of vigilantism. A series of painful visions began to plague him, ones of crimes yet to be committed. He discovered that if he took steps to prevent them or to bring their perpetrators to justice, the painful visions would recede. Compelled by the knowledge that he would continue to suffer unless he found a way to help others, Max embarked on a years-long trek around the globe in his teens. He learned every form of martial arts known to man, studied philosophy in the Mountains of Tibet, and mastered most known sciences. On the day he first created the identity of The Rook, Max Davies felt a sense of liberation take hold. It was as if he were a bird taking flight for the first time.

And those who slithered in darkness found a new enemy, one who would never stop until every innocent could sleep safely in their own bed.

Hansome sat on the edge of his bed, dressed in a white dressing gown and slippers. His hands were shaking badly enough that the cup of warm milk he was holding threatened to spill. His tongue darted out, wetting his upper lip. He didn't understand why the others weren't taking this more seriously – even though he hadn't done the horrible deed, he had more than enough secrets that could be exposed by an investigation.

Even more troubling was the nagging question that resided in the back of Hansome's mind: What if one of the others **was** the murderer? He didn't think that Groseclose would do such a thing and Melvin was too old and feeble to have overpowered a healthy young girl… but what about Phillips? The man was brawny and had a temper. Maybe Phillips had tried to force himself on the girl and, when she refused, he'd gotten so angry that he'd cut her to pieces. Phillips had claimed to have an alibi, but Hansome knew those could be faked. Lots of things could be faked, which was something that both Hansome and Phillips knew well.

The lawyer drank the last of the milk and stood up, preparing to set the empty container on the nightstand and crawl into bed. He froze in place as the door to his bedroom unexpectedly open and a masked figure stepped into the room, a handgun held in his right hand. Hansome dropped the glass, jumping when it shattered on the floor.

"Merle Hansome," The Rook said, taking several steps closer to the nervous attorney. "Men call me The Rook. Have you heard of me?"

"Yes," Hansome answered, his voice barely above a whisper. "You're that vigilante who kills people."

"I kill bad people. Are you a bad person, Mr. Hansome?"

"No."

"Then you have nothing to fear from me." The Rook made a show of lowering his weapon and placing it inside a holster under his right arm. "I want to talk to you about the death of Claudia Schuller."

"I have sex with men." Hansome's hands flew up over his mouth and his eyes opened wide. He wasn't sure why he'd said that. It was like his nervousness had somehow caused him to admit his deepest secret in the hopes that it would somehow protect him.

The Rook seemed unfazed by the comment. "I know. And I know that you're not the killer. I'm not here to investigate **you**. I want you to help me investigate **them**."

Hansome relaxed somewhat though it wasn't in his nature to completely be at ease. "Are you talking about my business partners? Because if you are, the man you need to be looking at is Robert Phillips. I'd bet my last dollar that it's him."

"I don't think it is — at the very least, if he is involved, he wasn't involved in all the murders. He didn't move to the city until after the first girl was killed."

Hansome looked confused. "First girl? Are you saying that Schuller wasn't the first to die?" As he asked these questions, Hansome seemed to grow even more nervous. He seemed on the verge of sharing something with The Rook but was obviously hesitant to do so.

The Rook nodded. "That's exactly what I'm saying. What I want from you is access to their personal information — you handle all of them as clients, don't you?"

"Well, Mr. Melvin has his own lawyers so I only assist with the Sovereign affairs that he has. But for the others, yes." Hansome's tongue darted out, touching his upper lip. "But there's a matter of confidentiality. I can't just open their records to you."

"Not even if innocent women are dying?" Hansome hesitated and the Rook continued, "And what about if a prolonged investigation ends up revealing a lot of your dirty laundry? We wouldn't want that, would we?"

Hansome exhaled. "All right. What do you need to know?"

The Rook was about to provide a list of files that he wanted to see when the distinctive sound of footsteps moving stealthily up the stairs gave him pause. The Rook knew from the look on Hansome's face that the man wasn't expecting any company. He held a finger to his lips, indicating that Hansome should remain quiet, and drew his pistol once more.

The gun looked like a common automatic but it was actually proof of The Rook's remarkable scientific acumen. The chamber had been specially modified so that it could hold dozens of miniaturized bullets. It was whispered in the Underworld that The Rook's guns never ran out of bullets but that wasn't quite true — it was simply that each gun held so many shells that few ever saw him reload. The small size of the bullets said nothing about their power, however. Each one packed enough punch to send a large man tumbling backward, meaning that he rarely needed to hit a target more than once.

The Rook crept to the bedroom door and grasped the handle with his free hand. He yanked it open and came face-to-face with a man dressed all in black, save for a crimson mask. The mask was carved of wood and painted with vibrant red. It was a devil's leering face, a tongue jutting forth in a mockery of laughter. In the man's right hand was a long, curving dagger that gleamed in the light. The terrible sight was made all the more terrifying because of the man's great size: he was a veritable bear.

The Rook squeezed the trigger of his automatic, but the first blast went awry as the devil-faced man swung out with his knife, forcing The Rook to back away from the blow. The Rook was well versed in fighting but the man he was now facing was quick and quite skilled in the use of a blade. The Rook found himself ducking under another swipe of the blade and then hurrying to throw up an arm to prevent another. The sharp edge of the knife dug through flesh on the underside of The Rook's arm and blood began to drip onto the floor.

The Rook responded with a karate chop to the stranger's throat, causing the other man to squawk in pain and stagger back. The Rook then grabbed hold of the arm that held the dagger, applying enough pressure to the wrist that the masked man dropped the knife.

"Who are you?" The Rook demanded, driving an elbow into the side of the man's head.

"Call me Devil Face," the man answered, using a peculiar high-pitched voice that was obviously disguised. "And I'm not here for you. I just want the faggoty man. Give him to me and I'll let you live."

The Rook slammed a knee into Devil Face's midsection and for a moment, he thought he'd won the day. The masked man appeared to nearly lose his footing and The Rook made the mistake of letting up on his assault. It was then that Devil Face reached down to his right ankle and freed a second blade that he'd hidden in his sock. Devil Face sprang upward, stabbing The Rook in the left shoulder. Devil Face pushed on, using all his strength to slam the vigilante against the wall. The back of The Rook's head cracked against the wall and his vision began to swim. He slid to the floor, his eyes fluttering. Over the throbbing in his head, he heard the sounds of a scuffle, followed by a piercing cry. The Rook struggled to rise but he found himself unable to find his footing. He lost consciousness, the last sight he saw being that of Devil Face dragging Hansome's limp form out of the room.

Chapter III
Assistance Unlimited

Morgan Watts was a former confidence man, a lackey for more crime bosses than he cared to remember. But his life had taken a change for the better when he'd met Lazarus Gray. He'd realized that the emptiness he'd carried inside him for so long was his sense of morality. It was an empty cup, waiting to be filled. And Lazarus Gray soaked it to overflowing.

Morgan was seated in the briefing room of Assistance Unlimited's expansive headquarters. It was an old hotel that had been retrofitted to their purposes but some of the rooms retained the feeling of impermanence, as if no one was truly meant to call this place home. It was a building designed for fleeting visits.

Lazarus was standing in front of a flannel board upon which photos of the various suspects, along with the known victims of the killer, had been hung. "Morgan, you said that Phillips was at home at the time of the killing?"

"Apparently so. He returned home after the party at Groseclose's and found a car in front of his house with a flat tire. He helped get them patched up – he even produced the name and address of the man he helped."

"And you checked into that?"

"I did. Mr. Thomas Murphy of 1455 Hancock Street. Verifies everything Phillips said. Maybe a little too perfectly, to be honest. They both remember every detail in a way that doesn't usually happen."

Eun Jiwon, the young Korean member of the team, was seated between Morgan and Samantha. He leaned forward, staring hard at his employer's impassive face. "I know Mr. Phillips, Chief. He's a Grade A goon, just dressed up in a business suit. I don't know if he could kill a woman, but I know he's got a temper."

"You mean you knew him before all this began?" Samantha asked.

Eun nodded. He was a handsome young man but after an awkward initial series of flirtations, Samantha had realized they weren't really attracted to each other. In fact, Eun didn't care for women sexually at all, though it took some time before he trusted everyone enough to confirm that. "When I first moved to Sovereign with my parents, they had to jump through hoops to get Phillips to sign off on the permits they needed to build their store. It was pretty obvious that he didn't care for immigrants."

Lazarus turned to the board, staring at the images of the men there: Groseclose, Davies, Melvin, Phillips, and Hansome were all men highly respected in their fields. He knew that sometimes respectability was just a veneer that hid a sociopath's true nature, but he found it hard to believe any of these men were capable enough to have pulled off a series of murders like this. In the case of Phillips, he hadn't even moved to the city when the first of them began.

"Whoever did this is skilled with a blade," he said aloud, tapping his chin. "They also know enough about police work to know how to cover their tracks, washing away all the evidence that might implicate them."

"I don't think it's Hansome," Morgan stated. "The guy's way too nervous to have pulled this off. The guy folds under the least bit of pressure."

"Funny thing to say about a lawyer," Eun said. "They lie for a living, don't they?"

"Not the good ones," Lazarus replied. "But I agree with Morgan. I think we can cross Hansome off our list, at least in terms of being the killer. Nothing in his background suggests that he would be capable of this. Having said that, he might be still be involved as an accomplice somehow."

"Well," Samantha said, leaning forward with interest, "if it's not Hansome and it's not Phillips – since he wasn't in town when the murders began – that only leaves a couple of them as suspects, especially if you still believe that Max Davies isn't one of them. We're just left with Melvin and Groseclose."

"That's not quite true."

All eyes turned to the doorway, where The Rook stood, his body outlined in silhouette. He moved into view, his blood splattered form drawing a gasp from Samantha.

Eun moved around the table, intending to attack this intruder, but Morgan caught him by the sleeve. "Hold off," the older man warned. "I think I've heard of this guy."

The Rook nodded at Morgan before fixing his eyes on Lazarus. "Sorry for not knocking on my way in."

"How did you get past our locks and security devices?"

"What can I say? I'm amazing." The Rook flashed a crooked grin. "But I wanted to let you know that Hansome is missing. He was just kidnapped out from under my nose by a masked man calling himself Devil Face. I'm willing to bet that Devil Face is our killer… and he was far too fit and youthful seeming to be either Groseclose or Melvin."

"Then we're back to square one," Samantha said with an air of disappointment.

DARKNESS, SPREADING ITS WINGS OF BLACK

"You're forgetting about Smithson," The Rook answered, sliding his weary form into one of the spare seats at the table. "Young and fit, if I recall correctly. Maybe he's doing the dirty work on his employer's behalf. Or maybe he's flying solo on this."

"Do you have any proof that it's Smithson?" Samantha inquired.

"No. He's just the only one not on that list." The Rook noticed that Eun remained tense and he gave what he hoped would be a reassuring smile. "I'm not your enemy. I'm here for the same reasons you are: to help the innocent."

Eun sneered. "Only you choose to do it while hiding behind a mask."

"I have reasons for hiding my identity."

"All I know," Eun continued, "is that you're wanted on charges of murder, assault, and resisting arrest." The young Korean glanced at Lazarus, his entire body tense. "Tell me why we aren't arresting him, Lazarus. Please."

The Rook struck quickly, spinning the legs of his chair so that his body was now turned toward Eun. He drove the heel of one shoe hard into the younger man's stomach but Eun recovered quickly, having been trained in the martial arts since childhood. He grabbed hold of The Rook's ankle and drove an elbow down hard against it, nearly shattering the delicate bones.

The Rook gritted his teeth but continued with his planned moves. He had anticipated Eun's reaction and knew that it was a gamble to expose his ankle to such an attack, but it left Eun completely exposed up top. The Rook reached into an inner pocket sewn into his jacket and produced a small capsule that snapped open between his fingers. A fine brown mist exploded into the air and The Rook leaned forward, blowing the mist straight into Eun's face. The Korean dropped his hold on the vigilante's foot and began coughing, his eyes watering so badly that he was virtually blind.

By now, Morgan and Samantha were on their feet. Morgan was reaching for his gun when The Rook held up a hand. "I didn't come here to fight. I can give Eun an antidote for the dust I just sprayed him with – or he can wait an hour for it to clear up on its own. I just wanted to show you that there are multiple reasons for not trying to bring me in."

Lazarus spoke up, having made no move to interfere during this entire exchange. Though the battle had taken only a few seconds, Lazarus was fast enough that he could have intervened. "I assume reason number one is that you're innocent of all charges."

"I only kill people who deserve it and who leave me no other choice." The Rook retrieved a second capsule and shoved it into Eun's hand. "Crack this open and wave it under your eyes and nose," he directed.

Morgan, still glaring daggers at The Rook, released his hold on his pistol, leaving it holstered at his waist. "And what's reason number two?"

"I would have thought that would have been obvious," The Rook stated, a bit of arrogance creeping into his voice. "None of you are capable of taking me down."

Samantha crossed her arms over her chest. "If you're so high-and-mighty, why do you need us at all, then? Is this Devil Face really so tough that you can't handle him yourself?"

The Rook hesitated before lowering his shoulders. "I'm sorry. None of this is coming out the way I'd intended. I really do try to help people: that's why I'm here in Sovereign and that's why I went to visit Hansome earlier tonight. I wanted access to the private files he held on his clients. Like all of you, I assumed that one of the men whose names were in that packet was the murderer. But I don't think that's the case any longer. I can't guarantee that it's Smithson, but I think it bears looking into."

Eun was blinking away tears now, having regained the ability to see after using the second capsule. "In a fair fight, I think I could take you," he muttered.

"Maybe," The Rook said, trying to make a peace offering. "But I'd rather not find out."

Lazarus stepped around the table, his eyes flicking toward the clock mounted on the wall. It was late, nearing midnight, but he didn't feel they had any time to waste. "Morgan, I want you and Eun to pay a visit to Mr. Melvin. I'm fairly certain that he'll keep his secretary close to him at all times so they should be in adjoining rooms at their hotel. Samantha, please remain here to coordinate our efforts."

The Rook caught a nod from Lazarus, who was heading toward the door. Falling into step alongside the enigmatic founder of Assistance Unlimited, The Rook lowered his voice and asked, "Where are **we** going?"

Lazarus led the masked man toward an elevator at the end of the hall. "Our first stop will be the medical lab downstairs. I don't think your wounds warrant calling in a physician but you need some patching up. It should take no more than five minutes. I hate to waste even that amount of time, but we may need to be at full strength."

"And then?"

"Then we're going to look for Mr. Hansome."

"I don't have any clue where Devil Face has taken him!" The Rook muttered. "What are you proposing? That we drive around town in hopes of spotting them somewhere?"

"Not quite," Lazarus answered. "All of my aides regularly ingest a radioactive isotope that allows me to easily trace them should they vanish while performing their duties. It's quite harmless. Earlier today, I took action to ensure that all of the men on our list of suspects ingested those same isotopes."

The Rook stopped just inside the fully stocked medical lab. "Including me?"

"Including you."

"How in the world--?"

"It was different for each of you – but for you, I slipped it into the scotch you poured back at your hotel room. You barely sipped any of it, but you still managed to swallow enough for me to trace you."

The Rook's lips spread into a grin. "I just realized you just tricked me into revealing my identity."

"It wasn't hard to figure out," Lazarus said in all honesty, leading The Rook toward a chair. After the vigilante was seated and Lazarus had begun treating his injuries, he continued, "The authorities in Boston have nearly uncovered your dual identities on several occasions. You've been so sloppy that it almost seems like you want to be caught."

The Rook winced as Lazarus dabbed antiseptic into his knife wound. "Yeah, I've been told that before. It's just so hard to balance a personal life with my private war... Considering how my father was killed because his enemies knew who he was, I thought it was important to keep my own identity secret. But when push has come to shove, I've erred on the side of catching bad guys, even when it meant that my identity might be compromised."

"I understand about the nature of dual lives," Lazarus admitted. He was normally a taciturn individual, but he sensed that Max Davies was someone who could fully understand the difficulties he faced. "Not long ago, I was a man named Richard Winthrop. I was a member of an international cartel with their fingers in every occult conspiracy you can think of. When I turned against them, I was killed... but here in Sovereign City, I was reborn. Now I find elements of my old life encroaching upon the new with disturbing regularity."

The Rook seemed to sense that he was being honored with this show of familiarity. He reached out and squeezed the other man's arm. "Maybe we can help each other. You can give me advice when it looks like I'm skating on thin ice with my secret identity... and I can offer you assistance in dealing with those old friends of yours."

Lazarus pulled away, reaching under a counter where he retrieved a gauze bandage. "I just might take you up on that."

"I don't like him," Eun said for about the fifteenth time. He glanced over at Morgan, who was leading the way down the hotel lobby. They had used their status as members of Assistance Unlimited to convince the desk clerk downstairs to tell them what rooms belonged to Mr. Melvin and his secretary. To Morgan's surprise, Melvin wasn't in the penthouse – rather, he was in one of the rooms on the fourth floor. Smithson, as Lazarus had surmised, was in an adjoining suite.

Morgan reached up and rubbed his fingertips over the slicked pencil-thin moustache that covered his upper lip. "Eun, give it a rest. The Rook is on our side."

"He's wanted for murder."

"I've killed more men than I care to remember," Morgan pointed out. "Most of them were back in my criminal days but it doesn't change the fact that I'm a murderer. At least The Rook supposedly hasn't offed anyone who didn't deserve it."

Eun didn't bother responding but from the sour look on his face, there was no need to. Morgan knew he was smarting more from his hurt pride than anything else. Hoping that the younger man would get past his distrust of The Rook, Morgan stopped outside Melvin's door and gave it a hard rap.

There was movement from within and the door opened and revealed Melvin, dressed in a smoking jacket and slippers. He seemed alert, despite the hour. "Yes?" he asked.

"My name's Morgan Watts. I work for Assistance Unlimited. You've heard of us?"

"Of course. Who hasn't?" Understanding seemed to dawn in the old man's eyes and he stepped back, allowing them entrance. "This is about that horrible murder, isn't it? The Schuller girl?"

Morgan stepped inside but Eun hung back. "My friend's going to speak to your secretary. He's next door?"

"Yes. But I can access his room with our adjoining door."

"We'd rather speak to each of you separately." Morgan nodded at Eun, who moved toward Smithson's room. Morgan took the door from Melvin and shut it. "You're right about us being here about the murder. I wanted to ask you how well you know Mr. Smithson."

"I'd trust him with my life. If you're going to accuse him of some wrongdoing, you're just going to end up with egg on your face. He's morally upstanding." Melvin took several steps toward a table where a half empty bottle of vodka sat next to an empty glass. Morgan had thought he'd detected the smell of alcohol on Melvin's breath and now he knew his senses had been correct. "Can I get you a drink?" Melvin asked, sitting down with creaking knees.

"Normally, I'd like nothing better, but I can't afford that right now. I'm working." Morgan sat down across from Melvin, his eyes flicking toward the door that led into the adjoining room. If The Rook was correct and Smithson was the murderer, Eun might be in grave danger. At the first sign of danger, Morgan would burst into that room, guns blazing.

"What makes you think that Smithson is the murderer?" Melvin asked, pouring himself a glass. He tilted the bottle until the liquid reached the lip of the glass, threatening to overflow.

"We're not accusing anyone," Morgan said. "As a matter of fact, Smithson's name wasn't one of those found on the dead girl's body. But most of the others either have alibis or have other elements to their lives that preclude them from being part of the killings."

"Killings?" Melvin asked, his eyes shining. "There's been more than one?"

"Yes. The press and the local police don't seem to have noticed, but Schuller wasn't the first girl to be killed. There have been several over the past few years, mostly prostitutes and the like. We think we're dealing with a modern day Jack the Ripper."

"Oh, my," Melvin whispered, the color draining from his face.

"What's wrong?"

Melvin suddenly seemed very fragile. "I think I might know something about all of this, after all…"

Morgan leaned forward with interest. It was at that moment that the sounds of gunfire rang out from Smithson's apartment.

Eun knew that he was being wrongheaded but he couldn't bring himself to change his opinion with regards to The Rook. The man was trouble with a capital T as far as Eun was concerned. He was still pondering this as Morgan shut the door to Melvin's room and Eun began to knock on Smithson's. There was no answer and Eun repeated the procedure, applying a bit more force to the knocking this time.

When Smithson still did not appear, Eun reached down and tried the doorknob. It was locked and Eun pondered for a moment what to do. He could enter Melvin's room and try to cross over through the adjoining door, but he didn't want to expose the old man to any danger if Smithson was the killer.

According to the clerk, both Smithson and Melvin were supposedly in their rooms but only one of them was answering – and while it would have made sense for the elderly Melvin to be hard of hearing, it defied logic for Smithson to be the same.

Eun took a step back and raised his right foot. He drove it hard against the door, repeating the blow twice more before the barrier cracked and swung open. Eun heard movement from within and he hurried inside, saying, "Mr. Smithson? Don't be alarmed."

The first thing that Eun noticed was that the room was illuminated by a single lamp, which sat next to the bed. Lying on top of the sheets was Smithson, but any hopes that he might shed some light on the murders was smashed when Eun spotted the pool of crimson that lay beneath him. A bullet hole over his heart was the source from which the blood had flowed and Eun knew immediately that Smithson was dead and had been for at least an hour.

A rustle of fabric drew Eun's attention away from the body. Standing in front of the open sliding glass door that led to the balcony was a dark figure. Eun remembered The Rook's description of Devil Face and quickly realized that this man did not match that look at all. This man wore a white shirt covered by a gray vest, black tie, and an ebony jacket. Over all of this was slung a dark opera-style cape that was clasped about his neck. With black slacks and shoes, as well as leather gloves and a top hat, the figure looked like he might be on his way to a fancy ball. But the presence of an automatic in his right hand and a large domino-style mask made it quite clear to Eun that the man's presence was a sinister one.

"I know how this looks," the man began, "but it's not quite what you think."

Eun grinned and sprang toward the man, eager to redeem his earlier defeat against The Rook. He moved so quickly that the well-dressed man was unprepared for the first blow that came: Eun caught him flat on the side of the skull with a closed fist. The younger Korean followed with a knee to the man's midsection that knocked the air from the man's lungs.

Eun felt a sense of elation, realizing that he might be about to singlehandedly solve the entire case. If this man was the killer, then perhaps he was working with Devil Face – or, just as likely, The Rook had made up the whole thing and was working with this man.

The well-dressed man recovered faster than Eun would have thought possible. He raised his pistol and squeezed off two quick shots. The first whistled past the Korean's ear and passed through the sheet rock behind him. The second stuck Eun in the left thigh and caused him to grit his teeth in pain.

Eun had taken bullets before and refused to give in. He was about to strike back when the masked man pistol-whipped him, cracking Eun's lip and sending a spray of blood against the wall.

"I'm not the killer," the masked man said. "I came here for the same reasons you did: to talk to that man. I found him like that just minutes before you showed up."

"I don't believe you," Eun hissed. "I've had it up to here with masked men telling me lies."

"Not sure what you're talking about, friend, but I'm called The Dark Gentleman. And I'm working to clean up the cesspool that Sovereign City's become."

At that moment, the adjoining door to Melvin's room burst open. Morgan sprinted through, throwing himself into a rolling ball. He popped up next to the bed and, with barely a glance at the corpse in the bed, opened fire at The Dark Gentleman.

The masked man cried out in surprise, hurling himself backwards. He landed against the balcony railing and quickly twisted so that his legs were up and over it. He dropped out of sight, leaving Eun and Morgan to rush forward in hopes of catching a glimpse of his fate.

Down below, the city streets were empty. It was a three-story drop but there was no sign of The Dark Gentleman.

Morgan took note of his friend's bleeding shoulder and mouth. "What the hell happened?"

"That guy in the mask that you just shot at – he calls himself The Dark Gentleman. I'm starting to think that those names on that girl's body weren't suspects… they were targets. Hansome missing, Melvin's secretary killed… maybe these men know something and that's why they're being bumped off now."

"Something that's tied to the murders of all those girls?"

DARKNESS, SPREADING ITS WINGS OF BLACK

Eun shrugged. He turned back toward the bed, where Melvin was now standing. The old man was staring at the body of his confidante. Melvin looked horrified and one liver-spotted hand came up to cover his own mouth, as if he wanted to stifle a scream.

"Mr. Melvin, we're going to summon the police," Eun said. "Can you remain here and wait for them?"

Numbly, Melvin nodded. He turned away from the corpse and seemed to regain some of his strength now that he wasn't faced with his secretary's body. "He was a good man, almost like a son to me."

Morgan caught Eun by the sleeve. "How about making that call and then staying here with Melvin? I can go looking for that guy without you."

"No," Eun answered firmly. "I'm not being left behind."

"You're hurt."

"I'm fine."

Morgan sighed and nodded. He was pretty sure that The Dark Gentleman hadn't left them any kind of trail worth mentioning, but they had to make sure. He was about to step out into the hall with Eun when he remembered that Melvin had been about to say something to him before the shooting began. He hesitated a moment, gesturing for Eun to go on without him.

"Mr. Melvin... You were about to tell me that you might know something about these murders?"

Melvin didn't bother looking at Morgan. He simply shook his head and whispered, "Nothing. I have nothing to say."

Chapter IV
Angels & Demons

"So that's how he did it!" Samantha sat back with a satisfied grin on her face. Ever since The Rook had interrupted their meeting, she'd wondered how he'd managed to bypass the security at Assistance Unlimited headquarters. It had taken a bit of digging through the archival footage to figure out what security flaw the masked man had uncovered but now she had it: he'd broken into one of the abandoned storefronts facing the old hotel that Assistance Unlimited used as their base. From there, he'd managed to travel through one of the underground tunnels that linked every building on the street. Everyone knew that Lazarus Gray had bought the entire block for purposes of secrecy but very few knew that they were all linked together, essentially transforming it into one giant headquarters.

Samantha still wasn't sure how The Rook had known about the underground tunnels, but at least she knew how he'd accessed the main building: he'd come in through the basement.

She was still marveling over the panache needed to break into their headquarters when Morgan and Eun entered the room. Eun looked pale, his shirtless body covered by bandages.

Samantha moved to fuss over his wounds but Eun waved her away and sat down heavily in a chair. "There's another masked man in town," he said. "Calls himself The Dark Gentleman."

Samantha straightened up. "That's odd. Sovereign's had its share of vigilantes in recent years, but most of them don't bother hiding their identities."

"Now we have two," Eun muttered, obviously still smarting from his wounded pride.

Morgan allowed the two younger members of the team to continue the discussion while he stepped into an adjacent room. He picked through some of the papers they'd accumulated on the various suspects. Something was bothering him, but he wasn't sure what… Obviously Melvin had thought about sharing something with them and then changed his mind. Was there some connection between Smithson and Hansome that they hadn't picked up on? And if so, how did it all play into the horrific murders of those girls?

He tapped a photo of Hansome and whispered, "I hope Lazarus can find you, shyster. I'm betting you have the answers we need."

The duo of Lazarus Gray and The Rook had traced the radioactive isotopes in Hansome's bloodstream, following the trail to a small rental property on the outskirts of town. A sign in the front yard indicated that the A-frame house was for rent by the owner and Lazarus noted that the painted phone number on the sign had peeled away, leaving only the first couple of digits.

"This is a front," The Rook said, standing outside the front door. There were no streetlights around and the interior of the house was dark, so both men held sterling silver penlights.

"What do you mean?"

"Nobody's really trying to rent this property. If they were, they would have repaired that sign. And the house itself is filthy… smells like something's died here. Recently."

Lazarus knew what his friend was implying and he moved forward, taking up position to the right of the door. The Rook took the left and they nodded at each other before Lazarus took a few steps back and lowered his shoulder. He crashed against the door, using all his impressive strength to shatter the barrier.

The interior was cloaked in an almost stygian darkness and the odor of death was far thicker than before. The Rook followed Lazarus into the house, using his penlight to locate a small lamp. He turned it on, bathing the living room in a dull yellow glow. What they saw was stomach churning and, even for men as used to the unusual as these two were, shocking.

There were human, dog, and cat skeletons nailed to the blood-red wallpaper, many of them arranged in obscene positions. In between the bones, the wallpaper had been covered with odd drawings of horned demons, acts of bestiality, and crying faces.

The skeleton of a human male, its bones held together by twine, dangled from the center of the ceiling. Large wings forged of leather and wood had been attached to the skeleton's back and goat horns had been glued to the top of the skull.

A long table was set against the back wall. It was waist-high and carved from some form of shiny blood-colored wood. Its bowed legs were carved to resemble great serpents, their fanged mouths reached upward. At each of the four corners was a black candle resting in bronze holder. The holders were shaped like skulls, the lower the jaw of each protruding out to hold the candle in place. A stone basin lay in the center of the table and as Lazarus approached it, he recognized the presence of human bones and dried blood.

The scene was disturbingly familiar to Lazarus. In his old life, he'd witnessed things like this as a member of The Illuminati. It had been horrors like this that had led him to turn against his friends, eventually bringing about his death and resurrection in Sovereign City.

The Rook allowed Lazarus to investigate the strange table and its horrible contents. He opened the other doors, finding a bedroom that looked like it had never been touched; a kitchen that was so filthy that it nearly caused him to retch; and a bathroom that contained a very nasty surprise.

"Lazarus," The Rook said, placing the back of a gloved hand over his nose and mouth. "I found Hansome."

Lazarus appeared almost instantly, looking past the masked man at the lumps of flesh that lay in the tub. The soapy water was filled with bleach, cleaning away much-needed evidence. Hansome's body had been neatly cut up into six pieces: his head, his torso, his arms, and his legs. Several large buckets filled with the man's blood lay outside the tub and plastic tubing rested on the counter top next to the sink.

"There goes any doubts about Hansome's kidnapper being related to the girls' killer," The Rook murmured. "Guess he's branching out to the other gender."

Lazarus knelt beside the tub, holding a handkerchief over his nose. His eyes watered from the strong bleach fumes that hung in the air, but he wanted to check on a suspicion he had. He grabbed hold of Hansome's head and lifted it from the bath, carrying it out of the room and setting it gently atop the bloodstained table in the living room. While The Rook watched in mounting curiosity, Lazarus pulled up a chair and sat facing the dead man's terror-stricken face. After pulling out a magnifying glass, he leaned so close to the decapitated head that their noses were almost touching.

"What are you doing?" The Rook asked, no longer able to contain himself.

"Are you familiar with the work of Willy Kühne, professor of physiology at Heidelberg?"

The Rook searched his memory and slowly nodded, beginning to see where his companion was going with this. "He studied retinal chemistry, didn't he?"

"Yes. He theorized that the retina behaves not only like a photographic plate but like an entire photographic workshop, in which the artist continually renews the plate by laying on new light-sensitive material, while simultaneously erasing the old image. By using the pigment epithelium, which bleaches in the light, he set out to prove that it might be possible to take a picture with the living eye. He called the process optography and its resulting products optograms."

The Rook found himself getting wrapped up in the science behind the matter. "And the rabbit's eyes held an image of the bars," he whispered to himself.

Kühne had created a famous optogram by using an albino rabbit, whose head had been fastened so that it faced a barred window. From this position the rabbit could only see out onto a cloudy sky. The rabbit's head had been alternately covered with a cloth, to allow its eyes to acclimate to the dark, and then exposed to bright light. After this, the rabbit was decapitated, with its eye removed and cut open along the equator. The rear half of the eyeball, containing the retina, was laid in a solution of alum to set. The next day, Kühne had seen printed upon the retina a picture of the window with the clear pattern of its bars. This had been repeated in other experiments, leading Kühne to state that the final image viewed before death would be fixed forever, like a photo. If death were to occur at a moment when the pupils of the eyes were hugely dilated – because of fear, anger, surprise, or some other strong emotion – the retinal optograms of the deceased would be even more detailed.

"Do you see anything," The Rook asked.

Lazarus nodded, his eyes staring into those of the dead man. Reflected there, as clear as day, was the face of the devil.

Theodore Groseclose couldn't sleep. He was sitting in his study, a glass of warm milk in his hand, unable to stop thinking about the events of the past few days. He'd liked Claudia. She was smart and pretty, the sort of combination he always enjoyed having around the office. It was hard for him to visualize her body having been violated in the ways he'd heard. What sort of monster could do that? Who could snuff out a beautiful girl's light like that?

Groseclose looked up as he heard the unmistakable sound of the front door being unlocked. He set down his milk and moved to the foyer, his eyes widening as his 24-year old son Michael entered the house, looking disheveled. Michael was blessed with his mother's good looks and his father's intellect… but there were whispers that he was squandering both since dropping out of college two years before. Since then, he'd lurked in the shadows, vanishing for days on end with no explanation.

"What the hell are you doing?" his father demanded, all the frustrations of the past few days finding a new target. "I swear to heaven, I don't think you care what the community thinks, do you?"

Michael's jaw clenched, as if he were barely able to hold back his own anger. "I was out on business."

"At this hour of the night? I don't believe you. I believe you were out drinking and whoring, that's what I think!"

Michael shook his head and stepped around his father. "I'm going to bed."

"The hell you are!" Theodore bellowed, grabbing hold of his son's arm and clenching it tight. "I've had enough of you. You're my son! And that means people are going to look at you differently than if you were some ragamuffin off the street!"

Michael whirled around, bringing his face close to his father's. Had Theodore not been so wrapped up in his anger, he would have realized that there was not a trace of alcohol on his son's breath. "You know what, Dad? I've had enough of you, too. You sit in your office and you print your stories but what do you really know about life in this city? Have you walked its streets? Have you seen all the joy and happiness sucked out of its people because they can't believe in the system anymore? Do you know that there are dozens of mobs out there, all vying for power? And that the men in charge turn a blind eye to it because they're too scared or to crooked to do what's right?" Michael yanked his arm free. "Oh, but you would know about that last part, wouldn't you? You're the one helping make sure good people are being put out on the street so your buddies can build their high-rises."

Theodore's mouth moved silently for a moment before his anger gave him new voice. "How dare you?"

"I know a lot more about this town than you give me credit for. And I'm actually doing something about it." Michael spun on his heels and jogged upstairs, regretting the anger he'd shown his father, but refusing to back down. He slammed the door to his room shut and then sagged down onto his bed. He needed to get his own place if he wanted to really make a difference. Sneaking in and out of his own house was just one more headache that he didn't need.

Michael had trained for months, preparing to take to the streets as The Dark Gentleman… but what had happened on his first night out? He'd run into not one, but two members of Assistance Unlimited, both of whom now thought he was a murderer. He'd meant to question Smithson about the men whose names were linked to Claudia's death… but whoever had killed him had come and gone before Michael had arrived.

Claudia had been a lovely girl and one that would have normally attracted Michael's intense interest. But he'd been so single-minded as of late that he'd never bothered approaching her.

Michael stood up quickly and began pacing. He wanted to do something, wanted to prove that the past few weeks hadn't been some pointless lark. He could help Sovereign City, he was sure of it.

He suddenly realized that he needed to clear the air with Assistance Unlimited. Right now, they were probably wasting valuable time hunting him down when they could be going after the real killer.

Michael forced himself to stop. He had to get some rest. In the morning, he could go down to Robeson Avenue and make peace with them. Maybe they'd even agree to let him assist them in the case.

A smile suddenly blossomed on his lips. Michael realized he was beginning to feel like a kid hoping to fall in with the popular crowd at school. He needed to rest before he did anything reckless – more reckless than putting on a top hat and mask.

DARKNESS, SPREADING ITS WINGS OF BLACK

Devil Face stared in the mirror, marveling at the beauty of his visage. This was the true expression of his inner self, come to life in the form of a wooden depiction of Satan himself. The leering mouth, the jutting tongue, the crimson tint... They were everything that he so desperately wanted to be. They were far truer than the face he wore every day to the office, where he pretended to be so much less than he truly was.

It had been years since he'd moved to Sovereign City, this cesspool of immorality. The place had called to him and he'd recognized it as home. He had felt it in his blood and in the dark little corner of his mind where the Devil resided. At first, he'd tried to be good, tried to silence the voices that screamed for bloody murder... and he'd almost succeeded. But then he'd seen those whores, all made up like pretty dollies – they'd forced him to do what he'd done. He'd punished them for their sins, for using their breasts and their buttocks to tantalize and tease. Who knew how many boys they'd corrupted with their offers of love? He'd killed them and washed them, not to remove traces of his identity as the police had assumed: but to cleanse them of their filth.

Claudia had been different than the rest and she was the cause of all of Devil Face's current problems. She'd been so sweet and desirable, nothing like those tarts he'd killed in the past. Claudia was a good girl. She'd sobbed to him in the end, begging him to spare her. She claimed she was a virgin and Devil Face almost believed her – he'd wanted so badly to believe her. But he knew she'd gone to Max's apartment and they'd done *things*... dirty things that caused butterflies to swim about in his stomach when he imagined them. This made him realize that even if she wasn't a whore yet, she was well on her way. So he'd punished her for the sins she'd yet to commit.

And then had come the guilt, so quick that it had surprised him. He'd borrowed Max's address book during a brief visit to the other man's hotel room. At the time, he'd merely wanted to find out more about Davies, who had seemed to be more than he claimed to be. Davies had this way of looking at everyone as if he could see through him or her. It was almost as if he was looking at Devil's Face's real features, which had been both exciting and infuriating.

After Claudia's death, though, the idea of leaving the address book on her body had seemed the proper way to assuage his guilt. A part of him wanted the world to know who he really was and this dangerous game of leaving clues to his identity served his need for self-punishment.

But after her body had been discovered, the Devil had taken hold and a sense of self-preservation had emerged. Hansome knew his real identity, which meant he'd had to die. Hansome's sexual interests had forced Devil Face to give him the same treatment he usually reserved for the whores: after all, Hansome probably would have offered his body if he'd thought it would have saved him. It was sickening, what Hansome would have done if given the chance....

Smithson was another problem. Too smart for his own good, Smithson had discovered Devil Face's secret and actually sought to blackmail him. Devil Face didn't think that Melvin knew the truth, but he couldn't be sure. Smithson and the old man were very close. Since Smithson wasn't a sex fiend like Hansome or the girls, Devil Face had killed him like an animal. It was the first time he'd ever killed without using the precious ritual – the ceremonial cutting, the washing of the flesh, reducing the body to chunks of flesh.

Devil Face turned away from the mirror, reaching up to peel away his mask. He hated to look at the face he showed the world on a regular basis. It was so ugly, with every crease and line containing a litany of sins. It was only when his true face was on display that he felt truly confident.

After placing the devil mask in a box under his bed, he headed downstairs to have a drink. Killing those men hadn't left him as ecstatic as cleansing the whores usually did. Normally he would have been humming a song to himself and feeling like he was on top of the world: instead, he felt tense and paranoid. How long before Smithson's body was discovered? Would they find the gun he'd discarded in the trash bin outside the hotel? Could it be linked back to him? And what about Hansome? His body was still in one of Devil Face's many safe houses but with Assistance Unlimited on the prowl, who could say that it wouldn't be discovered?

He paused as the phone in the study began to ring. He looked up at the clock and realized that it was nearly dawn. Where had the night gone?

Walking quickly to pluck up the receiver, the killer took a moment to make sure he used the proper voice. His day-to-day voice was deeper than the one he used when wearing the Devil Face mask. "Hello?"

Theodore Groseclose sounded on edge. "You need to come over to my house. Immediately."

"What's wrong?" he asked, though he knew what the answer would be. How could he not?

"Smithson and Hansome… they're both dead. Melvin's already here and I'm about to call Max. We could all be in danger – what if the killer's planning to kill everyone associated with Schuller?"

"Calm down," he soothed. He caught a glimpse of himself in the mirror and paused. His hair and beard looked unkempt and his eyes were wild. He didn't look much like Robert Phillips at the moment: he'd have to clean himself up before he went over to Groseclose's. "I'll be there soon."

Devil Face hung up the phone and reached up to smooth his hair. Had Smithson told Melvin about what he'd learned? If he had, then the old man would have to die, too… and then there was Groseclose. The man was a journalist and he might start digging on his own. If he found out that Phillips had moved to Sovereign and adopted a new identity for himself with Hansome's help, then all the dirty secrets might come out.

Phillips hurriedly bathed and dressed in fresh clothing, creeping down the stairs to the locked basement door before leaving for Groseclose's. He entered the finished basement, the coppery smell of blood filling his nostrils as he opened the door. Inside were 13 canisters filled with the blood of the women he'd killed over the years, dating back to before he'd come to Sovereign and adopted his current identity. He needed to kill only one more and then he'd be ready to leave this prison of flesh behind.

"Something troubles you, my love?"

The soft, purring voice of Lady Death echoed in his head. The temperature seemed to drop twenty degrees or more and his breath suddenly became visible in tiny cloudbursts that escaped his mouth. He turned to face the woman of his dreams, the only one who was pure in all things. He was the only one who could see her, the only one who heard her voice.

She was a few inches over five feet in height, her lush curves shifting beneath a hooded black robe. Her skin was a milky white that always reminded him of moonlight on water. Her ruby red lips and the lower half of her face was all that could be seen beneath the darkness of her hood, but he had seen her naked beauty before. The upper half of her skull was exposed, her eyes nothing more than two deep sockets of shadow that seemed to suck him right into their depths.

"My enemies are closing in on us," Devil Face answered, using the higher-pitched voice he normally saved for when he was masked. "I'm worried that they might stop me before I've accomplished my goal."

Lady Death reached out and touched his face, her icy grip making him shiver. "I am proud of you. You have done so much in my name… and now you only have to find one more whore, one more woman who needs to have her sins washed away. And then you'll be mine, in body and soul."

Devil Face leaned into her hand, his face lighting up like an excited puppy's. "I can go find another girl tonight!"

"No. You'll know her when you see her. There are only certain ones who fit our needs."

Lady Death pulled away, vanishing into the dark shadows of the basement. Devil Face reached after her, desperate to touch her skin once more but there was nothing there any longer.

Chapter V
But For the Grace of God

Max Davies woke up at six in the morning and immediately indulged in his daily ritual. He had a cup of warm tea followed by an hour-long session of yoga and Tai chi chuan. When he was done with his exercises, he dressed in a casual suit and placed the beak-like mask of The Rook over the bridge of his nose. He'd spent the night in the headquarters of Assistance Unlimited, enjoying the comforts that the former hotel offered. He felt a bit silly continuing to hide his identity – Lazarus knew who he was and he trusted the man implicitly. The fact that Lazarus in turn trusted his aides should have meant that Max did as well... but it wasn't quite that simple. The dark stares The Rook continued to receive from Eun were evidence that he wasn't fully accepted by all.

The Rook wandered downstairs to the team's meeting room and found that everyone else was already there. Morgan and Samantha were seated beside each other, their voices lowered to mere whispers. Morgan said something that Samantha found funny and she coyly covered her mouth as she laughed. Eun was leaning against the wall, looking as surly as ever. Lazarus himself was standing with his hands clasped behind his mask. His impassive face was pointed toward the window and the ray of sunlight that fell upon it accentuated his strong chin.

"Any breaks in the case?" The Rook asked, ignoring the way Eun muttered under his breath in response.

Lazarus looked toward him and gave a brief nod. "Perhaps. Groseclose is holding a private meeting at this hour with Phillips and Melvin. I understand they attempted to get in contact with Max Davies, but he's not at his hotel."

The Rook paused, a smile on his lips. "I might be able to reach Max and convince him to go to this little party. It would help us to know what was going on."

"That would be quite useful," Lazarus admitted. "We'll be waiting to hear

DARKNESS, SPREADING ITS WINGS OF BLACK

back from you."

Michael Groseclose was pulling out of the driveway just as the taxicab carrying Max Davies was coming to a stop in front of the house. Michael and Max locked eyes for a brief second before their travels carried them away from each other and Max was struck once more by how intelligent the young man seemed. They'd only met briefly at the party thrown by the elder Groseclose, but Max had felt a kinship to the youth.

Max was led into the house by a taciturn butler who looked almost as harried as Max felt. He wore on his lapel a miniscule listening device that would allow Lazarus to overhear every word that was said. Max was more impressed with Assistance Unlimited at every turn. The various skills of the aides were impressive enough, but combined with the various inventions and designs of their leader, they had become one of the most formidable organizations on earth.

Max found Groseclose in the sitting room, seated with his head hanging between his knees. Phillips, looking like an angry bear that had been roused from his winter's nap, was pacing in front of the fireplace. Melvin, looking older and frailer than Max could ever remember, sat pensively on a small couch, his eyes staring off into unfocused space.

Phillips stopped and stared, his mouth clamped into a thin line beneath his beard. "Davies. We were beginning to wonder if Devil Face had gotten to you."

"Devil Face?" Max asked, allowing a smile to appear on his face. He looked over at Groseclose, who had leaned back in his chair.

"According to a statement released by Assistance Unlimited, that's the name of the lunatic who's committing the murders," Groseclose said.

Max noticed that Melvin looked up sharply, his gaze shifting from Max to Phillips and back again. "You know about Smithson, don't you?" he asked. "They say Devil Face killed him, too, but he didn't mutilate him like he did the others."

Max knelt in front of Melvin and took the old man's hands. "I did hear and I'm sorry. I know he was like a son to you."

"He was. I don't know how I'm going to continue on without him. I'm not as young as I used to be."

Phillips growled like the animal he resembled. "I'm surprised the police don't have us all under protection. Two of the men whose names were on that dead girl's body have been murdered! We're important people, damn it!"

"Smithson's name wasn't in the packet," Max pointed out, drawing another dangerous stare from Phillips.

"I imagine they're planning to put us under protection," Groseclose said. "But I'm not sure that's going to be enough. Any man who could have evaded detection for as many years as this Devil Face has… I'm not sure he's human."

Melvin looked at him in surprise. "What do you mean?"

"Just that there are a lot of awful things in this world and not all of them can be explained by men. I haven't run half the rumors I've heard about Assistance Unlimited and the kinds of jobs they take on: demons, devil-worshipping cults, women who can kill men just by looking at them."

"Poppycock!" Phillips bellowed, though Max thought he saw a shadow of doubt pass over the big man's face. "Sounds to me like you've been paying too much attention to Gray's own rumor mongering. It's all an attempt to stir up an air of mystery around the man so he can charge more for his services!"

Max stood up and adjusted the sleeves of his coat. "Do we have any sort of plan here? Or is this meeting simply to share our concerns?"

Melvin struggled to his feet. "I'm leaving town. I only came to finalize our plans for the project and I daresay that they're on hold for now. I need to return home and inform Smithson's family about what's happened. I'm sure they've heard the news, but I want to tell them what the papers may not have."

"You can't leave town," Groseclose said sadly. "The police want us all to stay in Sovereign. We're persons of interest in the investigation."

Phillips stormed over to the table that sat in front of Groseclose's chair. He plucked up the morning newspaper and stared at the front page. It showed an old photograph of Lazarus Gray and his aides, under the headline **ASSISTANCE UNLIMITED HUNTS 'DEVIL FACE' KILLER!**

"Glory hounds," Phillips whispered, his eyes lingering on the pretty face of Samantha Grace. His lips moved a few more times, as if he were continuing to mouth words, but none of the other men could hear what he said. He abruptly threw the paper back on the table and stepped back, his eyes wide. "I hope for the best for you gentlemen. I don't plan to wait for either you or the police to come up with a scheme to protect me, however. I'll handle that quite well on my own!"

Max put a hand on the big man's arm, preventing him from walking toward the door. "Don't go off half-cocked, Phillips. The last thing any of us need to do is go out and get ourselves into trouble."

Phillips glared at Max, pulling his arm free as he did so. "You will be well advised to never touch me again," he said in a menacing tone.

"I'm just trying to help," Max answered, refusing to wilt before the bigger man's gaze. As they stared each other down, Max felt a tremor of recognition pass through him. He'd been face-to-face with Phillips before and never realized it. He'd be willing to bet his last dollar that it had been Phillips behind the Devil Face mask when they'd squared off in Hansome's bedroom. At the same moment that Max realized whom his enemy truly was, Phillips narrowed his own eyes, having come to the same realization.

"I don't need your help," Phillips hissed. "Just stay out of my way."

Max stared at the man's back as he exited the room. A moment later and they all heard the loud slam of the front door.

"Just let him be," Groseclose said wearily. "He's always been an aggressive sort and I imagine all this just makes him feel helpless. Lord knows that's how I feel."

Max looked over at Melvin, who was still standing in place. "Do you still want to leave?"

Melvin shrugged, looking pained with every breath. "I'd love to but I don't think it's very wise, do you? I can't leave the city and I don't want to stay at the hotel. Smithson was killed there so I wouldn't feel safe." He chewed his bottom lip for a moment before saying, "Smithson didn't like Phillips. Said he was dangerous. He warned me not to be alone with him. But he said something very strange to me just a few hours before he died. I thought about mentioning it to that fellow from Assistance Unlimited but then thought better of it. It sounds so foolish."

"What was it?" Max did his best to avoid looking overeager.

"Smithson said that Phillips was the same kind of man as Jack the Ripper: that he looked at other people, particularly at women, as slabs of meat. Mr. Watts of Assistance Unlimited compared the killer to Jack the Ripper, too. It reminded me of what Smithson had said." Melvin looked at Max and shook his head with a sad smile. "But Phillips is a respected businessman, just like I am. We don't do such things. Do we?"

Michael Groseclose checked his appearance for the tenth time, ensuring that his top hat was perched just so atop his head and that his gloves were tugged on to a tight fit over his hands. He tried to ignore the feeling that he was a kid playing dress up as he strode toward the front door of Assistance Unlimited. He'd never worn the mask during the daytime hours before and it all felt a little silly in the light of day.

Before he'd reached the door, Eun Jiwon and Morgan Watts were waiting to greet him. Eun stood with fists clenched at his sides and Morgan's hand drifted close to the interior of his coat, where a gun obviously lay in wait.

The Dark Gentleman raised both hands and came to a halt. "Like I said last night, I'm on your side."

Eun raised his chin. "Then tell us why you're wearing that mask, Mr. Groseclose."

The Dark Gentleman flinched as if struck. His hands lowered immediately and he didn't even bother trying to hide his dismay. "You know who I am?"

"We have cameras mounted all over this entire block," Eun explained, triumph in his voice. "While you parked down the street and started changing into your getup, I was looking to see who those licensed plates belonged to. If you're getting into the vigilante game, you need to learn the ropes."

"Damn." The Dark Gentleman shook his head, unsure how to continue past this point. He was saved the trouble when Morgan relaxed his stance and pulled the door open.

"Come on in, kid. Let's hear your story."

Samantha Grace had been charged with the task of watching the exterior of the Groseclose home during Max's meeting with the others. She had sat in a dark sedan across the street, listening in as the others back at Assistance Unlimited were doing. When Phillips had stormed out, she'd been forced to make a decision: should she wait where she was or should she follow the bearlike man who obviously had a temper? In the end, her female intuition told her to stick with Phillips, so she followed him at a distance as he drove back to his house. She drove past as she pulled into his driveway, circling back around the block and finally parking a few hundred feet from the front door. To her surprise, she saw that the entrance was standing wide open and that one of the potted plants just outside the steps had been overturned.

Never one to shy away from danger, Samantha was out of the car in a flash. Given the fact that both Smithson and Hansome were dead, it stood to reason that Phillips might be another target.

The petite blond hurried across the street, a small handgun clutched in her right hand. Her heels clicked on the asphalt and she was glad that she'd worn slacks today. She enjoyed the feeling of femininity that came with skirts and dresses, but they were difficult to fight in.

Samantha crept up the stairs toward the open door. "Mr. Phillips? Are you in there? I'm with Assistance Unlimited."

Stepping inside, Samantha noticed no signs of a struggle. She was about to raise her voice and identify herself again when she heard the creak of the door behind her. She whirled around to see Devil Face lunging for her, blade in hand. That it was Phillips was undeniable – the build and the fact that he still wore the same clothing made that quite clear. But the mask, with its distorted demon's features, was disconcerting.

Samantha pulled the trigger but her shot went wild, passing harmlessly over Devil Face's shoulder. Well versed in jujitsu, Samantha was able to quickly evade a swipe of the blade, but her position in the foyer didn't allow her much room to work with and Devil Face was so large that she was immediately pressed up against the wall.

"I'm going to help you," the killer said, speaking in a voice that was much higher-pitched than the one she had heard Phillips use earlier. "Don't be afraid."

If the situation hadn't been so terrifying, Samantha would have laughed. Was he really telling her not to be afraid, even as he was stabbing wildly at her with a sharpened blade? Men were always confusing to her but killers were the worst: the natural inclinations men had toward being dense were amplified by madness.

DARKNESS, SPREADING ITS WINGS OF BLACK

Samantha jammed her knee into the big man's crotch and she was rewarded with a squeal of pain from him. She drew up her pistol, pressing the barrel directly against the forehead of the mask but before she could fire, a white-hot pain sliced through her midsection. She felt rapidly spreading warmth spiral out from her stomach and she didn't have to look down to realize that the killer's knife was deep inside her.

If I die, I'm taking you with me, she thought, pulling hard on the trigger. Devil Face's head jerked back as the bullet struck his mask and he staggered back in shock. Samantha reached down and gripped the hilt of the knife, growing dizzy as she began to extract the blade from her stomach. She tossed the weapon down and blinked away the stars that were obscuring her vision. As she sagged to her knees, she realized that Devil Face had recovered and was standing over her. His mask had protected him from the full impact but it had split in two and the pieces now lay on the floor. Phillips was staring at her, a tiny dot of blood between his eyes. His hands continually opened and closed and he was breathing heavily, as if he were teetering on the verge of anger or tears.

"You bitch," he hissed. "You broke my face."

Samantha struggled to lift her gun again, but her strength was fading nearly as quickly as the blood was gushing from her midsection. She heard the sound of Devil Face's fist rushing through the air toward her head but she never saw it. The blow slammed her skull against the wall and rushed her into blessed darkness.

Phillips watched her for a moment before bending down and almost reverently picking up the broken pieces of his mask. "You have a lot of sins that are going to be washed away," he said, casting his gaze over Samantha's bloody form. "Just remember: pain is the crucible that will forge the perfect you."

The Dark Gentleman tried to maintain his composure but it was hard to, seated as he was in the headquarters of the famous Assistance Unlimited, with no less than Lazarus Gray himself facing him across the table. Morgan and Eun stood behind their employer, wearing very different expressions. Morgan looked bemused while Eun seemed to grow more annoyed by the minute. The face of Lazarus was so impassive that the Dark Gentleman had no idea what the man was thinking.

"So I'm here because I want to help. I'm not looking to join Assistance Unlimited, but I thought that we could pool our resources."

Eun barked out a laugh. "What resources do you have that we don't?"

"Enough," Lazarus said and Eun fell silent. "Michael, I admire your desire to help this city. It takes a special kind of man to put his life on the line for strangers. Nevertheless, it's foolhardy to go into situations like this without proper training and know-how."

"I've done the best I could," Michael retorted. "It's not like there's a vigilante school where I could enroll."

"Understandable," Lazarus admitted. "But you're just as likely to get yourself killed or get an innocent killed… if you'll permit me, I'd be willing to tutor you in various skills."

Michael couldn't hide the pleasure he felt. "I'd be honored."

Just then, a phone rang in the next room and Morgan went to answer it. He returned in less than a minute. "That was Davies. He says that the meeting's broken up at Groseclose's. But get this: Samantha's gone, car and all. He thinks she went off after Phillips."

Eun glanced up at the clock. "She should have reported in by now."

All of them had overheard Melvin's words at the meeting and understood what they meant. But the arrival of The Dark Gentleman had prevented them from going off in pursuit of Phillips for questioning.

Now Gray was in motion and it was a terrible thing to behold. His emerald-colored eye shone like a gem while the brown one seemed to smolder. His normally impassive face was now set in grim determination and from the way his jaw continually clenched and released, it was obvious that a cauldron of emotion was now at play. He stood up and began barking orders that were impossible to ignore.

"Morgan, bring the car around. Eun, tell Max to meet us at Phillips' house. Michael, you're with us."

The Dark Gentleman tried -- and failed -- to keep from grinning. "I'm ready."

"We'll see if you are," Gray responded.

The Rook didn't need to be told where to go. He was already in flight before Eun ever made it to the telephone. He borrowed Groseclose's car without asking and burned rubber through the rain-slicked city streets. Before arriving in Sovereign, Max had heard the jokes about how often it rained here, but he'd quickly learned that it wasn't hyperbole. It was as if God himself were constantly shedding tears for what had become of Sovereign.

The Rook tried to ignore the pounding in his head, but it was strong enough to force him to grit his teeth. His vision was swimming as the world around him intermingled with possible futures. The visions of future crimes that he often saw were far more of a curse than a boon and he'd prayed numerous times to be rid of them. He was forced to pull over to the curb, knowing that he had to ride it out before he could safely continue on his way.

The vision became clearer, obliterating everything else. The Rook saw a dark basement, the walls stained with gore. There were barrels or canisters of some kind, filled with the blood of Devil Face's victims. Samantha was there,

DARKNESS, SPREADING ITS WINGS OF BLACK

her nude body dangling from the ceiling, her arms stretched above her head. Devil Face was preparing his blades but he wasn't alone, there was another in the shadows, nearly invisible. The Rook, who routinely walked along the dark and narrow passage that lay between the sane world and the supernatural, felt like he recognized this figure: he knew she was female and that her stench had been a constant companion to him over the years.

With a shiver that rocked his spine, The Rook realized that Lady Death herself was there in that room. She was no simple manifestation of Phillips' madness, this was the dark lady herself, the one who kissed all men at the end of their days.

Lady Death stepped into view, her body hidden by her robes. She moved forward until she dominated The Rook's vision and he could see the curve of her jaw beneath her hood. She opened her mouth and spoke, her voice sounding so seductive that Max nearly forgot what an awful thing she was: he had spent his whole life fighting to avoid her and to save others from her embrace but now, he realized how easy it would be to fall into her arms. "Max," she whispered, "come to me. It's time."

A rapping on the driver's side window of his car snapped The Rook out of his reverie. He turned his head to see a police officer standing there, obviously having come to check on him. When the officer saw that The Rook wore a mask, his eyes widened. Before anything else could happen, The Rook floored the accelerator and left a trail of burning rubber in his wake. There was no time to waste now: Samantha Grace was in the presence of Death herself.

Chapter VI
Darkness

Samantha woke up to a world of pain. The joints in her shoulders felt like they were on fire and as her mind cleared, she realized that she was shackled by her wrists to the ceiling of Phillips' basement. Her clothing was gone and her nude body was covered by a fine sheen of sweat. The back of her head throbbed and her mouth felt abnormally dry and tasted tinny. She realized that she had bitten her tongue before falling unconscious and swallowed a good bit of blood.

Devil Face was about ten feet away from her, humming a song to himself as he polished a series of sharp knives and bone saws. His mask had been crudely repaired with glue and even in the dim lighting, Samantha could see that it hadn't fully dried yet - bubbles of glue glistened in the candlelight. Even as she tested the strength of her bonds, Samantha recognized the tune that Devil Face was humming: *Smoke Gets In Your Eyes* by Paul Whiteman. She suddenly realized she was never going to like that song ever again.

Devil Face heard the rattling of the chains and glanced over at her. His eyes traveled up her toned legs, past the mound of Venus between her legs, over the flat stomach and pert breasts. He caught his breath, hating the way she made him feel. It was the way of women: to tantalize men with their bodies until the spirit was made weak. He would very much enjoy purifying her. He would cut away all the pieces that teased him and then he would drain her of blood, lovingly washing every bit of her until she was as pure as the driven snow.

"I was worried you weren't going to wake up," Devil Face purred, moving toward her with a scalpel in his right hand. His foot brushed a bucket filled with tubing and Samantha swallowed hard, not wanting to imagine what it was for. "You're going to be my thirteenth. That's a sacred number."

Samantha grimly regarded the killer, refusing to show even the tiniest bit of fear. She trusted that Lazarus and the others would find their way there – and if they didn't, she'd just have to free herself. "Should I feel honored?"

"Yes. You should."

"Let me go, Phillips. You're in enough trouble as it is. Hurt me and I can't promise that they'll even let the police take you in. Lazarus might just skin you alive."

"I doubt that. I've read all about your employer. He's committed to bringing criminals to justice. He'd actually blame himself if anything happened to me."

"Morgan won't beat himself up for putting a bullet in your brain," Samantha said with a smile. That, at least, wasn't a lie. Morgan carried quite a torch for her and she knew that he'd stop at nothing to avenge her.

Devil Face brought the scalpel up to Samantha's cheek and drew it slowly across the skin, leaving a thin trail of blood. "You're so beautiful," he whispered. "I wish you weren't such a whore... but if you weren't we couldn't share this moment together, could we? So maybe I'm secretly glad."

Samantha flinched at the onset of new pain, but she said nothing. Her eyes caught the flicker of movement over Devil Face's shoulder and she gasped. "Is someone else here with us?" she asked, unable to maintain her silence any longer.

Devil Face stepped back, his eyes wide with surprise beneath his mask. "You can see her?"

Samantha peered into the shadows but saw nothing at all. "I thought," she began, but then fell quiet again with a shake of her head. "It was nothing."

Devil Face smiled, momentarily taken aback but now once more in control. No one else had ever seen Lady Death, not even the girls who had rested on the precipice between the world of the living and of the dead. "Well, it's time we began in earnest. You're the last one."

"What does that mean?" Samantha asked, as Devil Face turned away from her. He moved over to the tray of sharp implements and set down his scalpel, plucking up one of the bone saws and examining the teeth on the blade.

"Thirteen girls have to die," he said, not caring if she knew his secrets. It was too late for her and he was too close to achieving ultimate power. What could it hurt? "And then Lady Death will cross over onto this plane and she'll make me her consort."

Samantha heard the dreamy nature of his voice and couldn't help but think he was absolutely insane. But she'd seen some very strange things as a member of Assistance Unlimited, so she wasn't prepared to discount it completely.

"I'm not sure why being Death's lover would be a good thing," she said, hoping to keep Devil Face talking long enough to allow her friends to find them.

"You haven't felt her touch," Devil Face replied. He turned toward her with the bone saw in hand. As he approached, he bent down and grabbed the bucket filled with tubing and carried it in his other hand. He set the bucket down next to her dangling feet. "But you will soon enough."

Samantha slammed her foot against Devil Face in an attempt to hurt him, but her position didn't allow her to put any real strength behind the blow and it elicited nothing more than a chuckle from the madman.

"Don't fight," Devil Face warned. "It will only make things harder for you."

The next moment was one that Samantha would long remember. Devil Face placed the sharp blade against her shoulder, obviously intending to remove her right arm with no anesthetic whatsoever. Just before he began his grisly task, a figure descended the stairs and threw himself at Devil Face's back. The impact knocked the villain aside, though the blade drug painfully across Samantha's arm, taking a long stretch of flesh with it.

Devil Face whirled about to see Lazarus Gray facing him, hands balled into fists. Rapidly moving into the room were Morgan, The Dark Gentleman and Eun, all of whom looked at Samantha with concern. Normally, she would have felt embarrassed by her nudity but at the moment she didn't care – her only desire was to be freed so she could help bring this killer to justice.

It was Morgan who reached her first, steadfastly keeping his eyes off her nakedness. He fumbled with the locks around her wrists, concern for her making him sloppy. "We'll get that cut sewn up," he said, as if her bleeding arm was important to her.

Eun saw that Morgan was busy with Samantha so he moved to assist his employer, The Dark Gentleman in tow. Devil Face was swinging his blade with great skill, forcing Lazarus to keep his distance.

"There's too many of them," Devil Face hissed. "Please – help me!"

The Dark Gentleman glanced around, wondering whom it was that Devil Face was talking to.

"He's talking to the woman over there," Lazarus explained, nodding his head in the direction of Lady Death.

"I don't see anyone!"

"She's there. Trust me." Lazarus knew that the woman before them was not human. His past experiences as a member of the Illuminati had included many forays into the supernatural. As such, his mind was open to perceiving things that most people could simply not accept. He could see Lady Death as clearly as Devil Face could – and, truthfully, so could all of his aides, but because of the unreality of the situation, their minds refused to accept what their eyes beheld. Thus, they could not acknowledge it.

Lazarus ducked under a swipe of Devil Face's blade and struck out with a karate chop that knocked the air from the man's lungs. Devil Face recovered quickly, however, driving the bone saw against Gray's neck an instant later. Blood spilled freely, but Lazarus knew that it would look worse than it really was: nothing vital had been struck.

Eun smelled something awful, like an ancient tomb had been thrown open. He gagged and backed away, his eyes widening as half a dozen figures emerged from the shadows, shambling toward them with open sores dotting their skins and portions of white bone protruding. These were the undead, summoned forth by Lady Death and their presence was a sign of just how close Devil Face was to completing his awful ritual. He had loosened the barriers between Death's realm and those of mortal man… and now her warriors were spilling through.

The first of the zombies uttered a long, guttural moan and reached for Eun. The young Korean batted the hand aside and unleashed a series of kick punches and kicks, most of which had no obvious effect. To Eun, it felt like he was attacking a side of beef. It wasn't until one of his fists crashed through the thing's ribs and was momentarily stuck that he realized the full danger he was in: these creatures were not alive and were thus immune to all forms of pain.

Eun looked about and saw that the monsters, all of which were grabbing at his clothes and hair, now surrounded him. One of them dug its claws into the meat of Eun's arm, tearing into the flesh and spilling blood.

The Dark Gentleman shared Eun's horror. Unlike the members of Assistance Unlimited, this was his first contact with the supernatural and it was almost enough to shake his sanity. But his sense of self-preservation was strong enough to propel him into combat, shooting several bullets into the torso of the nearest zombie. The impacts caused the undead creature to pause but didn't deter it from coming onward.

Lazarus knew that things were quickly spiraling out of control and made an effort to end his battle with Devil Face all the faster. He lowered his shoulder and charged like a maddened bull, slamming his bulk into the big man's chest. They tumbled back until the basement wall halted Devil Face's progress. Devil Face grunted hard and struck wildly with the bone saw. He repeatedly cut Gray's face and shoulders, but the leader of Assistance Unlimited ignored the pain and continued pummeling his enemy, breaking ribs, smashing a nose and finally fracturing Devil Face's hip.

The man who had lived as Robert Phillips these past few years, coasting on a fabricated past until he had achieved a position of power, now knew that his plans were swiftly coming to an end. He sagged to his knees, pain blotting out all rational thought. He saw The Rook entering the basement and he wanted to curse the unfairness of it all, but he knew that it was his own fault. He had stuck to a plan for years, killing only those girls who wouldn't be missed. But Schuller had been an impulse murder and it had led to his downfall.

"Don't give up hope just yet," Lady Death purred and her voice seeped directly into her follower's mind. "We may yet have our victory…."

The Rook stared about him in amazement. He saw the lovely young Samantha Grace being freed from her chains by Morgan Watts; Eun Jiwon was in danger of being ripped to shreds by a half dozen undead; Lady Death herself stood on the edge of it all, a haunting smile visible from beneath her hood; Devil Face was on the floor, flecks of blood on his lips; and – most surprisingly of all – a villain from his past.

Turning to face him was Doctor York, a madman who had tried to open a portal to Hell back in '33. The Rook had defeated him then but the incident had haunted him ever since, mostly because he knew how close he'd come to losing the battle.

The Rook drew one of his pistols and took careful aim. If York was involved in all this, then things were even more dangerous than he'd assumed.

Lazarus Gray could scarcely believe what he was seeing. Coming down the stairs in all his arrogant glory was Walther Lunt. Lunt was the German mastermind who had recruited Richard Winthrop into the Illuminati and he had eventually become Winthrop's greatest foe, overseeing the plot that led to Winthrop's "death" and "rebirth" as Lazarus Gray. Since then, the two had clashed repeatedly and Gray had come to know Lunt's ruined visage almost as well as he knew his own. Badly scarred by an acid attack years ago, the right side of Lunt's face was a mass of burned tissue and the ugliness had seeped into the man's very soul.

Suddenly things began to fall into place: no doubt Lunt was somehow the puppet master behind all of this, pulling Devil Face's strings in some elaborate plot to destroy Gray and his allies.

After casting one quick glance at Devil Face to ensure that he was in no shape to re-enter the fray, Lazarus threw himself toward his old enemy. He managed to drive Lunt against the wall but the other man responded with more skill than Lazarus remembered him possessing, slipping an arm under Gray's and using the bigger man's momentum to toss him to the ground.

Lunt slammed a foot down, narrowly missing Gray's skull when Lazarus rolled out of the way. Lazarus reached out and grabbed Lunt's leg, driving a fist just above the German's kneecap. A loud cracking sound indicated that Lazarus had successfully broken the man's leg and Lunt quickly joined Lazarus on the floor. They grappled now, hands wrapped around each other's throat. There was no letting up now and it was obvious to each that this would be their final battle.

The Rook was in the fight of his life. In their last meeting, Doctor York had shown none of the skills that he was now displaying. The made scientist had just broken one of The Rook's legs and he was now choking the life from him. The Rook had to exert all his will to remain conscious as he fought to take York down. Somewhere in all of this, The Rook's pistol had been knocked from his grip, but the vigilante had more pressing concerns at the moment.

DARKNESS, SPREADING ITS WINGS OF BLACK

Stars were beginning to appear before The Rook's eyes and he knew that he was literally seconds away from blacking out. He drew his head back and then slammed it forward, smashing his forehead directly into York's nose. Blood spurted from York's nostrils and his grip weakened enough for The Rook to pull free, gasping for air.

The Rook scrambled to his feet, his shoe bumping against something hard on the floor. Looking down, he spotted his pistol and he quickly snatched it up. His broken leg ached horribly and he was unable to put much weight on it but with one good shot, the battle would be over.

York was on his feet again and The Rook realized that he had a perfect shot: one bullet to the villain's head and the city would be safe.

Just as he was about to pull the trigger, he caught a glimpse of Lady Death. The hooded figure was watching the battle with obvious interest and The Rook momentarily assumed that it was because she was concerned for York's survival. But then something occurred to him: where was Lazarus Gray? His aides were here, actively battling the zombies – even poor Samantha, naked as the day she was born. But their erstwhile leader was nowhere to be seen.

The Rook suddenly realized that he'd been duped. He twisted, turning the barrel of the gun on Lady Death.

Lazarus had tensed, preparing for a potentially fatal shot to come from Lunt's gun. Blood was flowing freely from his nose, but Lazarus was ignoring it. If he didn't time his movements just so, he was about to die... and all that he'd accomplished with Assistance Unlimited was going to come to an end.

Lazarus caught Lunt's eyes shift to something over his shoulder and he risked a glance, wanting to make sure that Devil Face wasn't back in the fray. What he saw gave him pause: it was Lady Death, standing half in the shadows. Seeing her brought a bit of clarity to his mind – something about this situation did not feel right. The last time he'd checked on Lunt's whereabouts, he'd been in Europe... how had he managed to spearhead this plan involving Devil Face? Especially since the murders began before Lunt ever came to Sovereign in pursuit of Lazarus? Had he just taken over a pre-existing plot of some kind? Or was all of this just a bizarre illusion perpetrated by Lady Death?

Narrowing his eyes and focusing all of his amazing willpower allowed Lazarus to suddenly see the truth: the man before him was not Wilhelm Lunt at all. He had been battling The Rook for the past several minutes, while his aides fought for their survival.

Just as The Rook turned his gun on Lady Death, Lazarus turned and jumped into the middle of the scene involving the zombies and the other members of Assistance Unlimited. Samantha's body was covered with scratches and bruises.

She was fighting bravely, but was unarmed and had been backed into a corner by two of the undead. They tugged at her hair and opened their mouths in an attempt to catch her tender flesh between their teeth. Lazarus unsheathed the dagger he kept on the calf of his left leg and drove the blade through the head of one of the monsters, freeing Samantha to dispatch the other by gripping its skull in her hands and repeatedly driving it into the wall. When the thing's head had been reduced to a liquid pool of gore, Samantha shoved it away from her.

"Glad to have you back with us," she said with a smile. "I was wondering what was up with you and The Rook."

Lazarus removed his jacket and draped it around her shoulders. "A momentary lapse of rationality," he explained.

A gunshot rang out, sounding abnormally loud in the basement. All heads, even those of the remaining zombies, turned to see Lady Death stagger back. The bullet couldn't really destroy her, but it was enough to ruin her tenuous hold on this plane. Her body shimmered, turning to thin trails of smoky vapor that eventually dissipated. Devil Face cried out, a mournful sound that spoke of dashed hopes and lost love.

The four remaining zombies seemed uncertain now, their hungers no longer enough to drive them forward. They became easy prey for Morgan, The Dark Gentleman, and Eun, the three men using differing means to dispose of the beasts: Morgan and The Dark Gentleman put bullets through their brains while Eun preferred bashing their skulls in.

In the aftermath, the heroes stood silently for a moment, lost in their own thoughts. When enough time had passed for everyone to feel like they'd regained their footing in the real world, it was Lazarus who spoke first. "We should tie up Phillips and call the authorities."

The Rook cleared his throat, gun still in hand. "I think we should kill him. He's dangerous – and the police won't believe half of the truth, even if we decide to tell them. With his money and clout, he might pay somebody off in this town and get off scot-free. The best way to deal with a rabid dog is to put him down."

"That's not how I do things," Lazarus retorted. "I know that the justice system in Sovereign is corrupt, but we have to give it a chance to do the right thing."

The Rook's fingers shifted on the gun he held and he knew that no one would be able to stop him if he chose to end Devil Face's life here and now. But he liked Lazarus and didn't want to test their friendship in that way. He holstered his weapon and nodded toward The Dark Gentleman. "Decided to add a masked man to your team, Lazarus?"

The Dark Gentleman smiled. "I'm just helping out."

The Rook watched as Lazarus used a thin, almost invisible cord to wrap up Devil Face's hands. The killer was sobbing softly and put up no resistance. The cord was obviously of Gray's own design and The Rook knew there was no chance of the villain escaping, even if he came to his senses and tried.

DARKNESS, SPREADING ITS WINGS OF BLACK

The members of Assistance Unlimited crowded around one another now, sharing their experiences. The men were anxious to know that Samantha was mostly unharmed and she was grateful that none of them mentioned the fact that they'd seen her naked.

The Rook slowly ascended the stairs, preferring not to say goodbye. He had forged some friendships here, but he had other places to be and he had never been good with partings. He noticed that The Dark Gentleman had the same idea. The young man was making his way to the stairs when The Rook stepped out onto the first floor and hurried out into the Sovereign City streets.

To The Rook's surprise, the sun had come through the clouds. The darkness still clung to the edges of the sky, but it looked like they were being driven back by the rays of the sun. For a moment, The Rook thought he saw the face of Lady Death in one of the clouds but then it was gone, replaced by a beam of light that shot forth, like a spotlight.

For one day at least, the forces of good had won – and in a place like Sovereign, that was something to be proud of.

THE END

THE SCORCHED GOD
AN INTERVIEW WITH AUTHOR BARRY REESE

THE SCORCHED GOD
An Interview With Author Barry Reese

The Scorched God is the sixth installment in The Rook Chronicles but it's unique in that it's set in-between previous volumes. What made you decide to take that route?

I wasn't entirely pleased with how the fifth volume turned out, quite honestly. I thought I'd made things a bit too easy for Max with all the allies he'd accumulated and moved too far away from the core concepts of the series. So I came up with the idea of doing a story set in a "classic" era of The Rook, with all the coolest things still in place. So you've got his father, his marriage, his visions of the future, the branding of criminals, etc. – this is the story I'd hand to someone if they said they wanted to read only one Rook story to see what the fuss was all about.

Can you tell us about Sun Koh?

Sun Koh was an actual character that was quite popular in the 1930s Germany. His series ended in 1938, just prior to the outbreak of World War II. His stories haven't been translated into English, but folks like Jess Nevins and Art Sippo have done a wonderful job of keeping the character from being forgotten. I have to give major thanks to Art Sippo, who not only inspired me to use Sun Koh as the antagonist of this novel but who also gave permission for me to use a few characters he'd created for his own Sun Koh series in this book. If you haven't already read them, I highly recommend you seek out his Sun Koh books published by Age of Adventure. Very high quality stuff and a slightly different take on the "Nazi Doc Savage" than what I went with.

The Furies were a lot of fun – were they always meant to be part of this story?

I actually thought about using The Furies before I decided to include Sun Koh. The high concept of The Furies was that they were going to be the Axis version of Charlie's Angels. When I got Ed Mironiuk to do the cover, I knew they had to be featured there, since his stuff is oriented in those directions. I really liked the girls and felt kinda bad for killing them off.

The tie-in to the Un-Earth from Volume Three was interesting. What brought that about?

Basically, it occurred to me that Sun Koh was the embodiment of all the Aryan ideals – so much so, that it almost seemed unbelievable that he could be real. So what if he *wasn't?* What if some overzealous researcher on the Un-Earth Project created Sun Koh and then accidentally released him into the real world before his own creation? It was a paradox that I found interesting and helped preserve both the history of the world I'd set up for The Rook and the one presented in Sun Koh's own series.

The ending – with a vision of Sun Koh victorious – is that meant to be real? Did Sun Koh go to heaven? What's that about?

I'll leave that up to the reader to decide. It kind of wrote itself and I liked leaving things on an ambiguous note.

Any hints about Volume Seven?

The Rook is going on a very interesting journey in Volume Seven. In many ways.

THE ROOK

A TIMELINE

THE ROOK - A TIMELINE

Major Events specific to certain stories and novels are included in brackets. Some of this information contains **SPOILERS** *for The Rook, Lazarus Gray, Eobard Grace and other stories.*

1748 - Johann Adam Weishaupt is born.

1776 - Johann Adam Weishaupt forms The Illuminati. He adopts the guise of the original Lazarus Gray in group meetings, reflecting his "rebirth" and the "moral ambiguity" of the group.

1865 - Eobard Grace returns home from his actions in the American Civil War. Takes possession of the Book of Shadows from his uncle Frederick. [*"The World of Shadow," The Family Grace: An Extraordinary History*]

1877 - Eobard Grace is summoned to the World of Shadows, where he battles Uris-Kor and fathers a son, Korben. [*"The World of Shadow," The Family Grace: An Extraordinary History*]

1885 - Along with his niece Miriam and her paramour Ian Sinclair, Eobard returns to the World of Shadows to halt the merging of that world with Earth. [*"The Flesh Wheel," The Family Grace: An Extraordinary History*]

THE ROOK - A TIMELINE

1890 - Eobard fathers a second son, Leopold.

1895 - Felix Cole (the Bookbinder) is born.

1900 - Max Davies is born to publisher Warren Davies and his wife, heiress Margaret Davies.

1901 - Leonid Kaslov is born.

1905 - Richard Winthrop is born in San Francisco.

1908 - Warren Davies is murdered by Ted Grossett, a killer nicknamed "Death's Head". [*"Lucifer's Cage", the Rook Volume One, more details shown in "Origins," the Rook Volume Two*] Hans Merkel kills his own father. [*"Blitzkrieg," the Rook Volume Two*]

1910 - Evelyn Gould is born.

1913 - Felix Cole meets the Cockroach Man and becomes part of The Great Work. [*"The Great Work," Startling Stories # 5*]

1914 - Margaret Davies passes away in her sleep. Max is adopted by his uncle Reginald.

1915 - Felix Cole marries Charlotte Grace, Eobard Grace's cousin.

1916 - Leonid Kaslov's father Nikolai becomes involved in the plot to assassinate Rasputin.

1917 - Betsy Cole is born to Felix and Charlotte Grace Cole. Nikolai Kaslov is murdered.

1918 - Max Davies begins wandering the world. Richard Winthrop's parents die in an accident.

1922 - Warlike Manchu tutors Max Davies in Kyoto.

1925 - Max Davies becomes the Rook, operating throughout Europe.

1926 - Charlotte Grace dies. Richard Winthrop has a brief romance with exchange student Sarah Dumas.

1927 - Richard Winthrop graduates from Yale. On the night of his graduation, he is recruited into The Illuminati. Max and Leopold Grace battle the Red Lord in Paris. Richard Winthrop meets Miya Shimada in Japan, where he purchases The McGuinness Obelisk for The Illuminati.

1928 - The Rook returns to Boston.

1929 - Richard Winthrop destroys a coven of vampires in Mexico.

1932 - The Rook hunts down his father's killer [*"Origins," the Rook Volume Two*]

1933 - Jacob Trench uncovers Lucifer's Cage. [*"Lucifer's Cage", the Rook Volume One*] The Rook battles Doctor York [*All-Star Pulp Comics # 1*] After a failed attempt at betraying The Illuminati, Richard Winthrop wakes up on the shores of Sovereign City with no memory of his name or past. He has only one clue to his past in his possession: a small medallion adorned with the words Lazarus Gray and the image of a naked man with the head of a lion. [*"The Girl With the Phantom Eyes," Lazarus Gray Volume One*]

1934 - Now calling himself Lazarus Gray, Richard Winthrop forms Assistance Unlimited in Sovereign City. He recruits Samantha Grace, Morgan Watts and Eun Jiwon [*"The Girl With the Phantom Eyes," Lazarus Gray Volume One*] Walther Lunt aids German scientists in unleashing the power Die Glocke, which in turn frees the demonic forces of Satan's Circus [*"Die Glocke," Lazarus Gray Volume Two*]

THE ROOK · A TIMELINE

1935 - Felix Cole and his daughter Betsy seek out the Book of Eibon. [*"The Great Work," The Family Grace: An Extraordinary History*] Assistance Unlimited undertakes a number of missions, defeating the likes of Walther Lunt, Doc Pemberley, Malcolm Goodwill & Black Heart, Princess Femi & The Undying, Mr. Skull, The Axeman and The Yellow Claw [*"The Girl With the Phantom Eyes," "The Devil's Bible," "The Corpse Screams at Midnight," "The Burning Skull," "The Axeman of Sovereign City," and "The God of Hate," Lazarus Gray Volume One*] The Rook journeys to Sovereign City and teams up with Assistance Unlimited to battle Devil Face [*"Darkness, Spreading Its Wings of Black," the Rook Volume Six)*]

1936 - The Rook moves to Atlanta and recovers the Dagger of Elohim from Felix Darkholme. The Rook meets Evelyn Gould. The Rook battles Jacob Trench. [*"Lucifer's Cage", the Rook Volume One*]. Reed Barrows revives Camilla. [*"Kingdom of Blood," The Rook Volume One*]. Kevin Atwill is abandoned in the Amazonian jungle by his friends, a victim of the Gorgon legacy. [*"The Gorgon Conspiracy," The Rook Volume Two*]. Nathaniel Caine's lover is killed by Tweedledum while Dan Daring looks on [*"Catalyst," The Rook Volume Three*]

1937 - Max and Evelyn marry. Camilla attempts to create a Kingdom of Blood. The world's ancient vampires awaken and the Rook is 'marked' by Nyarlathotep. Gerhard Klempt's experiments are halted. William McKenzie becomes Chief of Police in Atlanta. The Rook meets Benson, who clears his record with the police. [*"Kingdom of Blood," the Rook Volume One*]. Hank Wilbon is murdered, leading to his eventual resurrection as the Reaper. [*"Kaslov's Fire," The Rook Volume Two*]

1938 - The Rook travels to Great City to aid the Moon Man in battling Lycos and his Gasping Death. The Rook destroys the physical shell of Nyarlathotep and gains his trademark signet ring. [*"The Gasping Death," The Rook Volume One*]. The jungle hero known as the Revenant is killed [*"Death from the Jungle," The Rook Volume Four*]

1939 - Ibis and the Warlike Manchu revive the Abomination. Evelyn becomes pregnant and gives birth to their first child, a boy named William. [*"Abominations," The Rook Volume One*]. The Rook allies himself with Leonid Kaslov to stop the Reaper's attacks and to foil the plans of Rasputin. [*"Kaslov's Fire," the Rook Volume Two*] Violet Cambridge and Will McKenzie become embroiled in the hunt for a mystical item known as The Damned Thing [*The Damned Thing*]

1940 - The Warlike Manchu returns with a new pupil -- Hans Merkel, aka Shinigami. The Warlike Manchu kidnaps William Davies, but the Rook and Leonid Kaslov manage to rescue the boy. [*"Blitzkrieg," the Rook Volume Two*] The Rook journeys to Germany alongside the Domino Lady and Will McKenzie to combat the demonic organization known as Bloodwerks. [*"Bloodwerks," the Rook Volume Two*] Kevin Atwill seeks revenge against his former friends, bringing him into conflict with the Rook [*"The Gorgon Conspiracy," The Rook Volume Two*]. The Rook takes a young vampire under his care, protecting him from a cult that worships a race of beings known as The Shambling Ones. With the aid of Leonid Kazlov, the cult is destroyed [*"The Shambling Ones," The Rook Volume Two*]

1941 - Philip Gallagher, a journalist, uncovers the Rook's secret identity, but chooses to become an ally of the vigilante rather than reveal it to the world [*"Origins," the Rook Volume Two*]. The Rook teams with the Black Bat and Ascott Keane, as well as a reluctant Doctor Satan, in defeating the plans of the sorcerer Arias [*"The Bleeding Hells"*]. The Rook rescues McKenzie from the Iron Maiden [*"The Iron Maiden," The Rook Volume Three*]

1942 - The Rook battles a Nazi super agent known as the Grim Reaper, who is attempting to gather the Crystal Skulls [*"The Three Skulls," The Rook Volume Three*]. The Rook teams with Ascott Keane and the Green Lama to defeat a monster that has escaped from The World of Shadows [*"The Gilded Beast," The Family Grace: An Extraordinary History*]. The Rook becomes embroiled in a plot by Sun Koh and a group of Axis killers known as The Furies. The Rook and Sun Koh end up in deadly battle on the banks of the Potomac River. [*"The Scorched God," The Rook Volume Six*]. In London, the Rook and Evelyn meet Nathaniel Caine (aka the Catalyst) and Rachel Winters, who are involved in stopping the Nazis from creating the Un-Earth. They battle Doctor Satan and the Black Zeppelin [*"Catalyst," The Rook Volume Three*]. Evelyn learns she's pregnant with a second child. The Rook solves the mystery of the Roanoke Colony [*"The Lost Colony," The Rook Volume Three*] The Warlike Manchu is revived and embarks upon a search for the Philosopher's Stone [*"The Resurrection Gambit," The Rook Volume Three*]

1943 - The Rook is confronted by the twin threats of Fernando Pasarin and the undead pirate Hendrik van der Decken [*"The Phantom Vessel," The Rook Volume Four*]. Evelyn and Max become the parents of a second child, Emma Davies. The Rook teams up with the daughter of the Revenant to battle Hermann Krupp and the Golden Goblin [*"Death from the Jungle," The Rook Volume Four*] The Rook battles Doctor Satan over possession of an ancient Mayan tablet [*"The Four Rooks," The Rook Volume Four*]. The Rook travels to Peru to battle an undead magician called The Spook [*"Spook," The Rook Volume Four*]. Baron Rudolph Gustav gains possession of the Rod of Aaron and kidnaps Evelyn, forcing the Rook into an uneasy alliance with the Warlike Manchu [*"Dead of Night," The Rook Volume Four*]. Doctor Satan flees to the hidden land of Vorium, where the Rook allies with Frankenstein's Monster to bring him to justice [*"Satan's Trial," The Rook Volume Four*].

1944 - The Rook organizes a strike force composed of Revenant, Frankenstein's Monster, Catalyst and Esper. The group is known as The Claws of the Rook and they take part in two notable adventures in this year: against the diabolical Mr. Dee and then later against an alliance between Doctor Satan and the Warlike Manchu [*"The Diabolical Mr. Dee" and "A Plague of Wicked Men", The Rook Volume Five*].

1946 - The Rook discovers that Adolph Hitler is still alive and has become a vampire in service to Dracula. In an attempt to stop the villains from using the Holy Lance to take over the world, the Rook allies with the Claws of the Rook, a time traveler named Jenny Everywhere, a thief called Belladonna and Leonid Kaslov. The villains are defeated and Max's future is revealed to still be in doubt. Events shown from 2006 on are just a possible future. The Rook also has several encounters with a demonically powered killer known as Stickman. [*"The Devil's Spear," The Rook*

Volume Five]. The Rook encounters a madman named Samuel Garibaldi (aka Rainman) and his ally, Dr. Gottlieb Hochmuller. The Rook and his Claws team defeat the villainous duo and seveal new heroes join the ranks of the Claws team -- Miss Masque, Black Terror & Tim and The Flame. [*"Resurrection Day," The Rook Volume Five*]

1953 - The Rook acquires the Looking Glass from Lu Chang. [*"Black Mass," The Rook Volume One*]

1961 - Max's son William becomes the second Rook. [*"The Four Rooks," The Rook Volume Four*]

1967 - The second Rook battles and defeats the Warlike Manchu, who is in possession of the Mayan Tablet that Doctor Satan coveted in '43. Evelyn Davies dies. [*"The Four Rooks," The Rook Volume Four*]

1970 - William Davies (the second Rook) commits suicide by jumping from a Manhattan rooftop. Emma Davies (Max's daughter and William's brother) becomes the Rook one week later, in February. [*"The Four Rooks," The Rook Volume Four*]

1973 - The third Rook is accompanied by Kayla Kaslov (daughter of Leonid Kaslov) on a trip to Brazil, where the two women defeat the Black Annis and claim the Mayan Tablet that's popped up over the course of three decades. Emma gives it to her father, who in turn passes it on to Catalyst (Nathaniel Caine) [*"The Four Rooks," The Rook Volume Four*]

~1985 - Max resumes operating as the Rook, adventuring sporadically. Due to various magical events, he remains far more active than most men his age. The reasons for Emma giving up the role are unknown at this time.

2006 - The Black Mass Barrier rises, enveloping the world in a magical field. The World of Shadows merges with Earth. Fiona Grace (descended from Eobard) becomes a worldwide celebrity, partially due to her failure to stop the Black Mass Barrier. [*"Black Mass," The Rook Volume One*]

THE ROOK · A TIMELINE

2009 - Ian Morris meets Max Davies and becomes the new Rook. He meets Fiona Grace. Max dies at some point immediately following this. [*"Black Mass," The Rook Volume One*]

2012 - The fourth Rook (Ian Morris) receives the Mayan Tablet from Catalyst, who tells him that the world will end on December 21, 2012 unless something is done. Using the tablet, Ian attempts to take control of the magic spell that will end the world. Aided by the spirits of the three previous Rooks, he succeeds, though it costs him his life. He is survived by his lover (Fiona Grace) and their unborn child. Max Davies is reborn as a man in his late twenties and becomes the Rook again. [*"The Four Rooks," The Rook Volume Four*]

BARRY REESE

ABOUT THE AUTHOR

Barry Reese has spent the last decade writing for publishers as diverse as Marvel Comics, West End Games, Wild Cat Books and Moonstone Books. Known primarily for his pulp adventure works like The Rook Chronicles, The Adventures of Lazarus Gray and Savage Tales of Ki-Gor, Barry has also delved into slasher horror (Rabbit Heart) and even the fantasy pirate genre (Guan-Yin and the Horrors of Skull Island). His favorite classic pulp heroes are The Avenger, Doc Savage, John Carter, Conan and Seekay. More information about him can be found at http://www.barryreese.net

Special thanks to Dr. Art Sippo for his assistance in the Sun Koh portion of the story and for the use of his original character, Ashanti Garuda.